HIT AND RUN

He twisted toward me in the seat and chopped at my head with the loaded butt of his gun. I went out, all the way. After a while the darkness where I lay was invaded by dreams. Huge turning wheels, like the interlocking wheels of eternity and necessity, resolved themselves into a diesel locomotive. I was lying limp across the tracks and the train was coming, swinging its Cyclops eye.

It honked its horn at me. It wasn't a train sound, though, and I wasn't lying on a track, and it was no dream. I sat up in the middle of the northbound lane of the highway. A truck lit up like a Christmas tree was bearing down on me, honking repeatedly.

Its brakes were shrieking too, but it wasn't going to be able to stop before it got to me. I lay down and watched it blot out the stars. . . .

THE
INSTANT
ENEMY

ROSS MACDONALD

BANTAM BOOKS
TORONTO • NEW YORK • LONDON • SYDNEY • AUCKLAND

THE INSTANT ENEMY
*A Bantam Book / published by arrangement with
Alfred A. Knopf, Inc.*

PRINTING HISTORY

Knopf edition published February 1968
Bantam edition / May 1969

2nd printing ...... May 1969	8th printing .... March 1971
3rd printing ...... June 1969	9th printing .. October 1971
4th printing ...... June 1970	10th printing .. January 1972
5th printing ...... July 1970	11th printing . December 1972
6th printing .. February 1971	12th printing ..... July 1974
7th printing .... March 1971	13th printing ..... June 1977
14th printing ... February 1985	

ISBN 0-553-24738-7

Published simultaneously in the United States and Canada

*Bantam Books are published by Bantam Books, Inc. Its trade-
mark, consisting of the words "Bantam Books" and the por-
trayal of a rooster, is Registered in U.S. Patent and Trademark
Office and in other countries. Marca Registrada. Bantam
Books, Inc., 666 Fifth Avenue, New York, New York 10103.*

PRINTED IN THE UNITED STATES OF AMERICA

H   23 22 21 20 19 18 17 16 15 14

To
Ping Ferry

Chapter 1

THERE WAS LIGHT early morning traffic on Sepulveda. As I drove over the low pass, the sun came up glaring behind the blue crags on the far side of the valley. For a minute or two, before regular day set in, everything looked fresh and new and awesome as creation.

I left the freeway at Canoga Park and stopped at a drive-in for a ninety-nine-cent breakfast. Then I went on up to the Sebastians' place in Woodland Hills.

Keith Sebastian had given me detailed instructions on how to find his house. It was an angular contemporary house cantilevered out over a slope. The slope ran steeply down to the edge of a golf course, green from the first of the winter rains.

Keith Sebastian came out of the house in shirt sleeves. He was a handsome man of forty or so, with thick curly brown hair frosted at the sides. He hadn't shaved yet, and his growth of beard looked like fibrous dirt that his lower face had been rubbed in.

"It's good of you to come right out," he said when I had introduced myself. "I realize it's an ungodly hour—"

"You didn't pick it, and I don't mind. I gather she hasn't come home yet."

"No, she hasn't. Since I called you I've found out something else is missing. My shotgun, and a box of shells."

"You think your daughter took them?"

"I'm afraid she must have. The gun cabinet wasn't broken, and nobody else knew where the key to it was. Except my wife, of course."

Mrs. Sebastian had appeared as if on cue at the open front door. She was thin and dark and rather beautiful in a haggard sort of way, and she was wearing fresh lipstick and a fresh yellow linen dress.

"Come in," she said to both of us. "It's *cold* out."

She made a shivery self-hugging gesture which didn't end when it should have. She went on shivering.

"This is Mr. Lew Archer," Sebastian was saying. "The private detective I called." He spoke as if he was presenting me to her as a kind of peace offering.

She answered him impatiently: "I guessed that. Come in, I've made some coffee."

I sat between them at the kitchen counter and drank the bitter brew from a thin cup. The place seemed very clean and very empty. The light pouring in through the window had a cruel clarity.

"Can Alexandria fire a shotgun?" I asked them.

"Anybody can," Sebastian said glumly. "All you have to do is pull the trigger."

His wife cut in. "Actually Sandy's a fair shot. The Hacketts took her quail hunting earlier this year. Much against my wishes, I might add."

"You might and did," Sebastian said. "I'm sure the experience was good for her."

"She hated it. She said so in her diary. She hates to kill things."

"She'll get over it. And I know it gave pleasure to Mr. and Mrs. Hackett."

"Here we go again."

But before they did, I said: "Who in hell are Mr. and Mrs. Hackett?"

Sebastian gave me a self-revealing look, partly offended, partly patronizing.

"Mr. Stephen Hackett is my boss. That is, he controls the holding company that controls the savings and loan company I work for. He owns quite a few other things, too."

"Including you," his wife said. "But not my daughter."

"That's unfair, Bernice. I never said—"

"It's what you do that counts."

I got up and walked around to the other side of the counter and stood facing them. They both looked a little startled and ashamed.

"All this is very interesting," I said. "But I didn't get out of bed at five o'clock in the morning to referee a family argument. Let's concentrate on your daughter Sandy. How old is she, Mrs. Sebastian?"

"Seventeen. She's in her senior year."

"Doing well?"

"She was until the last few months. Then her grades started slipping, quite badly."

"Why?"

She looked down into her coffee cup. "I don't really know why." She sounded evasive, unwilling even to give herself an answer.

"Of course you know why," her husband said. "All this has happened since she took up with that wild man. Davy what's-his-name."

"He isn't a man. He's a nineteen-year-old boy and we handled the whole thing abominably."

"What whole thing, Mrs. Sebastian?"

She held out her arms as if she was trying to encompass the situation, then dropped them in despair. "The business of the boy. We mishandled it."

"She means *I* did, as usual," Sebastian said. "But I only did what I had to do. Sandy was starting to run wild. Skipping school to have afternoon dates with this fellow. Spending her nights on the Strip and God knows where else. Last night I went out and hunted them down—"

His wife interrupted him. "It wasn't last night. It was the night before last."

"Whenever it was." His voice seemed to be weakening under the steady cold force of her disapproval. It shifted gears, to a kind of chanting shout. "I hunted them down in a weird joint in West Hollywood. They were sitting there in public with their arms around each other. I told him if he didn't stay away from my daughter I'd take my shotgun and blow his bloody head off."

"My husband watches a good deal of television," Mrs. Sebastian said dryly.

"Make fun of me if you want to, Bernice. Somebody had to do what I did. My daughter was running wild with a criminal. I brought her home and locked her in her room. What else could a man do?"

His wife was silent for once. She moved her fine dark head slowly from side to side.

I said: "Do you know the young man is a criminal?"

"He served time in the county jail for auto theft."

"Joy riding," she said.

"Call it what you like. It wasn't a first offense, either."

"How do you know?"

"Bernice read it in her diary."

"I'd like to see this famous diary."

"No," Mrs. Sebastian said. "It was bad enough for me to have read it. I shouldn't have." She took a deep breath. "We haven't been very good parents, I'm afraid. I'm just as much to blame as my husband is, in subtler ways. But you don't want to go into that."

"Not now." I was weary of the war of the generations, the charges and countercharges, the escalations and negotiations, the endless talk across the bargaining table. "How long has your daughter been gone?"

Sebastian looked at his wrist watch. "Nearly twenty-three hours. I let her out of her room yesterday morning. She seemed to have calmed down—"

"She was furious," her mother said. "But I never thought when she started out for school that she had no intention of going there. We didn't really catch on until about six o'clock last night when she didn't come home for dinner. Then I got in touch with her homeroom teacher and found out she'd been playing hooky all day. By that time it was dark already."

She looked at the window as if it was still dark, now and forever. I followed her glance. Two people were striding along the fairway, a man and a woman, both white-haired, as if they'd grown old in the quest for their small white ball.

"One thing I don't understand," I said. "If you thought she was going to school yesterday morning, what about the gun?"

"She must have put it in the trunk of her car," Sebastian said.

"I see. She's driving a car."

"That's one of the reasons we're so concerned." Sebastian pushed his face forward across the counter. I felt like a bartender being consulted by a drunk. But it was fear he was drunk on. "You've had some experience in these matters. Why would she take my shotgun, for heaven's sake?"

4

"I can think of one possible reason, Mr. Sebastian. You told her you'd blow her friend's head off with it."

"But she couldn't have taken me seriously."

"I do."

"So do I," his wife said.

Sebastian hung his head like a prisoner in the dock. But he said under his breath: "By God, I will kill him if he doesn't bring her back."

"Good thinking, Keith," his wife said.

Chapter 2

THE FRICTION BETWEEN the two was starting to rasp on my nerves. I asked Sebastian to show me his gun cabinet. He took me into a small study which was partly library and partly gun room.

There were light and heavy rifles standing upright behind glass in the mahogany gun cabinet, and an empty slot where a double-barreled shotgun had fitted. The bookshelves held a collection of best sellers and book-club editions, and one drab row of textbooks in economics and advertising psychology.

"Are you in advertising?"

"Public relations. I'm chief PR officer for Centennial Savings and Loan. Actually I should be there this morning. We're deciding on our program for next year."

"It can wait one day, can't it?"

"I don't know."

He turned to the gun cabinet, opening it and the drawer under it where he kept his shells. They unlocked with the same brass key.

"Where was the key?"

"In the top drawer of my desk." He opened the drawer and showed me. "Sandy knew where I kept it, of course."

"But anybody else could easily have found it."

"That's true. But I'm sure she took it."

"Why?"

"I just have a feeling."

"Is she gun-happy?"

"Certainly not. When you're properly trained in the use of guns, you don't become gun-happy, as you call it."

"Who trained her?"

"I did, naturally. I'm her father."

He went to the gun cabinet and touched the barrel of the heavy rifle. Carefully he closed the glass door and locked it. He must have caught his reflection in the glass. He backed away from it, scouring his bearded chin with his cupped palm.

"I look terrible. No wonder Bernice has been picking at me. My face is coming apart."

He excused himself and went away to put his face together. I took a peek at my own face in the glass. I didn't look too happy. Early morning was not my best thinking time, but I formulated a vague unhappy thought: Sandy was middle girl in a tense marriage and at the moment I was middle man.

Mrs. Sebastian came softly into the room and stood beside me in front of the gun cabinet.

"I married a boy scout," she said.

"There are sorrier fates."

"Name one. My mother warned me not to take up with a good-looking man. Marry brains, she told me. But I wouldn't listen. I should have stuck with my modeling career. At least I can depend on my own bones." She patted the hip nearest me.

"You have good bones. Also, you're very candid."

"I got that way in the course of the night."

"Show me your daughter's diary."

"I will not."

"Are you ashamed of her?"

"Of myself," she said. "What could the diary tell you that I can't tell you?"

"If she was sleeping with this boy, for instance."

"Of course she wasn't," she said with a little flash of anger. "Or anybody else."

"That's absurd." But her face went sallow.

"Was she?"

6

"Of course not. Sandy's remarkably innocent for her age."

"Or was. Let's hope she still is."

Bernice Sebastian retreated to higher ground. "I—we didn't hire you to pry into my daughter's morals."

"You didn't hire me, period. In a chancy case like this, I need a retainer, Mrs. Sebastian."

"What do you mean, chancy?"

"Your daughter could come home at any time. Or you and your husband could change your minds—"

She stopped me with an impatient flick of her hand. "All right, how much do you want?"

"Two days' pay and expenses, say two hundred and fifty."

She sat at the desk, got a checkbook out of the second drawer, and wrote me a check. "What else?"

"Some recent pictures of her."

"Sit down, I'll get you some."

When she was gone, I examined the checkbook stubs. After paying me my retainer, the Sebastians had less than two hundred dollars left in their bank account. Their smart new house cantilevered over a steep drop was an almost perfect image of their lives.

Mrs. Sebastian came back with a handful of pictures. Sandy was a serious-looking girl who resembled her mother in her dark coloring. Most of the pictures showed her doing things: riding a horse, riding a bicycle, standing on a diving board ready to dive, pointing a gun. The gun looked like the same .22 rifle as the one in the gun cabinet. She held it as if she knew how to use it.

"What about this gun bit, Mrs. Sebastian? Was it Sandy's idea?"

"It was Keith's. His father brought him up to hunt. Keith passed on the great tradition to his daughter." Her voice was sardonic.

"Is she your only child?"

"That's right. We have no son."

"May I go through her room?"

The woman hesitated. "What do you expect to find? Evidence of transvestitism? Narcotics?"

She was still trying to be sardonic, but the questions came through literally to me. I'd found stranger things than those in young people's rooms.

Sandy's room was full of sunlight and fresh sweet odors. I found pretty much what you'd expect to find in the bedroom of an innocent, serious high-school senior. A lot of sweaters and skirts and books, both high-school books and a few good novels like *A High Wind in Jamaica.* A menagerie of cloth animals. College pennants, mostly Ivy League. A pink-frilled vanity with cosmetics laid out on the top of it in geometrical patterns. The photograph of another young girl smiling from a silver frame on the wall.

"Who's that?"

"Sandy's best friend, Heidi Gensler."

"I'd like to talk to her."

Mrs. Sebastian hesitated. These hesitations of hers were brief but tense and somber, as if she was planning her moves far ahead in a high-stakes game.

"The Genslers don't know about this," she said.

"You can't look for your daughter and keep it a secret both at the same time. Are the Genslers friends of yours?"

"They're neighbors. The two girls are the real friends." She made her decision suddenly. "I'll ask Heidi to drop over before she goes to school."

"Why not right away?"

She left the room. I made a quick search of possible hiding places, under the pink oval lamb's-wool rug, between the mattress and springs, on the high dark shelf in the closet, behind and under the clothes in the chest of drawers. I shook out some of the books. From the center of *Sonnets from the Portuguese* a scrap of paper fluttered.

I picked it up from the rug. It was part of a lined notebook page on which someone had written in precise black script:

> Listen, bird, you give me a pain
> In my blood swinging about.
> I think I better open a vein
> And let you bloody well out.

Mrs. Sebastian was watching me from the doorway. "You're very thorough, Mr. Archer. What *is* that?"

"A little verse. I wonder if Davy wrote it."

8

She snatched it from between my fingers and read it. "It sounds quite meaningless to me."

"It doesn't to me." I snatched it back and put it in my wallet. "Is Heidi coming?"

"She'll be here in a little while. She's just finishing breakfast."

"Good. Do you have any letters from Davy?"

"Of course not."

"I thought he might have written to Sandy. I'd like to know if this verse is in his handwriting."

"I have no idea."

"I'm willing to bet it is. Do you have a picture of Davy?"

"Where would I get a picture of him?"

"The same place you got your daughter's diary."

"You needn't keep flinging that in my face."

"I'm not. I'd simply like to read it. It could give me a lot of help."

She went into another of her somber hesitations, straining her eyes ahead over the curve of time.

"Where is the diary, Mrs. Sebastian?"

"It doesn't exist any longer," she said carefully. "I destroyed it."

I thought she was lying, and I didn't try to conceal my thought. "How?"

"I chewed it up and swallowed it, if you must know. Now you've got to excuse me. I have a dreadful headache."

She waited at the doorway for me to come out of the room, then closed and locked the door. The lock was new.

"Whose idea was the lock?"

"Actually it was Sandy's. She wanted more privacy these last few months. More than she could use."

She went into another bedroom and shut the door. I found Sebastian back at the kitchen counter drinking coffee. He had washed and shaved and brushed his curly brown hair, put on a tie and a jacket and a more hopeful look.

"More coffee?"

"No thanks." I got out a small black notebook and sat beside him. "Can you give me a description of Davy?"

"He looked like a young thug to me."

"Thugs come in all shapes and sizes. What's his height, approximately?"

"About the same as mine. I'm six feet in my shoes."

"Weight?"

"He looks heavy, maybe two hundred."

"Athletic build?"

"I guess you'd say that." He had a sour competitive note in his voice. "But I could have taken him."

"No doubt you could. Describe his face."

"He isn't too bad-looking. But he has that typical sullen look they have."

"Before or after you offered to shoot him?"

Sebastian moved to get up. "Look here, if you're taking sides against me, what do you think we're paying you for?"

"For this," I said, "and for a lot of other dull interrogations. You think this is my idea of a social good time?"

"It's not mine, either."

"No, but it belongs to you. What color is his hair?"

"Blondish."

"Does he wear it long?"

"Short. They probably cut it off in prison."

"Blue eyes?"

"I guess so."

"Any facial hair?"

"No."

"What was he wearing?"

"The standard uniform. Tight pants worn low on the hips, a faded blue shirt, boots."

"How did he talk?"

"With his mouth." Sebastian's thin feelings were wearing thinner again.

"Educated or uneducated? Hip or square?"

"I didn't hear him say enough to know. He was mad. We both were."

"How would you sum him up?"

"A slob. A dangerous slob." He turned in a queer quick movement and looked at me wide-eyed, as if I'd just applied those words to him. "Listen, I have to get down to the office. We're having an important conference about next year's program. And then I'm going to have lunch with Mr. Hackett."

Before he left, I got him to give me a description of his daughter's car. It was a last year's Dart two-door, light green in color, which was registered in his name. He wouldn't let me put it on the official hot-car list. I wasn't to tell the police anything about the case.

"You don't know how it is in my profession," he said. "I have to keep up a stainless-steel front. If it slips, I slip. Confidence is our product in the savings and loan industry."

He drove away in a new Oldsmobile which, according to his check stubs, was costing him a hundred and twenty dollars a month.

Chapter 3

A FEW MINUTES LATER I opened the front door for Heidi Gensler. She was a clean-looking adolescent whose yellow hair hung straight onto her thin shoulders. She wore no makeup that I could see. She carried a satchel of books.

Her pale-blue gaze was uncertain. "Are you the man I'm supposed to talk to?"

I said I was. "My name is Archer. Come in, Miss Gensler."

She looked past me into the house. "Is it all right?"

Mrs. Sebastian emerged from her room wearing a fluffy pink robe. "Come in, Heidi dear, don't be afraid. It's nice of you to come." Her voice was not maternal.

Heidi stepped inside and lingered in the hallway, ill at ease. "Did something happen to Sandy?"

"We don't know, dear. If I tell you the bare facts, I want you to promise one thing: you mustn't talk about it at school, or at home, either."

"I wouldn't. I never have."

"What do you mean by that, dear: 'You never have'?"

Heidi bit her lip. "I mean—I don't mean anything."

Mrs. Sebastian moved toward her like a pink bird with a

keen dark outthrust head. "Did you know what was going on between her and that boy?"

"I couldn't help it."

"And yet you never told us? That wasn't very friendly of you, dear."

The girl was close to tears. *"Sandy* is my friend."

"Good. Fine. Then you'll help us get her safely home, won't you?"

The girl nodded. "Did she run away with Davy Spanner?"

"Before I answer that, remember you have to promise not to talk."

I said: "That's hardly necessary, Mrs. Sebastian. And I really prefer to do my own questioning."

She turned on me. "How can I know you'll be discreet?"

"You can't. You can't control the situation. It's out of control. So why don't you go away and let me handle this?"

Mrs. Sebastian refused to go. She looked ready to fire me. I didn't care. The case was shaping up as one on which I'd make no friends and very little money.

Heidi touched my arm. "You could drive me to school, Mr. Archer. I don't have a ride when Sandy isn't here."

"I'll do that. When do you want to go?"

"Any time. If I get there too early for my first class I can always do some homework."

"Did Sandy drive you to school yesterday?"

"No. I took the bus. She phoned me yesterday morning about this time. She said she wasn't going to school."

Mrs. Sebastian leaned forward. "Did she tell you where she *was* going?"

"No." The girl had put on a closed, stubborn look. If she did know anything more, she wasn't going to tell it to Sandy's mother.

Mrs. Sebastian said: "I think you're lying, Heidi."

The girl flushed, and water rose in her eyes. "You have no right to say that. You're not my mother."

I intervened again. Nothing worth saying was going to get said in the Sebastian house. "Come on," I told the girl, "I'll drive you to school."

We went outside and got into my car and started downhill toward the freeway. Heidi sat very sedately with her satchel of books between us on the seat. She'd probably remembered that she wasn't supposed to get into an automobile with a strange man. But after a minute she said: "Mrs. Sebastian blames *me*. It isn't fair."

"Blames you for what?"

"For everything Sandy does. Just because Sandy tells me things doesn't mean I'm responsible."

"Things?"

"Like about Davy. I can't run to Mrs. Sebastian with everything Sandy says. That would make me a stool pigeon."

"I can think of worse things."

"Like for instance?" I was questioning her code, and she spoke with some defiance.

"Like letting your best friend get into trouble and not lifting a finger to prevent it."

"I didn't *let* her. How could I stop her? Anyway, she isn't in trouble, not in the way you mean."

"I'm not talking about having a baby. That's a minor problem compared with the other things that can happen to a girl."

"What other things?"

"Not living to have a baby. Or growing old all of a sudden."

Heidi made a thin sound like a small frightened animal. She said in a hushed voice: "That's what happened to Sandy, in a way. How did you know that?"

"I've seen it happen to other girls who couldn't wait. Do you know Davy?"

She hesitated before answering. "I've met him."

"What do you think of him?"

"He's quite an exciting personality," she said carefully. "But I don't think he's good for Sandy. He's rough and wild. I think he's crazy. Sandy isn't any of those things." She paused in solemn thought. "A bad thing happened to her, is all. It just *happened*."

"You mean her falling for Davy?"

"I mean the other one. Davy Spanner isn't so bad compared with the other one."

"Who's he?"

"She wouldn't tell me his name, or anything else about him."

"So how do you know that Davy's an improvement?"

"It's easy to tell. Sandy's happier than she was before. She used to talk about suicide all the time."

"When was this?"

"In the summer, before school started. She was going to walk into the ocean at Zuma Beach and swim on out. I talked her out of it."

"What was bothering her—a love affair?"

"I guess you could call it that."

Heidi wouldn't tell me anything further. She'd given Sandy her solemn oath never to breathe a word, and she had already broken it by what she'd said to me.

"Did you ever see her diary?"

"No. I know she kept one. But she never showed it to anybody, ever." She turned toward me in the seat, pulling her skirt down over her knees. "May I ask you a question, Mr. Archer?"

"Go ahead."

"Just what happened to Sandy? This time, I mean?"

"I don't know. She drove away from home twenty-four hours ago. The night before, her father broke up a date she was having with Davy in West Hollywood. He dragged her home and locked her up overnight."

"No wonder Sandy left home," the girl said.

"Incidentally, she took along her father's shotgun."

"What for?"

"I don't know. But I understand Davy has a criminal record."

The girl didn't respond to the implied question. She sat looking down at her fists, which were clenched in her lap. We reached the foot of the slope and drove toward Ventura Boulevard.

"Do you think she's with Davy now, Mr. Archer?"

"That's the assumption I'm going on. Which way?"

"Wait a minute. Pull over to the side."

I parked in the sharp morning shadow of a live oak which had somehow survived the building of the freeway and the boulevard.

"I know where Davy lives," Heidi said. "Sandy took me to his pad once." She used the shabby word with a certain pride, as if it proved that she was growing up. "It's in the Laurel Apartments in Pacific Palisades. Sandy told me he gets his

14

apartment free, for looking after the swimming pool and stuff."

"What happened when you visited his place?"

"Nothing happened. We sat around and talked. It was very interesting."

"What did you talk about?"

"The way people live. The bad morals people have today."

I offered to drive Heidi the rest of the way to school, but she said she could catch a bus. I left her standing on the corner, a gentle creature who seemed a little lost in a world of high velocities and low morals.

Chapter 4

I LEFT SEPULVEDA at Sunset Boulevard, drove south to the business section of Pacific Palisades, and made a left turn on Chautauqua. The Laurel Apartments were on Elder Street, a slanting street on the long gradual slope down to the sea.

It was one of the newer and smaller apartment buildings in the area. I left my car at the curb and made my way into the interior court.

The swimming pool was sparkling. The shrubs in the garden were green and carefully clipped. Red hibiscus and purple princess flowers glowed among the leaves.

A woman who sort of went with the red hibiscus came out of one of the ground-floor apartments. Under her brilliant housecoat, orange on black, her body moved as though it was used to being watched. Her handsome face was a little coarsened by the dyed red hair that framed it. She had elegant brown legs and bare feet.

In a pleasant, experienced voice that hadn't been to college she asked me what I wanted.

"Are you the manager?"

"I'm Mrs. Smith, yes. I own this place. I don't have any vacancies at the moment."

I told her my name. "I'd like to ask you some questions if I may."

"What about?"

"You have an employee named Davy Spanner."

"Do I?"

"I understood you did."

She said with a kind of weary defensiveness: "Why don't you people leave him alone for a change?"

"I've never laid eyes on him."

"But you're a policeman, aren't you? Keep after him long enough and you'll push him over the edge again. Is that what you want?" Her voice was low but full of force, like the mutter of a furnace.

"No, and I'm not a policeman."

"Probation officer then. You're all the same to me. Davy Spanner's a good boy."

"And he's got at least one good friend," I said, hoping to change the tone of the interview.

"If you mean me, you're not wrong. What do you want with Davy?"

"Just to ask him a few questions."

"Ask me instead."

"All right. Do you know Sandy Sebastian?"

"I've met her. She's a pretty little thing."

"Is she here?"

"She doesn't live here. She lives with her parents, some-place in the Valley."

"She's been missing from home since yesterday morning. Has she been here?"

"I doubt it."

"What about Davy?"

"I haven't seen him this morning. I just got up myself." She peered up at the sky like a woman who loved the light but hadn't always lived in it. "So you are a cop."

"A private detective. Sandy's father hired me. I think you'd be wise to let me talk to Davy."

"I'll do the talking. You don't want to set him off."

She led me to a small apartment at the rear beside the entrance to the garages. The name "David Spanner" had been

inscribed on a white card on the do♦
hand as the verse that had fallen out of S♦

Mrs. Smith knocked lightly and when s♦
called out: "Davy."

There were voices somewhere behind the door♦ ♦g
man's voice and then a girl's which set my heart po♦ ♦ing
for no good reason. I heard the soft pad of footsteps. The
door opened.

Davy was no taller than I was, but he seemed to fill the
doorway from side to side. Muscles crawled under his black
sweatshirt. His blond head and face had a slightly unfinished
look. He peered out at the sunlight as if it had rejected him.

"You want me?"

"Is your girl friend with you?" Mrs. Smith had a note in
her voice which I couldn't quite place. I wondered if she was
jealous of the girl.

Apparently Davy caught the note. "Is there something the
matter?"

"This man seems to think so. He says your girl friend is
missing."

"How can she be missing? She's right here." His voice was
flat, as though he was guarding his feelings. "Her father sent
you, no doubt," he said to me.

"That's right."

"Go back and tell him this is the twentieth century, second
half. Maybe there was a time when a chick's old man could
get away with locking her up in her room. The day's long
past. Tell old man Sebastian that."

"He isn't an old man. But he's aged in the last twenty-four
hours."

"Good. I hope he dies. And so does Sandy."

"May I talk to her?"

"I'll give you exactly one minute." To Mrs. Smith he said:
"Please go away for a minute."

He spoke to both of us with a certain authority, but it was
a slightly manic authority. The woman seemed to feel this.
She moved away across the court without an argument or a
backward glance, as if she was deliberately humoring him. As
she sat down by the pool I wondered again in exactly what
capacity she employed him.

...locking the doorway with his body, he turned and called to the girl: "Sandy? Come here a minute."

She came to the doorway wearing dark glasses which robbed her face of meaning. Like Davy, she had on a black sweatshirt. Her body thrust itself forward and leaned on Davy's with the kind of heartbroken lewdness that only very young girls are capable of. Her face was set and pale, and her mouth hardly moved when she spoke.

"I don't know you, do I?"

"Your mother sent me."

"To drag me back home again?"

"Your parents are naturally interested in your plans. If any."

"Tell them they'll find out soon enough." She didn't sound angry in the usual sense. Her voice was dull and even. Behind the dark glasses she seemed to be looking at Davy instead of me.

There was some kind of passion between them. It gave off a faint wrong smoky odor, like something burning where it shouldn't be, arson committed by children playing with matches.

I didn't know how to talk to them. "Your mother's pretty sick about this, Miss Sebastian."

"She'll be sicker."

"That sounds like a threat."

"It is. I guarantee that she'll be sicker."

Davy shook his head at her. "Don't say anything more. Anyway his minute is up." He made an elaborate show of checking his wrist watch, and I caught a glimpse of what went on in his head: large plans and intricate hostilities and a complicated schedule which didn't always jibe with reality. "You've had your minute. Good-bye."

"Hello again. I need another minute, or maybe two." I wasn't deliberately crossing the boy, but I wasn't avoiding it, either. It was important to know how wild he really was. "Do me a favor, Miss Sebastian. Take off your glasses so I can see you."

She reached for her glasses with both hands, and lifted them from her face. Her eyes were hot and lost.

"Put them back on," Davy said.

She obeyed him.

"You take orders from me, bird. From nobody else." He turned on me. "As for you, I want you to be out of sight in one minute. That's an order."

"You're not old enough to be giving orders to anybody. When I leave, Miss Sebastian goes along."

"You think so?" He pushed her inside and shut the door. "She's never going back to that dungeon."

"It's better than shacking up with a psycho."

"I'm not a psycho!"

To prove it he swung his right fist at my head. I leaned back and let it go by. But his left followed very quickly, catching me on the side of the neck. I staggered backward into the garden, balancing the wobbling sky on my chin. My heel caught on the edge of the concrete deck around the pool. The back of my head rapped the concrete.

Davy came between me and the sky. I rolled sideways. He kicked me twice in the back. I got up somehow and closed with him. It was like trying to wrestle with a bear. He lifted me clear off my feet.

Mrs. Smith said: "Stop it!" She spoke as if he really was some half-tamed animal. "Do you want to go back to jail?"

He paused, still holding me in a bear hug that inhibited my breathing. The redheaded woman went to a tap and started a hose running. She turned it full on Davy. Some of the water splashed on me.

"Drop him."

Davy dropped me. The woman kept the hose on him, aiming at the middle of his body. He didn't try to take it away from her. He was watching me. I was watching a Jerusalem cricket which was crawling across the deck through the spilled water, like a tiny clumsy travesty of a man.

The woman spoke to me over her shoulder: "You better get the hell out of here, troublemaker."

She was adding insult to injury, but I went. Not very far: around the corner where my car was parked. I drove around the block and parked it again on the slanting street above the Laurel Apartments. I couldn't see the inner court or the doors that opened onto it. But the entrance to the garage was clearly visible.

I sat and watched it for half an hour. My hot and wounded

feelings gradually simmered down. The kick-bruise in my back went right on hurting.

I hadn't expected to be taken. The fact that I had been meant I was getting old, or else that Davy was pretty tough. It didn't take me half an hour to decide that both of these things were probably true.

The name of the street I was parked on was Los Baños Street. It was a fairly good street, with new ranch houses sitting on pads cut one above another in the hillside. Each house was carefully different. The one across the street from me, for example, the one with the closed drapes, had a ten-foot slab of volcanic rock set into the front. The car in the driveway was a new Cougar.

A man in a soft leather jacket came out of the house, opened the trunk of the car, and got out a small flat disk which interested me. It looked like a roll of recording tape. The man noticed my interest in it and slipped it into the pocket of his jacket.

Then he decided to make something more of it. He crossed the street to my side, walking with swaggering authority. He was a large heavy man with a freckled bald head. In his big slack smiling face the sharp hard eyes came as a bit of a shock, like gravel in custard.

"You live around here, my friend?" he said to me.

"I'm just reconnoitering. You call it living around here?"

"We don't like strangers snooping. So how would you like to move along?"

I didn't want to attract attention. I moved along. With me I took the license number of the Cougar and the number of the house, 702 Los Baños Street.

I have a good sense of timing, or timing has a good sense of me. My car had just begun to move when a light-green compact backed out of the garage of the Laurel Apartments. As it turned downhill toward the coastal highway, I could see that Sandy was driving and Davy was with her in the front seat. I followed them. They turned right on the highway, went through a yellow light at the foot of Sunset, and left me gritting my teeth behind a red light.

I drove all the way to Malibu trying to pick them up again, but I had no luck. I went back to the Laurel Apartments on Elder Street.

Chapter 5

THE CARD ON THE DOOR of Apartment One said: "Mrs. Laurel Smith." She opened the door on a chain and growled at me:

"You drove him away. I hope you're satisfied."

"You mean they're gone for good?"

"I'm not talking to you."

"I think you'd better. I'm not a troublemaker by choice, but trouble can be made. If Davy Spanner's on probation, he broke it when he swung on me."

"You were asking for it."

"That depends on which side you're on. You're obviously on Davy's side. In which case you better cooperate with me."

She thought about this. "Cooperate how?"

"I want the girl. If I get her back in reasonable shape, in a reasonable period of time—like today—I won't bear down hard on Davy. Otherwise I will."

She unhooked the chain. "Okay, Mr. God. Come in. The place is a mess but then so are you."

She smiled with one side of her mouth and one eye. I think she wanted to be angry with me, but so many things had happened in her life that she couldn't stay angry. One of the things that had happened to her, I could tell by her breath, was alcohol.

The clock on her mantel said it was half past ten. The clock was under a bell jar, as if to shield Laurel Smith from the passage of time. The other things in the living room, the overstuffed furniture and the gewgaws and the litter of magazines, had an unlived-with feeling. It was like a waiting room where you couldn't relax, for fear that the dentist would call you in any minute. Or the psychiatrist.

The small television set in one corner of the room was on, with the sound turned off. Laurel Smith said apologetically:

"I never used to watch TV. But I won this thing in a contest a couple of weeks ago."

"What kind of a contest?"

"One of those telephone contests. They called me up and asked me what was the capital of California. I said Sacramento, and they told me I'd won a portable TV set, just like that. I thought it was a gag, but within the hour they turned up here with the set."

She switched it off. We sat facing each other at opposite ends of the chesterfield.

There was a cloudy glass on the coffee table between us. The picture window behind us was full of blue sky and blue sea.

"Tell me about Davy."

"There isn't much to tell. I took him on a couple of months ago."

"In what sense took him on?"

"To do the clean-up work around the place. He needed a part-time job, he's planning to start at junior college the first of the year. You wouldn't know it the way he acted this morning, but he's an ambitious young man."

"Did you know he'd been in jail when you hired him?"

"Naturally I did. That's what got me interested in his case. I've had my own share of troubles—"

"Troubles with the law?"

"I didn't say that. And let's not talk about me, eh? I've had a little luck in real estate, and I like to spread the luck around a little. So I gave Davy a job."

"Have you talked to him at any length?"

She let out a short laugh. "I'll say I have. That boy will talk your arm off."

"What about?"

"Any subject. His main subject is how the country is going to the dogs. He may be right at that. He says his time in jail gave him a worm's-eye view of the whole business."

"He sounds like a poolroom lawyer to me."

"Davy's more than that," she said defensively. "He's more than just a talker. And he isn't the poolroom type. He's a serious boy."

"What's he serious about?"

"He wants to grow up and be a real man and do something useful."

"I think he's conning you, Mrs. Smith."

"No." She shook her artificial head. "He isn't conning me. He may be conning himself a little. God knows he's got his problems. I've talked to his probation officer—" She hesitated.

"Who is his probation officer?"

"I forget his name." She went to the telephone directory in the hall and consulted the front of it. "Mr. Belsize. Do you know him?"

"We've met. He's a good man."

Laurel Smith sat down nearer me. She seemed to be warming up slightly, but her eyes were still watchful. "Mr. Belsize admitted to me that he was taking a chance on Davy. Recommending him for probation, I mean. He said Davy might make it and then again he might not. I said I was willing to take my chances, too."

"Why?"

"You can't just live for yourself. I found that out." A sudden smile lit her face. "I sure picked a hot potato, didn't I?"

"You sure did. Did Belsize say what was the matter with him?"

"He has emotional trouble. When he gets mad he thinks we're all his enemies. Even me. He never lifted his hand against me, though. Or anybody else until this morning."

"That you know of."

"I know he's been in trouble in the past," she said. "But I'm willing to give him the benefit. You don't know what that boy's been through—orphanages and foster homes and getting kicked around. He never had a home of his own, he never had a father or a mother."

"He still has to learn to handle himself."

"*I* know that. I thought you were beginning to sympathize."

"I do sympathize, but that won't help Davy. He's playing house and other games with a young girl. He's got to bring her back. Her parents could hang a rap on him that would put him away until he's middle-aged."

She pressed her hand against her breast. "We can't let that happen."

"Where would he have taken her, Mrs. Smith?"

"I don't know."

She raked her dyed head with her finger, then rose and went to the picture window. With her back to me, her body was simply an object, an odalisque shape against the light. Framed in dark-red curtains, the sea looked old as the Mediterranean, old as sin.

"Has he brought her here before?" I said to her black-and-orange back.

"He brought her to introduce her to me last week—week before last."

"Were they planning to get married?"

"I don't think so. They're too young. I'm sure Davy has other plans."

"What are his plans?"

"I told you, about going to school and all. He wants to be a doctor or a lawyer."

"He'll be lucky if he just stays out of jail."

She turned to me, clutching and pulling at her hands. Their friction made a dry anxious sound. "What can *I* do?"

"Let me search his apartment."

She was silent for a minute, looking at me as if she found it hard to trust a man.

"I guess that is a good idea."

She got her keys, a heavy clinking loop like an overgrown charm bracelet. The card with "David Spanner" written on it was missing from his door. That seemed to imply that he wasn't coming back.

The apartment was a single room with two convertible beds at right angles in a corner. Both beds had been slept in and left unmade. Mrs. Smith pulled back the covers and examined the sheets.

"I can't tell if they were sleeping together," she said.

"I assume they were."

She gave me a worried look. "The girl isn't Quentin quail, is she?"

"No. But if he takes her someplace against her will—or if she wants out and he uses force—"

"I know, that's kidnapping. But Davy wouldn't do that to her. He likes her."

I opened the closet. It was empty.

"He didn't have much in the way of clothes," she said. "He didn't care about clothes and things like that."

"What did he care about?"

"Cars. But on probation he isn't allowed to drive. I think that's one reason he took up with the girl. She has a car."

"And her father had a shotgun. Davy has it now."

She turned so quickly that the skirt of her housecoat flared out. "You didn't tell me that before."

"What makes it so important?"

"He might shoot somebody."

"Anyone in particular?"

"He doesn't *know* anybody," she said foolishly.

"That's good."

I went through the rest of the place. There were sliced ham and cheese and milk in the little refrigerator in the kitchenette. I found a few books on the desk by the window: *The Prophet,* and a book about Clarence Darrow, and one about an American doctor who had built a hospital in Burma. Meager wings to fly on.

Tacked up over the desk was a list of ten "Don'ts." They were written out in the precise hand I recognized as Davy's:

1. *Don't drive cars.*
2. *Don't drink alcoholic beverages.*
3. *Don't stay up too late—the night is the bad time.*
4. *Don't frequent crummy joints.*
5. *Don't make friends without careful investigation.*
6. *Don't use dirty language.*
7. *Don't use 'ain't' and other vulgarisms.*
8. *Don't sit around and brood about the past.*
9. *Don't hit people.*
10. *Don't get mad and be an instant enemy.*

"You see what kind of a boy he is?" Laurel said at my shoulder. "A real trier."

"You're fond of him, aren't you?"

She didn't answer directly. "You'd like him, too, if you only got to know him."

"Maybe." Davy's list of self-regulations was kind of touching, but I read it with a different eye from Laurel's. The boy was beginning to know himself, and didn't like what he saw.

I went through the desk. It was empty except for a sheet of paper jammed into the back of the bottom drawer. I spread it out on the desk top. It was covered with a map, crudely drawn in ink, of a ranch or large estate. Its various features were labeled in a girlish unformed hand: "main house," "garage with L.'s apt.," "artificial lake and dam," "road from highway" passing through a "locked gate."

I showed the map to Laurel Smith. "Does this mean anything to you?"

"Not a thing." But her eyes had grown small and intent. "Should it?"

"It looks as if they've been casing some joint."

"More likely they were just doodling."

"Some doodle." I folded the map and put it in my inside pocket.

"What are you going to do with that?" she said.

"Find the place. If you know where it is you could save me a lot of trouble."

"I don't," she said abruptly. "Now if you're finished in here, I've got other things to do."

She stood by the door till I went out. I thanked her. She shook her head gloomily; "You're not welcome. Listen, how much would you take to lay off Davy? Lay off the whole damn business?"

"I can't."

"Sure you can. I'll give you five hundred."

"No."

"A thousand? A thousand cash, no taxes to pay."

"Forget it."

"A thousand cash and me. I look better without my clothes on." She nudged my arm with her breast. All it did was make my kidneys hurt.

"It's a handsome offer but I can't take it. You're forgetting about the girl. I can't afford to."

"To hell with her and to hell with you." She walked away to her apartment, swinging her keys.

I went into the garage. Against the dim rear wall was a workbench littered with tools: hammer, screwdrivers, pliers, wrenches, a hacksaw. A small vise was attached to the bench. Under it and around it, bright new iron filings mixed with sawdust were scattered on the concrete floor.

The filings suggested a queer idea to my mind. I made a further search, which ended up in the rafters of the garage. Wrapped in a dirty beach towel and a rolled-up carpet remnant I found the two barrels and the stock which Davy had sawed off the shotgun. They gave me an ugly moment: they were like the leavings of a major amputation.

Chapter 6

I PUT THE SEVERED BARRELS and stock in the trunk of my car and drove to my office on Sunset. From there I phoned Keith Sebastian at Centennial Savings and Loan. His secretary told me he had just gone out for lunch.

I made an appointment with Sebastian for early afternoon. In order not to waste the noon hour I put in a call to Jacob Belsize before I left my office.

Belsize remembered me. When I mentioned Davy Spanner's name, he agreed to meet me for lunch at a restaurant near his building on South Broadway.

I found him waiting for me in a booth. I hadn't seen Jake Belsize in several years, and he had aged in the interval. His hair was almost white now. The lines around his mouth and eyes reminded me of the fissured clay surrounding desert water holes.

The Special Businessman's Dollar Lunch was a hot beef sandwich with French frieds and coffee. Belsize ordered it, and so did I. When the waitress had taken our order, he spoke under the clatter and buzz of eating, talking men:

"You weren't too clear on the phone. What's Davy been up to?"

"Aggravated assault. He stomped me in the kidneys."

Jake's dark eyes jumped. He was one of the good ones who never could stop caring. "You going to press charges?"

"I may. But he's got heavier charges to worry about. I

can't mention names because my client won't let me. His daughter is a high-school girl. She's been gone for a day and a night—a night which she spent with Davy in his apartment."

"Where are they now?"

"Driving around in her car. When I lost them, they were on the coast highway headed for Malibu."

"How old is the girl?"

"Seventeen."

He took a deep breath. "That isn't good. But it could be worse."

"It is worse, if you knew all the details. It's much worse."

"Tell me the details. What kind of a girl is she?"

"I saw her for two minutes. I'd say she's a nice girl in serious trouble. This seems to be her second go-round with sex. The first go-round made her suicidal, according to a friend of hers. This time could be worse. I'm guessing, but I'd say that the girl and Davy are spurring each other on to do something really wild."

Belsize leaned across the table toward me. "What do you think they might do?"

"I think they're building up to some kind of crime."

"What kind of crime?"

"You tell me. He's your boy."

Belsize shook his head. The lines in his face deepened, like cracks in his conception of himself. "He's mine in a very limited sense. I can't follow him down the street or out on the highway. I have a hundred and fifty clients, a hundred and fifty Davy Spanners. They walk through my dreams."

"I know you can't make it for them," I said, "and nobody's blaming you. I came here to get your professional judgment on Davy. Does he go in for crimes against the person?"

"He never has, but he's capable of it."

"Homicide?"

Belsize nodded. "Davy's pretty paranoid. When he feels threatened or rejected he loses his balance. One day in my office he almost jumped *me*."

"Why?"

"It was just before his sentencing. I told him I was recommending that he be sent to jail for six months as a condition of probation. It triggered something in him, something from the past, I don't know what. We don't have a complete history on Davy. He lost his parents and spent his early years in an orphanage, until foster parents took him on. Anyway, when I told him what I was going to do, he must have felt abandoned all over again. Only now he was big and strong and ready to kill me. Fortunately I was able to talk him back to his senses. And I didn't revoke my recommendation for probation."

"That took faith."

Belsize shrugged. "I'm a faith healer. I learned a good many years ago that I have to take my chances. If I won't take a chance on them, I can't expect them to take a chance on themselves."

The waitress brought our sandwiches, and for a few minutes we were busy with them. At least I was busy with mine. Belsize picked at his as if Davy and I had spoiled his appetite. Finally he pushed it away.

"I have to learn not to hope too much," he said. "I have to school myself to remember that they have two strikes on them before I ever see them. One more and they're whiffed." He raised his head. "I wish you'd give me all the facts about Davy."

"They wouldn't make you any happier. And I don't want you putting out an alarm for him and the girl. Not until I talk to my client, anyway."

"What do you want me to do?"

"Answer a few more questions. If you were high on Davy, why did you recommend six months in jail?"

"He needed it. He'd been stealing cars on impulse, probably for years."

"For sale?"

"For joy riding. Or grief riding, as he calls it. He admitted when we'd established rapport that he had driven all over the state. He told me he was looking for his people, his own people. I believed him. I hated to send him to jail. But I thought six months in a controlled situation would give him a chance to cool off, time to mature."

"Did it?"

"In some ways. He finished his high-school education and did a lot of extra reading. But of course he still has problems to work out—if he'll only give himself the time."

"Psychiatric problems?"

"I prefer to call them life problems," Belsize said. "He's a boy who never really had anybody or anything of his own. That is a lot of not-having. I thought, myself, a psychiatrist could help him. But the psychologist who tested him for us didn't think he'd be a good investment."

"Because he's semi-psychotic?"

"I don't pin labels on young people. I see their adolescent storms. I've seen them take every form that you could find in a textbook of abnormal psychology. But often when the storms pass, they're different and better people." His hands turned over, palms upward, on the table.

"Or different and worse."

"You're a cynic, Mr. Archer."

"Not me. I was one of the ones who turned out different and better. Slightly better, anyway. I joined the cops instead of the hoods."

Belsize said with a smile that crumpled his whole face: "I still haven't made my decision. My clients think I'm a cop. The cops think I'm a hood-lover. But we're not the problem, are we?"

"Do you have any idea where Davy would go?"

"He might go anywhere at all. Have you talked to his employer? I don't recall her name at the moment but she's a redheaded woman—"

"Laurel Smith. I talked to her. How did she get into the picture?"

"She offered him a part-time job through our office. This was when he got out of jail about two months ago."

"Had she known him before?"

"I don't believe so. I think she's a woman who wanted someone to help."

"And what did she expect in return?"

"You are a cynic," he said. "People often do good simply because it's their nature. I think Mrs. Smith may have had troubles of her own."

"What makes you think so?"

"I had an inquiry on her from the sheriff's office in Santa Teresa. This was about the time that Davy got out of jail."

"An official inquiry?"

"Semi-official. A sheriff's man named Fleischer came to my

office. He wanted to know all about Laurel Smith and all about Davy. I didn't tell him much. Frankly, I didn't like him, and he wouldn't explain why he needed the information."

"Have you checked Laurel Smith's record?"

"No. It didn't seem necessary."

"I would if I were you. Where did Davy live before he went to jail?"

"He'd been on his own for a year or more after he dropped out of high school. Living on the beaches in the summer, taking odd jobs in the winter."

"Before that?"

"He lived with foster parents, Mr. and Mrs. Edward Spanner. He took their name."

"Can you tell me where to find the Spanners?"

"They live in West Los Angeles. You can find them in the phone book."

"Is Davy still in touch with them?"

"I don't know. Ask them yourself." The waitress brought our checks, and Belsize stood up to go.

Chapter 7

THE CENTENNIAL SAVINGS building on Wilshire was a new twelve-story tower sheathed with aluminum and glass. An automatic elevator took me up to Sebastian's office on the second floor.

The violet-eyed secretary in the outer room told me that Sebastian was expecting me. "But," she added in an important tone, "Mr. Stephen Hackett is with him now."

"The big boss himself?"

She frowned and shushed me. "Mr. Hackett came back from lunch with Mr. Sebastian. But he likes to stay incognito.

This is just the second time I ever saw him myself." She sounded as if they were having a visit from royalty.

I sat on a settee against the wall. The girl got up from her typewriter desk and, to my surprise, came and sat down beside me.

"Are you a policeman or a doctor or something?"

"I'm a something."

She was offended. "You don't have to tell me if you don't want to."

"That's true."

She was silent for a time. "I'm concerned about Mr. Sebastian."

"So am I. What makes you think I'm a doctor or a cop?"

"The way he talked about you. He's very anxious to see you."

"Did he say why?"

"No, but I heard him crying in there this morning." She indicated the door of the inner office. "Mr. Sebastian is a very cool person in general. But he was actually crying. I went in and asked him if I could help. He said nothing could help, that his daughter was very ill." She turned and looked deep into my eyes with her ultraviolet ones. "Is that true?"

"It could be. Do you know Sandy?"

"I know her to see. What's the matter with her?"

I didn't have to offer a diagnosis. There was a soft scuffling of feet in the inner office. By the time Sebastian had opened the door the girl was back at her desk, looking as permanent as a statue in a niche.

Stephen Hackett was a well-kept man of forty or so, younger than I expected. His thick body borrowed some grace from his well-tailored tweeds, which looked like Bond Street. His scornful eyes flicked over me as if I was a misplaced piece of furniture. He gave the impression of wearing his money the way other men wear elevator shoes.

Sebastian clearly hated to see him go, and tried to follow him out to the elevator. Hackett turned at the door and gave him a quick handshake and a definite, "Good-bye. Keep up the good work."

Sebastian came back to me with bright dreaming eyes. "That was Mr. Hackett. He likes my program very very much." He was bragging to the girl as well as me.

"I knew he would," she said. "It's a brilliant program."

"Yeah, but you never can tell."

He took me into his office and closed the door. It wasn't large, but it was a corner room overlooking the boulevard and the parking lot. I looked down and saw Stephen Hackett step over the door of a red sports car and drive away.

"He's a terrific sportsman," Sebastian said.

His hero worship annoyed me. "Is that all he does?"

"He keeps an eye on his interests, of course. But he doesn't bother with active management."

"Where does his money come from?"

"He inherited a fortune from his father. Mark Hackett was one of those fabulous Texas oilmen. But Stephen Hackett is a moneymaker in his own right. Just in the last few years, for example, he bought out Centennial Savings and put up this building."

"Good for him. Jolly good for him."

Sebastian gave me a startled look and sat down behind his desk. On it were stand-up photographs of Sandy and his wife, and a pile of advertising layouts. The top one said in archaic lettering: "We respect other people's money just as profoundly as we respect our own."

I waited for Sebastian to shift gears. It took a while. He had to shift from the world of money, where being bought out by a millionaire was the finest thing you could hope for, back to his difficult private world. I liked Sebastian better since I learned that he had tears inside his curly head.

"I've seen your daughter within the last few hours."

"Really? Is she okay?"

"She seemed to be all right physically. Mentally, I don't know."

"Where did you see her?"

"She was with her friend in his apartment. I'm afraid she was in no mood to come home. Sandy seems to have quite a grudge against you and your wife."

I meant this to be a question. Sebastian picked up his daughter's photograph and studied it as if he could find the answer there.

"She always used to be crazy about me," he said. "We were real pals. Until last summer."

"What happened last summer?"

"She turned against me, against both of us. She practically stopped talking entirely, except when she flared up and called us bad things."

"I've heard she had a love affair last summer."

"A love affair? That's impossible at her age."

"It wasn't a happy love affair," I said.

"Who was the man?"

"I was hoping you could tell me."

His face underwent another change. His mouth and jaw went slack. His eyes were intent on something behind them, in his head.

"Where did you hear this?" he said.

"From a friend of hers."

"Are you talking about actual sexual relations?"

"There isn't much doubt that she's been having them, beginning last summer. Don't let it throw you."

But something had. Sebastian had a hang-dog look, and real fear in his eyes. He turned Sandy's picture face down on the desk as if to prevent it from seeing him.

I got out the amateurish map I'd found in Davy's desk and spread it out on top of Sebastian's desk. "Take a good look at this, will you? First of all, do you recognize the handwriting?"

"It looks like Sandy's writing." He picked up the map and studied it more closely. "Yes, I'm sure it's Sandy's. What does it mean?"

"I don't know. Do you recognize the place with the artificial lake?"

Sebastian scratched his head, with the result that one large curly lock fell down over one eye. It made him look furtive and a little shabby. He pushed the hair back carefully, but the shabbiness stayed on him.

"It looks like Mr. Hackett's place," he said.

"Where is it?"

"In the hills above Malibu. It's quite a showplace. But I don't know why Sandy would be drawing a map of it. Do you have any idea?"

"I have one. Before we talk about it I want you to see something. I got your shotgun back, or parts of it."

"What do you mean, parts of it?"

34

"Come down to the parking lot and I'll show you. I didn't want to bring it into the building."

We went down in the elevator and out to my car. I opened the trunk and unwrapped the sad amputated stock and barrels.

Sebastian picked them up. "Who did this?" He sounded shocked and furious. "Did Sandy do this?"

"More likely it was Davy."

"What kind of a vandal *is* he? That shotgun cost me a hundred and fifty dollars."

"I don't think this was vandalism. But it may lead to something worse. It almost certainly means that Davy's carrying a sawed-off shotgun. Put that together with Sandy's map of the Hackett place—"

"Good Lord, do you think they're planning to hold him up?"

"I think he should be warned of the possibility."

Sebastian made an abortive movement toward the building, then turned back toward me. He was full of anxiety, and some of it spilled. "We can't do that. You can't expect me to tell him my own daughter—"

"She drew the map. Does she know the place well?"

"Very well. The Hacketts have been very good to Sandy."

"Don't you think you owe them a warning?"

"Certainly not at this stage." He tossed the pieces of shotgun into the trunk, where they made a clanking noise. "We don't know for sure that they're planning anything. In fact, the more I think about it, the less likely it sounds. You can't expect me to go out there and ruin myself with the Hacketts —not to mention Sandy—"

"She'll really be ruined if her friend pulls a heist on the Hacketts. And so will you."

He went into deep thought, looking down at the asphalt between his feet. I watched the traffic go by on Wilshire. It usually made me feel better to watch traffic and not be in it. Not today.

"Does Hackett keep money and jewels in the house?"

"He wouldn't keep much money there. But his wife has diamonds. And they have a valuable art collection. Mr. Hackett has spent a lot of time in Europe buying pictures."

Sebastian paused. "What would you say to Hackett if you told him about this? I mean, could you keep Sandy out of it?"

"That's the whole point of what I'm trying to do."

"Why didn't you bring her home when you saw her?"

"She didn't want to come. I couldn't force her. I can't force you to go to Hackett with this information, either. But I think you should. Or else take it to the police."

"And get her thrown in jail?"

"They won't put her in jail if she hasn't done anything. Anyway, there are worse places than jail."

He looked at me with dislike. "You don't seem to realize, you're talking about my daughter."

"She's the only thing on my mind. You seem to have quite a few other things on yours. So here we stand while the whole thing slips away."

Sebastian bit his lip. He looked up at the metal and glass building as if for inspiration. But it was just a monument to money. He came closer to me and palpated my upper arm. He squeezed the muscles as if to compliment me and at the same time estimate my strength, in case we might come to blows.

"Look here, Archer, I don't see why you can't go out and talk to Mr. Hackett. Without telling him who's involved. You wouldn't have to mention my name *or* Sandy's."

"Is that what you want me to do?"

"It's the only sensible course. I can't believe that they're really planning anything drastic. Sandy's not a criminal."

"A young girl is whatever she runs with, usually."

"Not my daughter. She's never been in any kind of trouble."

I was tired of arguing with Sebastian. He was a man who believed whatever made him feel better at the moment.

"Have it your way. Was Hackett on his way home when he left you?"

"Yes, I think he was. You will go and see him then?"

"If you insist."

"And keep us out of it?"

"I may not be able to. Remember Hackett saw me in your office."

"Give him a story. You stumbled across this information and brought it to me because I work for his company. You and I are old friends, nothing more."

A good deal less. I made no promises. He told me how to find Hackett's place, and gave me his unlisted telephone number.

Chapter 8

I CALLED THE NUMBER from Malibu. A woman answered, and told me in a foreign accent that her husband wasn't home but she expected him at any moment. When I mentioned Sebastian's name she said she'd have someone meet me at the gate.

It was only a couple of miles from downtown Malibu. The gate was ten feet high, topped with barbed wire. On either side of it, a heavy wire fence plastered with "NO TRESPASSING" signs stretched off into the hills as far as I could see.

The man who was waiting for me at the gate was a lean Spanish type. His tight pants and loose haircut gave a youthful impression which his dark and ageless eyes repudiated. He made no attempt to conceal the heavy revolver in the belt holster under his jacket.

Before he opened the gate he made me show him the photostat of my license. "Okay, man. I guess it's okay."

He unlocked the gate and let me drive in, relocked it as I waited behind his jeep.

"Is Mr. Hackett here yet?"

He shook his head, got into his jeep, and led me up the private blacktop road. Once we had rounded the first curve, the place seemed almost as remote and untouched as backcountry. Quail were calling in the brush, and smaller birds were eating the red berries off the toyon. A couple of soaring vultures balanced high on a thermal were keeping an eye on things.

The road mounted a low pass and ran along the crest of

the wide earth dam which held back the water of the artificial lake. There were ducks on the water, pintails and cinnamon teal, and mud hens in the grass around its shore.

My escort drew his revolver and, without stopping his jeep, shot the nearest mud hen. I think he was showing off to me. All the ducks flew up, and all the mud hens but one ran like hell into the water, like little animated cartoons of terrified people.

The house was on a rise at the far end of the lake. It was wide and low and handsome, and it fitted the landscape so well that it looked like a piece of it.

Mrs. Hackett was waiting on the terrace in front of the house. She had on a brown wool suit, and her long yellow hair was done up in a loose bun at the nape of her neck. She was in her early thirties, pretty and plump and very fair. She called out angrily to the man in the jeep: "Was it you who fired that gun?"

"I shot a mud hen."

"I've asked you not to do that. It drives away the ducks."

"There's too many mud hens."

She went pale. "Don't talk back to me, Lupe."

They glared at each other. His face was like carved saddle leather. Hers was like Dresden porcelain. Apparently the porcelain won. Lupe drove away in the jeep and disappeared into one of the outbuildings.

I introduced myself. The woman turned to me, but Lupe was still on her mind. "He's insubordinate. I don't know how to handle him. I've been in this country for over ten years and I still don't understand Americans." Her accent was Middle European, probably Austrian or German.

"I've been here for over forty," I said, "and I don't understand Americans, either. Spanish-Americans are particularly hard to understand."

"I'm afraid you're not much help." She smiled, and made a small helpless gesture with her fairly wide shoulders.

"What's Lupe's job?"

"He looks after the place."

"Singlehanded?"

"It isn't as much work as you might think. We have a bonded maintenance service for the house and grounds. My husband dislikes to have servants underfoot. I miss having servants myself, we always had servants at home."

"Where's home?"

"'Bayerne,'" she said with heavy nostalgia. "Near München. My family has lived in the same house since the time of Napoleon."

"How long have you lived here?"

"Ten years. Stephen brought me to this country ten years ago. I'm still not used to it. In Germany the servant classes treat us with respect."

"Lupe doesn't act like a typical servant."

"No, and he isn't typical. My mother-in-law insisted that we hire him. He knows that." She sounded like a woman who needed someone to talk to. She must have heard herself. "I'm afraid I'm talking too much. But why are you asking me these questions?"

"It's a habit of mine. I'm a private detective."

Her eyes blurred with apprehension. "Has Stephen had an accident? Is that why he hasn't come home?"

"I hope not."

She looked at me accusingly. I was the messenger who brought bad news.

"You said on the telephone you were a friend of Keith Sebastian's."

"I know him."

"Has something happened to my husband? Is that what you're trying to say?"

"No. I suppose I'd better tell you why I'm here. May I sit down?"

"Of course. But come inside. It's getting cold out here in the wind."

She led me through a glass door, up a short flight of steps, and along a well-lit gallery hung with pictures. I recognized a Klee and a Kokoschka and a Picasso, and thought it was no wonder the place had a fence around it.

The living room commanded a broad view of the sea, which seemed from this height to slant up to the horizon. A few white sails clung to it like moths on a blue window.

Mrs. Hackett made me sit in an austere-looking steel-and-leather chair which turned out to be comfortable.

"Bauhaus," she said instructively. "Would you like a drink? Benedictine?"

She got a stone bottle and glasses out of a portable bar and poured small drinks for us. Then sat down confidentially with her round silk knees almost touching mine. "Now what is all this business?"

I told her that in the course of an investigation which I didn't specify, I'd stumbled on a couple of facts. Taken together they suggested that she and her husband might be in danger of robbery or extortion.

"Danger from whom?"

"I can't name names. But I think you'd be well advised to have the place guarded."

My advice was punctuated by a distant sound that resembled machine-gun fire. Hackett's red sports car came into view and scooted around the lake toward the house.

"Ach!" Mrs. Hackett said. "He's brought his mother with him."

"Doesn't she live here?"

"Ruth lives in Bel-Air. We are not enemies but neither are we friends. She is too close to Stephen. Her husband is younger than Stephen."

I seemed to have won Mrs. Hackett's confidence, and wondered if I really wanted it. She was handsome but a little fat and dull, and full of unpredictable emotions.

Her husband had stopped below the terrace and was helping his mother out of the car. She looked about his age, and dressed it. But if Hackett was forty, his mother had to be at least fifty-six or seven. As she came across the terrace on his arm, I could see the years accumulate behind her youthful façade.

Mrs. Hackett went to the window and waved at them rather lifelessly. The sight of her husband's mother seemed to drain her of energy.

The mother was introduced to me as Mrs. Marburg. She looked at me with the arithmetical eye of an aging professional beauty: would I be viable in bed?

Her son's eye was equally cold and calculating, but he was interested in other questions: "Didn't I see you in Keith Sebastian's office?"

"Yes."

"And you followed me out here? Why? I see you've made yourself cozy."

He meant the glasses on the coffee table. His wife flushed guiltily. His mother said in chiding coquetry: "I know you have a passion for privacy, Stephen. But don't be nasty, now. I'm sure the nice man has a very good explanation."

She reached for his hand. Hackett winced away from her touch, but it seemed to ground some of his static. He said in a more reasonable tone: "What *is* your explanation?"

"It was Sebastian's idea." I sat down and repeated the story I'd told his wife.

It seemed to upset all three of them. Hackett got a bottle of bourbon out of the portable bar and, without offering any of it around, poured himself a solid slug which he knocked back.

His German wife began to weep, without any sound, and then her hair came loose and flooded her shoulders. Hackett's mother sat down beside his wife and patted her broad back with one hand. The other hand plucked at her own throat where crepe had gathered in memory of her youth.

"It would help," Mrs. Marburg said to me, "if you'd lay out all the facts for us. By the way, I didn't catch your name."

"Lew Archer. I'm sorry I can't tell you much more than I have."

"But who are these people? How do we know they exist?"

"Because I say so."

Hackett said: "You could be angling for a bodyguard job."

"Guarding bodies isn't my idea of a decent job. I can give you the name of a good firm if you like." None of them seemed interested. "Of course you can do as you choose. People generally do."

Hackett saw that I was getting ready to leave.

"Now don't rush away, Mr. Archer. I really do appreciate your coming here." The whisky had humanized him, softening his voice and his perspective. "And I certainly don't mean to be inhospitable. Have a drink."

"One was enough, thanks." But I felt more friendly toward him. "You haven't had any threatening phone calls? Or letters asking for money?"

Hackett looked at his wife, and they both shook their

heads. He said: "May I ask a question? How do you know this-ah-criminal plot is directed against me?—against us?"

"I don't. But the people involved had a map of your place."

"*This* place, or the beach cottage?"

"This place. I thought that was good enough reason to come out here and talk to you."

"You're very thoughtful," Ruth Marburg said. Her voice was pleasant and a little coarse, a blend of Western drawls ranging from the Pacific Coast to the Gulf Coast. Under the sound of money, her voice remembered times when there hadn't been any. "I think we should pay Mr. Archer for his time."

Hackett got his wallet out and from the assortment of bills it contained selected a twenty. "This will take care of your time."

"Thanks, it's already taken care of."

"Go ahead, take it," Mrs. Marburg said. "It's good clean oil money."

"No thanks."

Hackett looked at me in surprise. I wondered how long it had been since anyone had refused a small piece of his money. When I made a move to leave he followed me into the gallery and started to name the artists represented.

"Do you like pictures?"

"Very much."

But Hackett's recital bored me. He told me how much each picture cost and how much it was worth now. He said he had made a profit on every picture he'd bought in the past ten years.

"Bully for you."

He cocked a pale eye at me. "Is that supposed to be funny?"

"No."

"That's good." But he was peeved. I'd failed to show proper respect for him and his money. "After all, you said that you were interested in paintings. These are some of the most valuable modern paintings in California."

"You told me."

"Very well, if you're not interested." He turned away, and then came back to me. "One thing I don't understand. Where does Keith Sebastian come in on all this?"

I told the lie I'd hoped to avoid telling: "I knew Keith worked for one of your companies. I went to him, and he sent me out here."

"I see."

Before Hackett saw too much, I got into my car and started for the gate. Lupe followed me in his jeep.

The ducks had not returned to the lake. The frightened mud hens had crossed to the far shore. In the distance they looked like a congregation of mourners.

Chapter 9

ON MY WAY BACK into the city I stopped at the Laurel Apartments to see if Davy and Sandy had come back there. The door of Laurel Smith's apartment was standing partly open. She didn't answer when I knocked. I listened, and heard the sound of snoring deep inside the place. I guessed that Laurel had drunk herself unconscious.

But when I went in and found her in the bathtub, I saw that she'd been hit by something heavier than alcohol. Her nose was bleeding and swollen; her eyes were puffed shut, her lips cut. The bathtub was dry, except for splashes of blood. Laurel still had on her orange and black housecoat.

I went to the phone and called the police, and asked at the same time for an ambulance. In the minutes before they arrived I gave the place a quick shakedown. The first thing I looked at was the portable television set. Laurel's account of winning it in a contest had sounded to me like a plant.

I took the back off. Glued to the inside of the cabinet was a plastic-encased bug, a miniature radio transmitter no larger than a pack of cigarettes. I left the bug where it was, and replaced the back of the set.

The other unusual thing I found was a negative fact. Nothing I came across in my hurried search suggested that Laurel

Smith had a personal history: no letters or old photographs or documents. I did find, in a purse in a bedroom drawer, a savings bank book with deposits totaling over six thousand dollars, and a dog-eared Social Security card in the name of Laurel Blevins.

The same drawer contained a sparsely populated address-book in which I found two names I recognized: Jacob Belsize, and Mr. and Mrs. Edward Spanner. I made a note of the Spanners' address, which wasn't too far from my own apartment in West Los Angeles. Then I put everything back in the drawer and pushed it shut.

I could hear the sound of the police siren rising from Pacific Coast Highway. It was a sound I hated: the howl of disaster in the urban barrens. It climbed Chautauqua and died like a wolf in Elder Street. The ambulance was whining in the distance.

I knew the two policemen who came in. Janowski and Prince were detective-sergeants from the Purdue Street station, men in their late thirties who were proud of their work and good at it. I had to tell them what I was doing there, but I suppressed Sandy's name. I gave them Davy Spanner's.

Prince said: "Did Spanner do that?" He jerked his thumb toward the bathroom, where by now two ambulance men were getting Laurel Smith onto a stretcher.

"I doubt it. They were good friends."

"How good?" Janowski said. He was a homely broad-faced Baltic type with a fair delicate skin.

"She gave him a job when he got out of jail."

"That's pretty good friends," Prince said. "What was he in for?"

"Car theft."

"So now he's doing postgraduate work in mayhem." Prince took crime personally. He was a former Golden Gloves welterweight who could have gone either way in his own life. Like me.

I didn't argue with them. If they picked up Davy, they'd probably be doing him a favor. And the afternoon was slipping away. I wanted to see the Spanners before it got too late.

We went outside and watched Laurel Smith being lifted into the ambulance. Three or four of the apartment dwellers, all women, had drifted out onto the sidewalk. Laurel was their landlady, and they undoubtedly knew her, but they didn't come too near. The snoring woman gave off the germs of disaster.

Janowski said to one of the attendants: "How bad is she hurt?"

"It's hard to say, with head injuries. She has a broken nose, and jaw, maybe a fractured skull. I don't think it was done with fists."

"With what?"

"A sap, or a truncheon."

Prince was questioning the women from the apartment building: none of them had heard or seen a thing. They were quiet and subdued, like birds when a hawk is in the neighborhood.

The ambulance rolled away. The women went into the building. Prince got into the police car and made a report in a low-pitched monotone.

Janowski went back into Laurel's apartment. I walked up to Los Baños Street for a second look at the house with volcanic rock built into the front. The drapes were still drawn. The Cougar was no longer in the driveway.

I wandered around to the back and found an unblinded sliding glass door. The room inside contained no furniture. I looked around the small back yard. It was overgrown with dry crabgrass, which the rains had failed to revive, and surrounded by a five-foot grapestake fence.

A woman looked over the fence from the next yard. She was an attempted blonde whose eyes were magnified by purple eye shadow.

"What do *you* want?"

"I'm looking for the man of the house."

"Big fellow with a bald head?"

"That's him."

"He left about an hour ago. It looked to me like he was moving out. Which would suit me just fine."

"How so?"

She threw me a sorrowful purple look over the grapestake fence. "You a friend of his?"

"I wouldn't say that."

"What do you want with him?"

45

"He was the one who wanted me. He called me out here to do some repairs."

"On that electronic equipment he had?"

"Right."

"You're too late. He took it with him. Piled it in the trunk of his car and took off. Good riddance, I say."

"Did he cause you any trouble?"

"Nothing you could put your finger on. But it was creepy having him next door, sitting all alone in an empty house. I think he's cracked myself."

"How do you know the house was empty?"

"I have my two good eyes," she said. "All he took in when he moved in was a camp cot and a folding chair and a card table and that radio equipment. And that was all he took out when he left."

"How long was he here?"

"A couple of weeks, off and on. I was getting ready to complain to Mr. Santee. It runs down the neighborhood when you don't put furniture in a house."

"Who's Mr. Santee?"

"Alex Santee. The agent I rent from. He's agent for that house, too."

"Where can I find Mr. Santee?"

"He has an office on Sunset." She pointed toward the Palisades downtown. "You've got to excuse me now, I've got something on the stove."

I went to the other side of the yard and looked downhill across several other back yards. I could see Laurel Smith's apartment. Her open door was in my direct line of vision. Detective-Sergeant Janowski came out and closed the door.

Chapter 10

ALEX SANTEE was a small middle-aged man with a bold stare masked by glasses. He was just closing his real-estate office when I arrived, but he was glad to stay open for a prospect.

"I only have a few minutes, though. I've an appointment to show a house."

"I'm interested in a house on Los Baños Street. 702, the one with the lava front."

"It is distinctive, isn't it? Unfortunately it's rented."

"Since when? It's standing empty."

"Since November 15 of this year. Do you mean the party hasn't moved in yet?"

"He's been and gone, according to the neighbors. Moved out today."

"That's peculiar." Santee shrugged. "Well, that's his privilege. If Fleischer has moved out, the house will be available for rental on the fifteenth of this month. Three hundred and fifty a month on a one-year lease, first and last months payable in advance."

"Maybe I better talk to him first. Did you say his name was Fleischer?"

"Jack Fleischer." Santee looked it up in his file and spelled it out. "The address he gave me was the Dorinda Hotel in Santa Monica."

"Did he say what business he was in?"

"He's a retired sheriff from someplace up north." He consulted the file again. "Santa Teresa. Maybe he decided to go back there."

The desk clerk at the Dorinda Hotel, a sad man with an exuberant pompadour hairpiece, didn't remember Jack Fleischer at first. After some research in the register he established that about a month ago, early in November, Fleischer had stayed there two nights.

In a passageway at the rear of the lobby, I found a phone booth and called the Spanners' number. A man's deep voice answered: "This is the Edward Spanner residence."

"Mr. Spanner?"

"Yes."

"This is Lew Archer. Mr. Jacob Belsize gave me your name. I'm conducting an investigation and I'd like very much to talk to you—"

"About Davy?" His voice had thinned.

"About Davy and a number of other things."

"Has he done something wrong again?"

"His employer has been beaten up. They just took her to the hospital."

"You mean Mrs. Smith? He never hurt a woman before."

"I'm not saying he did this. You know him better than anybody does, Mr. Spanner. Please give me a few minutes."

"But we were just sitting down to supper. I don't know why you people can't leave us alone. Davy hasn't lived with us for years. We never did adopt him, we're not legally responsible."

I cut him short: "I'll be there in half an hour."

The sun was setting as I left the hotel. It looked like a wildfire threatening the western edge of the city. Night comes quickly in Los Angeles. The fire was burnt out when I reached the Spanner house, and evening hung like thin smoke in the air.

It was a prewar stucco bungalow squeezed into a row of other houses like it. I knocked on the front door, and Edward Spanner opened it reluctantly. He was a tall thin man with a long face and emotional eyes. He had a lot of black hair, not only on his head but on his arms and on the backs of his hands. He was wearing a striped shirt with the sleeves rolled up, and gave off an old-fashioned impression, almost an odor, of soured good will.

"Come in, Mr. Archer. Welcome to our abode." He sounded like a man who had taught himself to speak correctly by reading books.

He took me through the living room, with its threadbare furnishings and its mottoes on the walls, into the kitchen

48

where his wife was sitting at the table. She wore a plain house-dress which emphasized the angularity of her body. There were marks of suffering on her face, relieved by a soft mouth and responsive eyes.

The Spanners resembled each other, and seemed very much aware of each other, unusually so for middle-aged people. Mrs. Spanner seemed rather afraid of her husband, or afraid for him.

"This is Mr. Archer, Martha. He wants to talk about Davy."

She hung her head. Her husband said by way of explanation: "Since you called me, my wife has made a little confession. Davy was here this afternoon while I was working. Apparently she wasn't going to tell me." He was speaking more to her than to me. "For all I know he comes here every day behind my back."

He'd gone too far, and she caught him off balance. "That isn't so, and you know it. And I was so going to tell you. I simply didn't want it to spoil your dinner." She turned to me, evading the direct confrontation with Spanner. "My husband has an ulcer. This business has been hard on both of us."

As if to illustrate her words, Spanner sat down at the head of the table and let his arms hang loose. A half-eaten plate of brown stew lay in front of him, glazing. I sat facing his wife across the table.

"When was Davy here?"

"A couple of hours ago," she said.

"Was anybody with him?"

"He had his girl friend with him. His fiancée. She's a *pretty* girl." The woman seemed surprised.

"What kind of a mood were they in?"

"They both seemed quite excited. They're planning to get married, you know."

Edward Spanner uttered a dry snortlike laugh.

"Did Davy tell you that?" I asked his wife.

"They both did." She smiled a little dreamily. "I realize they're young. But I was glad to see he picked a nice girl. I gave them a ten-dollar bill for a wedding present."

Spanner cried out in pain: "You gave him ten dollars? I cut ten heads of hair to clear ten dollars."

"I saved up the money. It wasn't your money."

Spanner shook his doleful head. "No wonder he went bad.

From the first day he came into our household you spoiled him rotten."

"I didn't. I gave him affection. He needed some, after those years in the orphanage."

She leaned over and touched her husband's shoulder, almost as if he and Davy were the same to her.

He rebounded into deeper despair: "We should have left him in the orphanage."

"You don't mean that, Edward. The three of us had ten good years."

"Did we? Hardly a day went by that I didn't have to use the razor strap on him. If I never heard of Davy again, I'd—"

She touched his mouth. "Don't say it. You care about him just as much as I do."

"After what he *did* to us?"

She looked across him at me. "My husband can't help feeling bitter. He put a lot of stock in Davy. He was a real good father to him, too. But Davy needed more than we could give him. And when he got into trouble the first time the Holy Brethren of the Immaculate Conception asked Edward to step aside as a lay preacher. That was a terrible blow to him, and with one thing and another we left town and moved here. Then Edward came down with his ulcer, and after that he was out of work for a long time—most of the last three years. Under the circumstances we couldn't do much for Davy. He was running loose by that time, anyway, running loose and living on his own most of the time."

Spanner was embarrassed by his wife's candor: "This is all ancient history."

"It's what I came to hear. You say you moved here from another town?"

"We lived most of our lives in Santa Teresa," she said.

"Do you know a man named Jack Fleischer?"

She looked at her husband. "Isn't that the name of the man who was here last month?"

I prompted them: "Big man with a bald head? Claims to be a retired policeman."

"That's him," she said. "He asked us a lot of questions about Davy, mainly his background. We told him what little we knew. We got him out of the Santa Teresa Shelter when he was six years old. He didn't have a last name, and so we gave him ours. I wanted to adopt him, but Edward felt we weren't up to the responsibility."

"She means," Spanner put in, "that if we adopted him the county wouldn't pay us for his board."

"But we treated him just like he was our own. We never had any children of our own. And I'll never forget the first time we saw him in the supervisor's office at the Shelter. He came right over to us and stood beside Edward and wouldn't go away. 'I want to stand beside the man,' was what he said. You remember, Edward."

He remembered. There was sorrowful pride in his eyes.

"Now he stands as tall as you do. I wish you'd seen him today."

She was quite a woman, I thought: trying to create a family out of a runaway boy and a reluctant husband, a wholeness out of disappointed lives.

"Do you know who his real parents were, Mrs. Spanner?"

"No, he was just an orphan. Some fieldworker died and left him in the tules. I found that out from the other man— Fleischer."

"Did Fleischer say why he was interested in Davy?"

"I didn't ask him. I was afraid to ask, with Davy on probation and all." She hesitated, peering into my face. "Do you mind if I ask you the same question?"

Spanner answered for me: "Mrs. Laurel Smith got beat up. I told you that."

Her eyes widened. "Davy wouldn't do that to Mrs. Smith. She was the best friend he had."

"I don't know what he'd do," Spanner said morosely. "Remember he hit a high-school teacher and that was the beginning of all our trouble."

"Was it a woman teacher?" I said.

"No, it was a man. Mr. Langston at the high school. There's one thing you can't get away with, and that's hitting a teacher. They wouldn't let him back in school after that. We didn't know what to do with him. He couldn't get a job. It's one reason we moved down here. Nothing went right for us after that." He spoke of the move as if it had been a banishment.

"There was more to it than hitting a teacher," his wife said. "Henry Langston wasn't a teacher really. He was what they call a counselor. He was trying to counsel Davy when it happened."

"Counsel him on what?"

"I never did get that clear."

Spanner turned to her: "Davy has mental trouble. You never faced up to that. But it's time you did. He had mental trouble from the time we took him out of the Shelter. He never warmed up to me. He was never a normal boy."

Slowly she wagged her head from side to side in stubborn negation. "I don't believe it."

Their argument had evidently been going on for years. Probably it would last as long as they did. I interrupted it: "You saw him today, Mrs. Spanner. Did he seem to have trouble on his mind?"

"Well, he's never cheerful. And he seemed to be pretty tense. Any young man is, these days, when he's getting ready to marry."

"Were they serious about getting married?"

"I'd say very serious. They could hardly wait." She turned to her husband: "I didn't mean to tell you this, but I guess it should all come out. Davy thought that maybe you would marry them. I explained you had no legal right, being just a lay preacher."

"I wouldn't marry him to anybody, anyway. I've got too much respect for the race of females."

"Did they say anything more about their plans, Mrs. Spanner? Where did they plan to get married?"

"They didn't say."

"And you don't know where they went after they left here?"

"No, I don't." But her eyes seemed to focus inward, as if she was remembering something.

"Didn't they give you some inkling?"

She hesitated. "You never answered *my* question. Why are you so interested? You don't really think he beat up Mrs. Smith?"

"No. But people are always surprising me."

She studied my face, leaning her elbows on the table. "You don't talk like a policeman. Are you one?"

"I used to be. I'm a private detective now—I'm not trying to pin anything on Davy."

"What *are* you trying to do?"

"Make sure the girl is safe. Her father hired me for that. She's only seventeen. She should have been in school today, not bucketing around the countryside."

No matter how unrewarding their own married lives may be, women seem to love the idea of weddings. Mrs. Spanner's wedding dream died hard. I watched it die.

"When I was out here in the kitchen making tea for them," she said, "I heard them talking in the living room. They were reading the wall mottoes out loud and making fun of them. That wasn't very nice, but maybe I shouldn't have been listening to them. Anyway, they made a joke about the Unseen Guest. Davy said that Daddy Warbucks was going to have an unseen guest tonight."

Spanner exploded: "That's blasphemy!"

"Was anything else said on the subject?"

"He asked the girl was she sure she could get him in. She said it would be easy, Louis knew her."

"Louis?" I said. "Or Lupe?"

"It could have been Lupe. Yes, I'm pretty sure it was. Do you know who they were talking about?"

"I'm afraid I do. May I use your telephone?"

"Long as it isn't long distance," Spanner said prudently.

I gave him a dollar and called the Hacketts' number in Malibu. A woman's voice which I didn't recognize at first answered the phone. I said:

"Is Stephen Hackett there?"

"Who is calling, please?"

"Lew Archer. Is that Mrs. Marburg?"

"It is." Her voice was thin and dry. "You were a good prophet, Mr. Archer."

"Has something happened to your son?"

"You're such a good prophet I wonder if it's prophecy. Where are you?"

"In West Los Angeles."

"Come out here right away, will you? I'll tell my husband to open the gate."

I left without telling the Spanners where I was going or why. On my way to Malibu I stopped at my apartment to pick up a revolver.

Chapter 11

THE HACKETTS' GATE was standing open. I expected to find police cars in front of the house, but the only car standing under the floodlights was a new blue Mercedes convertible. The young man who went with it came out of the house to meet me.

"Mr. Archer? I'm Sidney Marburg."

He gave me a hard competitive handshake. On second look he wasn't so very young. His smile was probably porcelain, and the smile-lines radiating from it could just as well have been worry-lines. His narrow black eyes were opaque in the light.

"What happened, Mr. Marburg?"

"I'm not too clear about it myself, I wasn't here when it happened. Apparently Stephen's been kidnapped. A young chick and a boy with a shotgun took him away in their car."

"Where was Lupe?"

"Lupe was here. He still is—lying down with a bloody head. The boy got out of the trunk of their car and held a sawed-off shotgun on him. The girl hit him over the head with a hammer or a tire iron."

"The girl did that?"

He nodded. "What makes it even queerer, it seems to be someone the family knows. My wife wants to talk to you."

Marburg took me into the library where his wife was sitting under a lamp, with a phone and a revolver at her elbow. She seemed calm, but her face had a look of chilled surprise. She forced a smile.

"Thank you for coming. Sidney's a charming boy, but he's not much practical use." She turned to him. "Now run along and play with your paints or something."

He stood resentfully between her and the door. His mouth opened and closed.

"Go on now like a good boy. Mr. Archer and I have things to discuss."

Marburg walked out. I sat on the leather hassock that matched her chair. "Where's Mrs. Hackett?"

"Gerda went to pieces—par for the course. Fortunately I always carry chloral hydrate. I gave her a couple of capsules and she cried herself to sleep."

"So everything's under control."

"Everything's busted wide open, and you know it. Are you going to help me put it back together?"

"I have a client."

She disregarded this. "I can pay you a good deal of money."

"How much?"

"A hundred thousand."

"That's too much."

She gave me a narrow, probing look. "I saw you turn down twenty dollars today. But nobody ever turned down a hundred grand."

"It isn't real money. You're offering it to me because you think I may be in on an extortion deal. No such luck."

"Then how did you know about it before it happened?"

"I came across the evidence. They left the map of this place lying around, almost as if they wanted to be stopped. Which doesn't make them any less dangerous."

"I know they're dangerous. I saw them. The two of them came right into the living room and marched Stephen out to their car. In their dark glasses they looked like creatures from another planet."

"Did you recognize either of them?"

"Gerda recognized the girl right away. She's been a guest here more than once. Her name is Alexandria Sebastian."

She turned and looked at me in surmise. I was glad the secret was coming out.

"Keith Sebastian is my client."

"And he knew about this?"

"He knew his daughter had run away. Then he knew what I told him, which wasn't much. Let's not get involved in recriminations. The important thing is to get your son back."

"I agree. My offer stands. A hundred thousand if Stephen comes home safe."

"The police do this work for free."

She pushed the idea away with her hand. "I don't want them. So often they solve the case and lose the victim. I want my son back alive."

"I can't guarantee it."

"I *know* that," she said impatiently. "Will you try?" She pressed both hands to her breast, then offered them to me, empty. Her emotion was both theatrical and real.

"I'll try," I said. "I think you're making a mistake, though. You should use the police."

"I've already said I wouldn't. I don't trust them."

"But you trust me?"

"Shouldn't I? Yes, I do, up to a point."

"So does Keith Sebastian. I'm going to have to check with him on this."

"I don't see why. He's one of our employees."

"Not when he's on his own time. His daughter is missing, remember. He feels about her just as strongly as you do about your son." Not quite, perhaps, but I gave Sebastian the benefit of the doubt.

"We'll get him out here." Abruptly she reached for the phone. "What's his number?"

"We're wasting time."

"I asked you for his number."

I looked it up in my black book. She dialed, and got Sebastian on the first ring. He must have been sitting beside the telephone.

"Mr. Sebastian? This is Ruth Marburg. Stephen Hackett's mother. I'm at his Malibu place now, and I'd very much like to see you . . . Yes, tonight. Immediately, in fact. How soon can you get here? . . . Very well, I'll look for you in half an hour. You won't disappoint me, will you?"

She hung up and looked at me quietly, almost sweetly. Her hand was still on the phone, as if she was taking Sebastian's pulse by remote control.

"He wouldn't be in on this with his daughter, would he? I know that Stephen isn't always popular with the hired help."

"Is that what we are, Mrs. Marburg?"

"Don't change the subject. I asked you a straight question."

"The answer is no. Sebastian doesn't have that kind of guts. Anyway he practically worships your son."

"Why?" she asked me bluntly.

"Money. He has a passion for the stuff."

"Are you *sure* he didn't put the girl up to this?"

"I'm sure."

"Then what in hell does she think she's doing?"

"She seems to be in revolt, against everyone over thirty. Your son was the biggest target within reach. I doubt that she picked the target, though. Davy Spanner's probably the main instigator."

"What does he want? Money?"

"I haven't figured out what he wants. Do you know of any connection between him and your son? This could be a personal thing."

She shook her head. "Maybe if you tell me what you know about him."

I gave her a quick rundown on Davy Spanner, son of a migrant laborer, orphaned at three or four and institutionalized, then taken by foster parents; a violent dropout from high school, a wandering teen-ager, car thief, jail graduate, candidate for more advanced felonies, possibly somewhat crazy in the head.

Ruth Marburg listened to me with a suspicious ear. "You sound almost sympathetic."

"I almost am," I said, though my kidneys were still sore. "Davy Spanner didn't make himself."

She answered me with deliberate roughness: "Don't give me that crap. I know these psychopaths. They're like dogs biting the hands that feed them."

"Has Spanner had previous contact with your family?"

"No. Not that I know of."

"But the girl has."

"Not with me. With Gerda, Stephen's wife. The girl was interested in languages, or pretended to be. Gerda took her under her wing last summer. She'll know better next time, if the family survives this."

I was getting impatient with the conversation. We seemed to have been sitting in the room for a long time. Book-lined, with the windows heavily draped, it was like an underground bunker cut off from the world of life.

Ruth Marburg must have sensed or shared my feeling. She went to one of the windows and pulled back the drapes. We looked out at the broken necklace of lights along the shore.

"I still can't believe it happened," she said. "Stephen has always been so careful. It's one reason they don't have servants."

"What's Lupe?"

"We hardly think of him as a servant. He's really the manager of the estate."

"A friend of yours?"

"I wouldn't say that, exactly. We get along." Her half-smile, and the way she held her body, gave the words a sexual connotation.

"May I talk to Lupe?"

"Not now. He's a pretty sick man."

"Should he have a doctor?"

"I'm going to get him one." She turned and faced me, visibly shaken by her own angry force. "You needn't take responsibility for things you're not responsible for. I'm hiring you to get my son back alive."

"You haven't hired me yet."

"And I may not." She turned back to the window. "What's keeping him?" She clenched her hands and rapped the knuckles together, making a noise which reminded me that she contained a skeleton.

As if he'd heard it, or felt her impatient will, Sebastian turned up almost immediately. His big car threw its lights up over the pass, came around the dark lake, and stopped under the floodlights.

"You took your time," Mrs. Marburg said at the door.

"I'm sorry. I had a phone call as I was leaving. I had to take it."

Sebastian seemed tremendously excited. He was pale and brilliant-eyed. He looked from the woman to me.

"What's up?"

Ruth Marburg answered grimly: "Come in, I'll tell you what's up." She led us into the library and closed the door emphatically, like a warder. "Your precious daughter has stolen my son."

"What do you mean?"

"She drove in here with her bully-boy hidden in the trunk of her car. Knocked out our manager with a tire iron. Walked into the house with bully-boy and marched Stephen out to their car and took him away."

"But that's insane."

"It happened."

"When?"

"Just before sundown. That was about five thirty. It's after eight now. The question is, what are you going to do about it?"

"Anything. I'll do anything."

A delayed rush of tears almost blinded him. He wiped them with his fingers, stood swaying in the light with his hands covering his eyes.

"You're *sure* it was Sandy?"

"Yes. My daughter-in-law knows her well. Mr. Archer here virtually predicted it was going to happen. Which brings me to the reason why you're here. I want Mr. Archer to get my son back for me."

"This means," I told him, "that you and I may be on opposite sides. Your daughter has helped to commit a major crime. I'm afraid I can't protect her from the consequences."

"But I'll expect you to cooperate with Archer," Mrs. Marburg told him. "If you hear from your daughter, for example, you've got to let him know."

"Yes." He nodded several times. "I promise I'll cooperate. Thank you for—thank you for telling me."

She waved him away, out of her sight.

"Well," she said to me when he had left the room, "do you think he put her up to it?"

"You know he didn't."

"Don't tell me what I know. People are capable of anything. Even the nicest people, and he's not one of them." She added: "Neither am I, in case you were in doubt."

"We're wasting time."

She had the last word: "You're on my time. On your way out, will you tell my husband to bring me a double Scotch. I'm as tired as death."

She slumped into her chair and let her face and body

droop like Plasticine. Her husband was in the lighted gallery looking at the pictures. I delivered her message to him.

"Thanks, old fellow. Don't work too hard on this assignment, will you? If Stephen doesn't come back, all this comes to Ruth and me. I love good paintings."

Marburg was half-serious, which was all he'd ever be. I went outside where Sebastian was waiting in my car. He was gnawing at a thumbnail. It was bleeding.

I got in behind the wheel. "Do you have something to tell me?"

"Yes. I was afraid to say it in front of her. That telephone call just before I left my house—it was from Sandy. She wanted me to come and get her."

"Where?"

"Santa Teresa. She was cut off before she could give me directions."

"Did she say where she was calling from?"

"No, but it was a collect call and the operator was able to trace it for me. Sandy used the office phone in the Power Plus station on this side of Santa Teresa. We've often driven up weekends, and stopped at that very station."

"I'd better get up there now."

"Take me along," he said. "Please."

I turned and looked into his face. I didn't like him much, or trust him very far. But I was liking him better as time passed.

"How well do you drive?"

"I don't have accidents, and I haven't been drinking."

"Okay, we'll take my car."

Sebastian left his in a Malibu parking lot next door to a drive-in. I had a quick sandwich, which tasted of highway fumes, while he phoned his wife. Then he phoned the Power Plus station in Santa Teresa.

"They're open till midnight," he told me. "And the man remembered Sandy."

My watch said nine fifteen. It had been a long day, and I expected to be up most of the night. I climbed into the back seat and went to sleep.

ROSS MACDONALD

Chapter 12

THE TURNING OFF of the engine woke me from dreams of supersonic flight. My car was standing beside the pumps in the hard white glare of the Power Plus station. A young man in coveralls came out of the office. He had one thin leg and wore a special boot. He moved with great rapidity, though it was late and his face was drawn.

"What can I do for you?" he asked Sebastian.

"I called you earlier. About my daughter." His voice was low and uncertain, like a beggar's.

"I see." The pain and fatigue in the attendant's face turned into sympathy, and altered the quality of the transaction. "Is she a runaway, something like that?"

"Something like that." I got out of the car to talk to him. "Was she driving a green compact?"

"Yeah. She stopped it right where your car is standing, asked me to fill the tank. It was nearly empty, it took over nineteen gallons."

"Did you see the others?"

"There was only the one other, the big fellow with the crew cut. He stayed in the car until he saw her phoning. She *said* she wanted to go to the ladies' room. I left the pump running and went to the office to get the key for her. Then she asked me if she could use the phone for a distance call. I said, if she made it collect, which she did. I stayed there to monitor her, like. Then the other one came charging in and made her quit."

"Did he use force?"

"He didn't hit her. He put his arms around her, more like a hug. Then she broke down and cried, and he took her back to the car. She paid for the gas and drove away herself, in the direction of town." He gestured toward Santa Teresa.

61

"You didn't see a gun?"

"No. She acted afraid of him, though."

"Did he say anything?"

"Just when he came charging into the office. He said she was crazy to call her folks, that they were her worst enemies."

Sebastian muttered something inarticulate.

"Hers, or his?" I said.

"Both of them. I think he said '*their* worst enemies.'"

"You're a good witness. What's your name?"

"Fred Cram."

I offered him a dollar.

"You don't have to pay me." He spoke with gentle force. "I'm sorry I couldn't do more. Maybe I should have tried to stop them, or called the police or something. Only I didn't think I had the right."

An old Chevrolet painted with brown undercoat rolled in from the street and stopped beside the pumps. A couple of teen-age boys occupied the front seat. The bare feet of two others projected from the rear window. The driver honked for service.

I asked Fred Cram again: "Are you sure there wasn't a third person in the car?"

He pondered the question. "Not unless you count the dog."

"What kind of a dog?"

"I don't know. It sounded like a big one."

"You didn't see it?"

"It was in the trunk. I could hear it breathing and kind of whining."

"How do you know it was a dog?"

"She said so."

Sebastian groaned.

"You mean it was a human being in there?" the young man said.

"I don't know."

Fred Cram gave me a long questioning look. His face saddened as he realized the depth of the trouble he had dipped into. Then the teen-ager honked again, imperiously, and he swung away on his mismatched legs.

"Jesus," Sebastian said in the car. "It really happened. We've got to get her back, Archer."

"We will." I didn't let him hear my doubts, the doubt that we could find her, the graver doubt that the law would let him keep her if we did. "The best contribution you can make is to get in touch with your wife and stay by a telephone. Sandy phoned home once, she may again."

"If he lets her."

But he accepted my suggestion. We checked into adjoining rooms in a beach motel near the center of Santa Teresa. It was the depth of the winter season, and the place was almost deserted. The yacht harbor under my window hung in the starlight like a dim white fantasy of summer.

The keyboy opened the door between our two rooms. I listened to Sebastian talking to his wife on the telephone. He told her with brisk cheerfulness that the case was progressing rapidly and she had nothing to worry about at all. The fine front he was putting on reminded me somehow of the young man with the thin leg, limping faster than other men could walk.

"I love you, too," Sebastian said, and hung up.

I went to the doorway. "How is your wife taking this?"

"Terrific. She's terrific."

But his gaze wandered around the room, taking in the details of his catastrophe: the lonely bed, the homeless walls, and my face watching him.

I tried to smile. "I'm going out for a bit. I'll check back with you later."

"What are you planning to do?"

"Pay a couple of visits to people in town."

"It's late for visiting."

"All the better. They're more likely to be home."

I went back into my room, got the directory out of the drawer in the telephone table, and looked up Henry Langston, the counsellor who had had a run-in with Davy Spanner. A young girl answered Langston's phone, and for a moment I thought by some remarkable coincidence it was Sandy.

"Who is that?" I asked her.

"Elaine. I'm just the baby-sitter. Mr. and Mrs. Langston are out for the evening."

"When do you expect them back?"

"They *promised* by midnight. You want to leave a message?"

"No thanks."

Coincidences seldom happen in my work. If you dig deep enough, you can nearly always find their single bifurcating roots. It was probably no coincidence that Jack Fleischer had taken off, presumably for his home in Santa Teresa, immediately after Laurel Smith was beaten. I looked him up in the directory and found his address: 33 Pine Street.

It was a street of older middle-class houses, appropriately pine-shaded, within walking distance of the courthouse. Most of the houses in the block were dark. I parked at the corner in front of an old church, and walked along the street looking for Fleischer's number with my flashlight.

I found two rusty metal three's attached to the porch of a two-story white frame house. There was light in the house, dim yellow behind drawn blinds. I knocked on the front door.

Uncertain footsteps approached the door and a woman's voice spoke through it: "What do you want?"

"Is Mr. Fleischer home?"

"No."

But she opened the door in order to peer out at me. She was a middle-aged blond woman whose face had been carefully made up at some point earlier in the day. Erosion had set in. In the midst of it her eyes regarded me with that steady look of hurt suspicion which takes years to develop.

There was gin on her breath, and it triggered an association in my mind. She looked enough like Laurel Smith to be her older sister.

"Mrs. Fleischer?"

She nodded grimly. "I don't know you, do I?"

"I'm better acquainted with your husband. Do you know where I can find him?"

She spread her hands. Under her quilted pink housecoat her body was sullen. "Search me."

"It's pretty important. I've come all the way from Los Angeles."

Her hand came out and clenched on my arm. I felt like a stand-in for Fleischer. "What's Jack been doing down there?"

"I'm afraid that's confidential."

"You can tell me. I'm his wife." She jerked at my arm. "Come in, I'll give you a drink. Any friend of Jack's—"

I let her take me into the large drab living room. It had an air of not being lived in, just being endured. The main ornaments of the room were Fleischer's shooting trophies on the mantel.

"What will you have? I'm drinking gin on the rocks."

"That will suit me."

She padded out of the room and came back with lowball glasses full of ice and gin.

I sipped at mine. "Cheers."

"Here, have a seat." She indicated a slip-covered davenport and sat down crowding me. "You were going to tell me what Jack is up to."

"I don't know all the ramifications. He seems to be doing an investigative job—"

She shut me off impatiently. "Don't let him fool you. And don't you cover up for him, either. There's a woman in it, isn't there? He's got another place in L.A. and that woman is living with him again. Isn't that right?"

"You know him better than I do."

"You bet I do. We've been married for thirty years, and for half of those thirty years he's been chasing the same skirt." She leaned toward me with an avid mouth. "Have you seen the woman?"

"I've seen her."

"Say I show you a picture of her," she said, "are you willing to tell me if it's the same woman?"

"If you'll help me locate Jack."

She gave my question serious thought. "He's headed for the Bay area, God knows why. I thought at least he'd be staying overnight. But he took a shower and changed his clothes and ate the dinner I cooked for him, and then he was off again."

"Where in the Bay area?"

"The Peninsula. I heard him call Palo Alto before he left. He made a reservation at the Sandman Motor Hotel. That's all I know. He doesn't tell me anything any more, and I know why. He's after that piece of skirt again. He had that light in his eye." Her voice buzzed with resentment, like a hornet caught in a web. She drowned it with gin. "I'll show you her picture."

She set down her empty glass on a table inset with polished

bits of stone, left the room and came back. She thrust a small photograph at me, and turned up the three-way lamp.

"That's her, isn't it?"

It was a full-face picture of Laurel Smith, taken when she was a dark-haired girl in her twenties. Even in this small and carelessly printed photograph, her beauty showed through. I remembered her beaten face as they lifted her into the ambulance, and I had a delayed shock, a sense of something valuable being destroyed by time and violence.

Mrs. Fleischer repeated her question. I answered her carefully: "I *think* it is. Where did you get this picture?"

"I got it out of Jack's wallet while he was taking his shower. He started carrying it again. It's an old picture he's had for a long time."

"How long?"

"Let's see." She counted on her fingers. "Fifteen years. It was fifteen years ago he picked her up. He kept her in Rodeo City, claimed she was a witness, that everything he did was strictly business. But the only crime *she* ever witnessed was Deputy Jack Fleischer taking off his pants."

There was sly satisfaction in her eyes. She was betraying her husband to me just as completely as he had betrayed her. And as an old cop's wife, she was betraying herself.

She took the picture and laid it on the table and picked up her glass. "Drink up. We'll have another."

I didn't argue. Cases break in different ways. This case was opening, not like a door or even a grave, certainly not like a rose or any flower, but opening like an old sad blonde with darkness at her core.

I emptied my glass, and she took it out to the kitchen for a refill. I think while she was out of the room she sneaked an extra drink for herself. Coming back she bumped the doorframe of the living room andd spilled gin on her hands.

I took both glasses from her and set them down on the stony table. She swayed in front of me, her eyes unfocused. She forced them back into focus, the cobweb of fine lines surrounding them cutting deep into her flesh.

"It's the same woman, isn't it?" she said.

"I'm pretty sure it is. Do you know her name?"

"She called herself Laurel Smith in Rodeo City."

"She still does."

"Jack's living with her in L.A., isn't he?"

"Nobody's living with her that I know of."

"Don't try to kid me. You men are always covering up for each other. But I know when a man's spending money on a woman. He took more than a thousand dollars out of our savings account in less than a month. And I have to beg him for twelve dollars to get my hair done." She pushed her fingers through her fine dry wavy hair. "Is she still pretty?"

"Pretty enough." I gathered my élan together, and paid her a compliment. "As a matter of fact, she looks quite a bit like you."

"They always do. The women he goes for always look like me. But that's no comfort, they're always younger." Her voice was like a flagellant's whip, turned against herself. She turned it against Fleischer: "The dirty creep! He has the almighty guts to spend our hard-earned money on that bag. Then he comes home and tells me he's investing it, going to make us rich for the rest of our lives."

"Did he say how?"

"*You* ought to know. You're one of his cronies, aren't you?"

She picked up her glass and drained it. She looked ready to throw the empty glass at my head. I wasn't her husband, but I wore pants.

"Drink up your drink," she said. "I drank up mine."

"We've had enough."

"That's what *you* think."

She carried her glass out of the room. Her mules slid along the floor and her body leaned as if she were on an irreversible slope, sliding away forever into the limbo of deserted women. I heard her smashing something in the kitchen. I looked in through the open door and saw her breaking dishes in the sink.

I didn't interfere. They were her dishes. I went back through the living room, took Laurel's picture from the table, and left the house.

On the porch next door, a white-haired man wearing a bathrobe stood in a listening attitude. When he saw me, he turned away and went into the house. I heard him say before he closed the door:

"Jack Fleischer's home again."

Chapter 13

HENRY LANGSTON'S one-story house was in a newer tract on the northern outskirts of the city. The lights were on, both inside and out. The doors of the attached garage were open but there was no car in it, only a child's tricycle standing against one wall.

A young woman wearing a fur-collared coat came out of the house. She had bright dark eyes and a piquant oval face. She stopped short before she reached me, ready to be alarmed.

"I'm looking for Mr. Langston," I told her.

"Why? Has something happened?"

"I've no reason to think so."

"But it's so *late*."

"I'm sorry. I tried to get him earlier. Is he home now?"

She glanced over her shoulder at the open front door. She was disturbed by me, as if I carried trouble like a communicable disease from the last house I had visited.

I smiled a midnight smile. "Don't get upset. This has nothing to do with you. I have some questions to ask him about one of his former students."

"I'm sure he won't want to talk to you tonight."

"I'm sure he will. Tell him it has to do with Davy Spanner."

"Him again." She tossed her head like a rival, then bit her lip. "Is Davy in trouble again, or is it still?"

"I prefer to discuss that with your husband. You *are* Mrs. Langston?"

"Yes, and I'm cold and tired and ready to go to bed, and we had a lovely evening with some friends, and now it's spoiled." Perhaps she had had a drink or two, but she was

68

deliberately indulging her feelings. She was pretty enough to do that.

"I'm sorry."

"If you're so sorry, go away."

She went inside and slammed the door with a carefully calculated degree of force, between six and seven on the Richter scale. I stood where I was on the flagstone walk. Mrs. Langston reopened the door, carefully, like somebody reopening a law case.

"I apologize. I know it must be important or you wouldn't be here. Are you a policeman?"

"A private detective. My name is Archer."

"Henry should be back any minute. He's just driving the baby-sitter home. Come in, it's a chilly night."

She backed into the living room. I followed her. The room was jammed with furniture and books. A closed baby grand piano was its central feature.

Mrs. Langston stood beside it like a nervous soloist. "Let me make you some coffee."

"Please don't bother. And please don't be afraid."

"It's not *your* fault. I'm scared of Davy Spanner."

"You were scared before his name came up."

"Was I? I guess you're right. You looked at me in such a strange way, as if I was going to die."

I didn't bother reminding her that she was going to. She took off her coat. She looked about six months pregnant.

"If you'll excuse me, I'm just plain going to bed. Please don't keep Henry up all night."

"I'll try not to. Good night."

She fluttered her fingers at me, leaving a kind of tremulous feeling in the room. When I heard the car in the driveway I went outside.

Langston got out, leaving his station wagon outside the garage with the headlights on and the engine running. A sense of alarm seemed to be in the air, and I could see it reflected in his face. He was a large, homely, sandy-haired young man with sensitive eyes.

"Is Kate all right?"

"Your wife is fine. She let me in and went to bed." I told him who I was. "Davy Spanner was in town tonight."

Langston's eyes seemed to withdraw, as if I'd touched invisible antennae. He went back to his wagon and turned off the engine and the headlights.

"We'll talk in the car, okay? I don't want to disturb her."

We got into the front seat, closing the doors without slamming them.

"You didn't see Davy tonight by any chance?"

He hesitated before answering. "Yes, I did. Briefly."

"Where?"

"He came here to my house."

"About what time?"

"Eight o'clock. Kate had gone to pick up Elaine—that's the high-school girl who sits with Junior—and I was just as glad she was out of the house. Fortunately he left before she got back. Davy upsets Kate basically, you know?"

"She isn't the only one."

Langston gave me a sideways look. "Has he been beating his head on the wall again?"

"If that's what you call it."

"Davy's a self-destroyer."

"It's the other people I'm worried about. Was the girl Sandy with him?"

"Very much so. She's one of the reasons he came to me tonight. He wanted me to look after her for him. Me and Kate, that is. He said that they were going to get married but first he had a job to do. It would take a day or two."

"Did he say what the job was?"

"No. I gathered it was going to be rough. He thought it would be nice if Sandy stayed with us until he got through with it."

"Why you?"

"It's what I often ask myself," he said with a quick wry smile. "Why me? The answer is, I asked for it. I got very deeply involved with Davy's problems, years ago, and once that happens it's very hard to, you know, wean your affections. It almost broke up my marriage at one point. Never again. I told him what he suggested was impossible. He took it hard, as if I was letting him down. But it was a question of who—of whom—I was going to let down, Davy or my own family."

"How did the girl react?"

"I never did get a chance to talk to her. I could see her

sitting in their car, looking rather pale and tense." He pointed with his thumb toward the street where my car was standing. "But I couldn't take the responsibility for her. The truth is I wanted them out of here before Kate returned. She's going to have another child, and she had a very hard time with the first—with Junior. I have to protect her from too much excitement—alarms and excursions."

"Of course."

"There have to be priorities," he went on. "Otherwise you spread yourself thin and the whole structure collapses." He sounded like an overconscientious man repeating a hard lesson he was trying to learn. But he couldn't help caring about the girl. "She really is his fiancée, isn't she?"

"They think so. She's a runaway, though, and only seventeen. Her parents originally hired me to get her back."

"And that's why you're here?"

"Partly. What other reasons did Davy have for coming to you?"

"Other reasons?"

"You said the girl was one reason. What were the others?"

"It had to do with history," he said rather obscurely. "He wanted some information, essentially information about himself. As I was saying, I delved pretty deeply into his case several years ago, when he was one of our students at the high school. I realize now I went too deep. I'd had some therapy when I was in college, and I thought I could use it to help him. But something happened, I don't know how to explain it."

His look was puzzled and inward, as if he were trying to explain the past to himself: "Something seemed to tear like a membrane in between us. There were times when our identities seemed to get mixed up. I could actually feel his feelings and think his thoughts, and I felt this terrible empathy—" He broke off. "Has that ever happened to you?"

"No. Unless you count women, in very special circumstances."

"Women?" he said in his puzzled way. "Kate is as strange to me as the mountains of the moon. That doesn't mean I don't love her. I worship her."

"Fine. You were going to tell me about Dave's history."

"He didn't have any history, that was the trouble. I

thought I could help him by providing some. But it turned out he couldn't handle it. Neither could I, really. I was the one who mishandled the situation, since I was the counselor and he was just a troubled sixteen-year-old."

Langston was troubled, too. His mind seemed to be struggling through magnetic fields of memory which put a twist on everything he said. I prompted him again: "Is it true his father was killed?"

He gave me a quick stabbing look. "You know about his father's death?"

"Just that. How did it happen?"

"I never did find out for sure. Apparently he fell under a train near Rodeo City. The train wheels passed over him and cut his head off." Langston drew his fingers across his own throat. "He was a young man, younger than I am now."

"What was his name?"

"Nobody seems to know. He wasn't carrying any identification. According to the theory of the deputy sheriff who handled the case—"

"Jack Fleischer?"

"Yes. Do you know him?"

"I'm looking forward to knowing him. What was his theory?"

"That the man was a migrant worker who was riding the rods and accidentally fell off. But there's one big trouble with that theory. He had a three-year-old boy with him and if *he* fell off the moving train, Davy must have fallen off, too. But he was unhurt, at least in the physical sense.

"In the psychic sense," he added, "Davy was badly hurt. I'm sure it's the root of his trouble. He sat beside the railroad tracks all night with that headless corpse." His voice had dropped so low I could barely hear him.

"How do you know that?"

"Deputy Fleischer found him beside the body. Davy confirmed this himself. I helped him to dredge up the memory. I thought it would be good for him. But I'm afraid it wasn't. I realize now I was playing God, practicing psychiatry without a license." His voice was contrite.

"He went completely wild and attacked me. We were in my office at the high school, and there wasn't any way I could keep it quiet. As a matter of fact he gave me quite a beating. The school expelled him, over my protests. It was all I could do to keep him out of reform school."

"Why did you want to?"

"I felt guilty, of course. I'd been playing with black magic —these repressed memories are as powerful as any magic—and the thing blew up in both our faces. He suffered permanent damage."

"That happened long before. You're still playing God," I said.

"I know the extent of my responsibility. I helped to bring that terrible memory back to his conscious mind. He's been fixed on it ever since."

"You don't know that."

"I do, though. That's the hell of it. He came here tonight and insisted I tell him exactly where his father's corpse was found. It's still the dominant thing in his mind."

"Did you tell him?"

"Yes. It was the only way to get rid of him."

"Can you take me to the place? Tonight?"

"I could. But it's at least an hour's drive up the coast." He looked at his watch. "It's past twelve thirty. If I take you, I won't get home before three. And I have to be at school at a quarter to eight."

"Forget about school. You said yourself there are priorities. This one has to do with a man's life or death."

"What man?"

I told Langston about the breathing in the trunk. "I thought at first it was a snatch for money. The people who pull them are getting younger all the time. But the motives for kidnapping are changing with the times, too. More and more of them are naked power plays, for the sheer sake of dominating another person. God knows what goes on in Davy's mind. Or the girl's, for that matter. They may be planning to re-enact his father's death."

I had Langston's full attention. He couldn't resist the psychological bait. "You may be right. He was terribly urgent about finding the right place. Are the police in on this?"

"No. The victim's family asked me to handle it myself."

"Who is he?"

"A Los Angeles financier. The girl's father works for one of his companies."

"It does sound more complex than a crime for money."

"Will you help me?" I said.

"I don't have much choice. We'll take your car, okay?"

"Whatever you say, Mr. Langston."

"Please call me Hank, everybody else does." He got out of the car. "Come into the house for a moment, won't you? I have to leave a note for my wife."

He wrote it on top of the baby grand while I looked over his books. They covered a surprising range including law and history. His psychology and sociology books emphasized the freer spirits in those fields: Erik Erikson and Erich Fromm, Paul Goodman, Edgar Z. Friedenberg.

He left the note to his wife on the music rack of the piano, with a small light shining on it. I read it on the way out:

> *Dearest:*
>
> *Just in case you wake up and wonder where I am, I've gone for a little spin with Mr. Archer. If anybody comes to the door, don't answer. Please don't worry. I love you with all my heart, in case you were wondering. Back soon.*
>
>

Love,

H.

(12:30 a.m.)

Chapter 14

I DROVE THE CAR, and told Langston he could sleep. He claimed that he wasn't sleepy, but soon after we got onto the highway he butted his cigarette and dozed off.

The highway left the sea for a while, looping inland through a mountain pass, and then returned to the sea. The railroad ran between the sea and the mountains, and I caught the gleam of the tracks from time to time.

There was very little traffic. This northern part of the county was mostly open country. On the ocean side a few oil stations and gas flares broke up the darkness. Inland, the fields sloped up to the rocky flanks of the headless mountains. There were cattle in the fields, as still as stones.

"No!" Langston said in his sleep.

"Wake up, Hank."

He seemed dazed. "Terrible dream. The three of us were in bed to—" He stopped in mid-sentence, and watched the night rush by.

"Which three of you?"

"My wife and I, and Davy. It was a rotten dream."

I said after some hesitation: "Are you afraid that Davy might go to your house?"

"The thought did occur to me," he admitted. "But he wouldn't do anything to anyone I love."

He was talking against the darkness. Perhaps I should have left him at home, I thought, but it was too late now. Since leaving his house I'd added over fifty miles to the odometer.

"How much further, Hank?"

"I can't say exactly. I'll know the place when I see it. You have to make a left turn onto a gravel road. It crosses the tracks." He peered ahead through the windshield.

"How long is it since you've visited the place?"

"About three years. Deputy Fleischer drove me up."

"Why did you go to all the trouble?"

"I wanted to know exactly what had happened. The people at the Shelter told me Davy was practically autistic when he was admitted—mute and almost unreachable. I wanted to know why. Fleischer hadn't told them much, if anything."

"Did he talk freely to you?"

"Policemen never do, do they? And I can understand an officer getting quite possessive about a case. At the time he brought me up here, he'd been working on this one for twelve years."

"Did he say so?"

"Yes."

"Then he couldn't have thought it was an accident."

"I don't know what he thought, really." Langston thrust his head forward. "Slow down. We're coming to the place."

Several hundred yards ahead in the lights of an approaching truck I could make out a gravel road sloping away to the left. A lonely hitchhiker was at the corner. It was a girl, standing with her back to us and frantically signaling to the truck driver. The truck passed her, and then us, without slackening speed.

I made a left turn onto the side road and got out. The girl was wearing sunglasses, as if the natural darkness wasn't deep enough for her. Her body made a jerky movement. I thought she was going to run. But her feet seemed to be stuck fast in the gravel.

"Sandy?"

She didn't answer me, except with a little moan of recognition. I had a vision of myself seen from above, a kind of owl's-eye view of a man moving in on a frightened girl at a deserted crossroads. Somehow my motives didn't enter the picture.

"What happened to the others, Sandy?"

"I don't know. I ran away and hid in the trees." She pointed toward a grove of Monterey pines on the far side of the railroad tracks. I could smell their odor on her. "He laid Mr. Hackett across the railroad tracks, and I got really scared. I thought he was pretending, until then. I didn't think he really meant to kill him."

"Is Hackett unconscious?"

"No, but he's all taped up—his hands and feet and mouth. He looked so helpless lying across the rail. He knew where he was, too, I could tell by the noises he made. I couldn't stand it, so I ran away. When I came back they were gone."

Langston moved up beside me. His feet crackled in the gravel. The girl shied away.

"Don't be afraid," he said.

"Who are you? Do I know you?"

"I'm Henry Langston. Davy wanted me to take care of you. It seems to be working out that way after all."

"I don't want to be taken care of. I'm all right. I can get a ride." She spoke with a kind of mechanical assurance which seemed to be unconnected with her real feelings.

"Come on," he said. "Don't be so stand-offish."

"Have you got a cigarette?"

"I have a whole pack."

"I'll come with you if you give me a cigarette."

He brought out his cigarettes and solemnly handed them over. She got a cigarette out of the pack. Her hands were shaking.

"Give me a light?"

Langston handed her a book of matches. She lit one and dragged deep. The end of her cigarette was reflected double like little hot red eyes in the lenses of her dark glasses.

"All right, I'll get into your car."

She sat in the front seat, with Langston and me on either side of her. She gulped her cigarette until it burned her fingers, then dropped it in the ashtray.

"You didn't have very good plans," I said. "Who made your plans?"

"Davy did, mostly."

"What did he have in mind?"

"He was going to kill Mr. Hackett, like I said. Leave him across the track and let the train cut him up."

"And you went along with this?"

"I didn't really believe he was going to do it. He didn't do it, either."

"We'd better check on that."

I released the emergency brake. The car rolled down the grade toward the crossing, which was marked by an old wooden sign with drooping crosspieces.

"Where did he put Mr. Hackett?"

"Right here beside the road." Sandy indicated the north side of the crossing.

I got out with my flashlight and looked over the railbed. There were fresh marks in the gravel which could have been gouged by heels. Still it was hard to imagine the scene that the girl had described.

I went back to the car. "Did Davy tell you why he picked this place?"

"He thought it would be a good place to kill him, I guess. Then he probably changed his mind when I ran away."

"Why did he choose Mr. Hackett as a victim?"

"I don't know."

I leaned in at the open door. "You must have some idea, Sandy. Mr. Hackett is or was a friend of your family."

"He's not my friend," she said guardedly.

"You've made that fairly clear. What did Hackett do, if anything?"

She turned to Langston. "I don't have to answer that, do I? I'm only a juvenile but I've got a right to a lawyer."

"You've not only got a right," I said. "You've got a need for one. But you're not going to help yourself by keeping quiet. If we don't head your boyfriend off, you'll end up going to trial with him for everything he pulls."

She appealed again to Langston, the cigarette king. "That isn't true, is it?"

"It could happen," he said.

"But I'm just a juvenile."

I said: "That's no protection against a capital charge. You already own a piece of a kidnapping. If Hackett gets killed, you'll be an accomplice in murder."

"But I ran away."

"That won't be much help, Sandy."

She was shocked. I think she was realizing that the place and the time were real, that this was her life and she was living it, badly.

I felt a certain empathy with her. The scene was becoming a part of my life, too: the grove of trees standing dark against the darkness, the rails reaching like iron strands of necessity from north to south. A late moon like an afterthought hung in the lower quarter of the sky.

Away off to the north the beam of a train's headlight was flung around a curve. It came toward us swinging, cutting the darkness into illegible patterns, pulling a freight train behind it. My own headlights were shining on the rails, and I could see them dip under the weight of the diesels. The overwhelming noise of the train completed the drastic reality of the scene.

Sandy let out a strangled cry and tried to fight her way past me. I forced her back into the car. She scratched at my face. I slapped her. We were both acting as if the noise had shut us off from the human race.

Langston said when the train had gone south: "Take it easy, now. There's no need for violence."

"Tell that to Davy Spanner."

"I have, many times. Let's hope it took." He said to the girl: "Mr. Archer is perfectly right, Sandy. If you can help us, you'll be helping yourself. You must have some idea where Davy went from here."

"He didn't know himself." She was breathing hard. "He did a lot of talking, about this place in the hills where he used to live. He didn't know where it was, though."

"Are you sure it existed?"

"*He* thought so. I don't know."

I got in behind the wheel. Our brief struggle had warmed her, and I could feel her body glowing beside me. It was too bad, I thought, that her parents hadn't been able to keep her on the back burner for another year or two. Too bad for her, and too bad for them.

I asked Sandy some further questions as we drove south. She was reticent about herself, and about her relations with Davy. But her answers established one thing to my own satisfaction: if Davy Spanner was the one who had beaten Laurel Smith, Sandy didn't know about it. And she had been with Davy right through the day, she said.

Chapter 15

IT WAS PAST THREE when we got back to Santa Teresa. I asked Langston to come along to the motel. He seemed to have a calming effect on the girl.

Sebastian heard us coming, and opened the door of his room before I could knock. Light spilled out over his daughter. She stood in it boldly with one round hip out.

He reached for her with open arms. She moved back abruptly. In a long-drawn-out gesture of contempt she lit a cigarette and blew smoke in his direction.

"I didn't know you smoked," he said lamely.

"I smoke pot when I can get it."

We all went into Sebastian's room, with me bringing up the rear. He turned to me.

"Where did you find her?" he asked.

"Up the highway a piece. This is Mr. Langston. He helped to locate her."

The two men shook hands. Sebastian said he was very grateful. But he looked at his daughter as if he wondered what he was grateful for. She sat on the edge of the bed with her knees crossed, watching him.

"We're still in trouble," I said. "And I'm going to make a few suggestions. First, take your daughter home and keep her there. If you and your wife can't control her, hire some help."

"What kind of help?"

"A psychiatric nurse, maybe. Ask your doctor."

"He thinks I'm crazy," Sandy said to the room. "*He* must be crazy."

I didn't look at her. "Do you have a good lawyer, Mr. Sebastian?"

"I don't have any lawyer. I've never really needed one."

"You need one now. Get someone to recommend a criminal lawyer, and give him a chance to talk to Sandy today. She's in serious trouble, and she's going to have to cooperate with the law."

"But I don't want her involved with the law."

"You don't have any choice."

"Don't tell me that. Mrs. Marburg told *you* to keep this whole thing private."

"I'm going to talk to Mrs. Marburg, too. The case is too big for me to handle alone."

Sandy made a break for the door. Langston caught her before she reached it, with one arm around her waist. She burned his wrist with her cigarette butt. He swung her around, pushed her down on the bed and stood over her panting. I could smell singed hair.

Somebody rapped on the other side of the wall. "Knock it off, swingers!"

Sebastian looked at his daughter with pained interest. She had suddenly grown up into a source of trouble. He must have been wondering how large the trouble was going to become.

"I think we better get out of here," I said. "Do you want to phone your wife?"

"I really should, shouldn't I?"

He went to the phone and after a good deal of receiver-banging managed to rouse the switchboard. His wife answered right away.

"I have wonderful news," he said in a shaky voice. "Sandy is with me. I'm bringing her home." The words brought mist to his eyes. "Yes, she's fine. We'll see you in a couple of hours. Get some sleep now."

He hung up and turned to Sandy. "Your mother asked me to give you her love."

"Who needs it?"

"Don't you care for us at all?"

She rolled over, face down on the bed, and lay stiff and silent. I went into the adjoining room to make a phone call of my own.

It was to Willie Mackey, who ran a San Francisco detective agency. His answering service took the call, but shifted it to Willie's California Street apartment. He answered in a sleep-fogged voice: "Mackey here."

"Lew Archer. Are you going to be free today?"

"I can make myself free."

"Good. I have a job on the Peninsula. It's just a tail job but it could turn out to be important. Got a pencil?"

"Hold it just a minute." Willie went away and came back. "Go ahead."

"You know the Sandman Motor Hotel in Palo Alto?"

"Yeah, it's on Camino Real. I've stayed there."

"A man named Jack Fleischer, a retired sheriff's deputy from Santa Teresa, is supposed to be checking in there some time tonight. I want to know why if possible. I want to know where he goes and who he talks to and what about. And I don't want you to lose him even if you have to spend some money."

"How much is some?"

"Use your own discretion."

"Do you want to tell me what it's all about?"

"Jack Fleischer may know. I don't, except that a man's life is at issue."

"Who's the man?"

"His name is Hackett. He's been kidnapped by a nineteen-year-old named Davy Spanner." I described the two of them, in case they turned up in Willie's territory. "Hackett is very well-heeled, but this doesn't seem to be a ransom kidnapping. Spanner's a sociopath with schizoid tendencies."

"They're always fun. I'll get right down to Palo Alto, Lew."

I went back into Sebastian's room. The girl was still lying face down on the bed with Langston standing over her.

"I'll drop you off at your house," I said to him. "I'm sorry I ruined the night for you."

"You didn't. I was glad to help, and that still goes. One thing. I feel I should talk to the local police."

"Let me handle that part. Okay?"

"Okay."

The girl got up when I told her to, and the four of us drove across town. The lights were on in Langston's house. His wife came running out to greet him, wearing a red Chinese robe.

"You shouldn't run," he told her. "Haven't you been to bed?"

"I couldn't sleep. I was scared something would happen to you." She turned on me. "You promised you wouldn't keep him up all night."

"No I didn't. Anyway it's only four."

"*Only* four!"

"You shouldn't be standing out here in the cold." Langston took her into the house, lifting his hand to me before he closed the door.

It was a dreary ride south to Malibu. The girl sat silent between me and her father. He made a few attempts to talk to her, but she pretended to be deaf.

One thing was clear. By changing the rules of the game to include outrage, she had gained an advantage over him. He had more to lose than she had. He was losing it, but he hadn't lost hope of holding on to something. She acted as if she had.

I dropped them off in the parking lot where Sebastian had

left his car. I waited until they were in it, and blue smoke puffed from its exhaust. Sandy made no attempt to run. Perhaps she realized there was no place to run to.

Below the narrow town a high tide was roaring on the beach. I caught glimpses of the breakers between the buildings, faintly phosphorescent in the beginning light.

It was too soon for another day to start. I checked into the first motel I came to.

Chapter 16

I WOKE UP PROMPTLY at eight. It was still too early, but my stomach was groaning. I went out and had a slice of grilled ham, two eggs fried over easy, a pile of toast, a side order of dollar-size pancakes with raspberry syrup, and several cups of black coffee.

By this time I felt as ready as I would ever feel to talk to Mrs. Marburg. Without phoning her in advance, I drove out to the Hackett place. The gate was standing open. I had a heavy *déjà-vu* feeling as I drove up past the artificial lake. The ducks had not returned, and the mud hens were still on the far side of the water.

A Cadillac coupe displaying a doctor's caduceus was standing in front of the house. A youthful-looking man with clever eyes and iron-gray hair met me at the door.

"I'm Dr. Converse. Are you from the police?"

"No, I'm a private detective working for Mrs. Marburg." I told him my name.

"She didn't mention you." He stepped outside and pulled the door shut behind him. "Exactly what has been going on around here? Has something happened to Stephen Hackett?"

"Didn't Mrs. Marburg tell you?"

"She gave me some intimations of disaster. But she seems to think she can undo the mischief by not talking about it.

She made a fearful row when I insisted on calling the police."

"What's her big objection to the police?"

"She has a fixed idea that they're corrupt and incompetent. I suppose she's entitled to it, after what happened to her previous husband."

"What happened to him?"

"I assumed you knew. He was shot to death on the beach about fifteen years ago. I'm not too clear about the details—it was before my time—but I don't believe the killer was ever found. Anyway, getting back to the present, I explained to Mrs. Marburg that the law requires physicians and hospitals to report all serious injuries."

"Are we talking about Lupe?"

"Yes. I called an ambulance and sent him to the hospital."

"Is he seriously hurt?"

"I wouldn't attempt to say. I'm an internist, not a brain surgeon, and these head injuries can be tricky. I'm putting him in the hands of a competent man, Dr. Sunderland at St. John's Hospital."

"Is Lupe conscious?"

"Yes, but he refuses to talk about what happened." The doctor's fingers tweezered my upper arm. He was wearing some piny scent which made me want to sneeze. "Do you know who hit him over the head?"

"It was a seventeen-year-old girl. Lupe's probably ashamed of it."

"Do you know her name?"

"Sandy Sebastian."

He frowned in a puzzled way. "Are you sure?"

"Yes."

"But Sandy isn't a rough girl at all."

"How well do you know her, doctor?"

"I've seen her once or twice, professionally. That was some months ago." His fingers tightened on me. "What happened with her and Lupe, anyway? Did he attempt to attack her?"

"You've got it turned around. Sandy and her boyfriend were on the attack. Lupe was defending himself and I assume Mr. Hackett."

"What's happened to Mr. Hackett? Surely you can tell me, I'm his physician." But Converse lacked authority. He looked and sounded like a society doctor who made his living by talking to money in the proper tone of voice. "Has he been injured, too?"

"He's been kidnapped."

"For ransom?"

"For kicks, apparently."

"And Miss Sebastian and her friend are responsible?"

"Yes. I caught Sandy last night and brought her home. She's with her parents in Woodland Hills. She's not in very good shape emotionally, and I think a doctor should see her. If you're her doctor—"

"I'm not." Dr. Converse let go of me and moved away as if I'd suddenly become contaminated. "I saw her just once, last summer, and I haven't seen her since. I can't call up her home and force my professional attentions on her."

"I suppose not. What did you treat her for last summer?"

"It would hardly be professional to tell you."

Communications had suddenly broken down. I went inside to talk to Mrs. Marburg. She was in the living room, half lying on a long chair with her back to the window. There were bluish bulges under her eyes. She hadn't changed her clothes since the night before.

"No luck, eh?" she said hoarsely.

"No. Did you sleep at all?"

"Not a wink. I had a bad night. I couldn't get a doctor to come out here. When I finally got Dr. Converse, he insisted on informing the police."

"I think it's a good idea. We should lay the whole thing out for them. They can do things I couldn't do if I hired a thousand men. They have a new statewide computer system for spotting cars, for example. The best chance we have is to pick up Sebastian's car."

She drew air hissingly between her teeth. "I wish I'd never heard of that creep or his wretched little daughter."

"I caught the girl, if that's any comfort to you."

Mrs. Marburg sat up straight. "Where is she?"

"At home with her mother and father."

"I wish you'd brought her to me. I'd give a good deal to know what goes on in her head. Did you question her?"

"Some. She won't talk freely."

"What was her motivation?"

"Sheer malice, as far as I can see. She wanted to hurt her father."

"Then why in God's name didn't they kidnap *him?*"

"I don't know. Did the girl have any trouble with your son?"

"Certainly not. Stephen treated her very well. It was Gerda who was her special friend, of course."

"Where is Mrs. Hackett?"

"Gerda's still in her room. She might as well sleep, she's no particular help to anybody. She's no better than Sidney."

She spoke with the fretful impatience of near-despair. Mrs. Marburg was evidently one of those stubborn souls who reacted to trouble by trying to take charge of a situation and make all the decisions. But the thing was slipping out of her hands, and she knew it.

"You can't stay up forever and do everything yourself. This could turn into a long siege. And it could end badly."

She leaned sideways toward me. "Is Stephen dead?"

"We have to face that possibility. Spanner isn't playing games. He's homicidal, apparently."

"How do you know that?" She was angry. "You're trying to frighten me, aren't you? So I'll cooperate with the police."

"I'm giving you the facts, so you can make a good decision. In the course of the night Spanner laid your son out across a railroad track. He intended to let a freight train run over him."

She looked at me in astonishment. "A freight train?"

"I know it sounds wild, but it happened. The girl saw it happen. She got scared and ran out on Spanner at that point, which makes it fairly certain she isn't lying."

"What happened to Stephen?"

"Spanner changed his mind when the girl got away. But he could try it again. There's a lot of railroad track in California, and freight trains are running all the time."

"What is he trying to do to us?"

"I doubt that he could tell you if you asked him. He seems to be acting out a childhood memory."

"That sounds like phony psychology to me."

"It isn't, though. I've talked to Davy Spanner's high-school counselor in Santa Teresa. His father was killed by a train at that same spot, when he was three. Davy saw it happen."

"Where is the place?"

"In the northern part of Santa Teresa County, near Rodeo City."

"I'm not familiar with that territory."

"Neither am I. Of course they may be hundreds of miles away from there by now. In northern California or out of the state in Nevada or Arizona."

She pushed my words away as if they were flies buzzing around her head. "You *are* trying to frighten me."

"I wish I could, Mrs. Marburg. You have nothing to gain by keeping this business private. I can't find your son by myself, I don't have the leads. The leads I do have should go to the police."

"I haven't had good luck with the local police."

"You mean in the death of your husband?"

"Yes." She gave me a level look. "Who's been talking?"

"Not you. I think you should. The murder of your husband and the taking of your son may be connected."

"I don't see how they could be. The Spanner boy couldn't have been more than four or five when Mark Hackett was killed."

"How was he killed?"

"He was shot on the beach." She rubbed her temple as if her husband's death had left a permanent sore spot in her mind.

"Malibu Beach?"

"Yes. We have a beach cottage, and Mark often went for an evening stroll down there. Someone came up behind him and shot him in the head with a handgun. The police arrested a dozen or more suspects—mostly transients and beach bums —but they never got enough evidence to lay charges."

"Was he robbed?"

"His wallet was taken. They never recovered it either. You can see why I'm not a great admirer of the local police."

"Still they have their uses, and they're coming out here anyway. I need your permission to talk to them, freely."

She sat still and solemn. I could hear her breathing, measuring out the slow seconds.

"I have to take your advice, don't I? If Stephen was killed because I decided wrong, I couldn't live with it. Go ahead, Mr. Archer, do what you want to do." She dismissed me with a wave of her hand, then called me back from the door. "I want you to stay with it, of course."

"I was hoping you would."

"If you do find Stephen yourself, and bring him home safely, I'm still prepared to pay you a hundred thousand. Do you need money for expenses, now?"

"It would help. I'm co-opting another man, a San Francisco detective named Willie Mackey. Do you want to advance me a thousand?"

"I'll write you a check. Where's my bag?" She raised her voice and called: "Sidney! Where's my bag?"

Her husband came from the adjoining room. He was wearing a paint-daubed smock and had a spot of red paint on his nose. His eyes looked through us as if we were transparent.

"What is it?" he said impatiently.

"I want you to find my bag."

"Find it yourself. I'm working."

"Don't use that tone on me."

"I wasn't aware of any particular tone."

"We won't argue. Go and find my bag. It will do you no harm to do something useful for a change."

"Painting is useful."

She half-rose from the long chair. "I said we wouldn't argue. Get my bag. I think I left it in the library."

"All right, if you want to make a major issue out of it."

He went and got her bag, and she wrote me a check for a thousand dollars. Marburg went back to his painting.

Then two deputies arrived from the sheriff's office, and Mrs. Marburg and I talked to them in the main living room. Dr. Converse stood listening just inside the door, his clever glance moving from face to face.

Later I talked to an officer of the highway patrol, and after that to a sheriff's captain named Aubrey. He was a big middle-aged man with a big man's easy confidence. I liked him. Dr. Converse was gone by this time, and with a single exception I held nothing back from Aubrey.

The single exception was the Fleischer angle. Jack Fleischer was a recently retired officer of the law, and officers of the law tend to hang together protectively in a pinch. I felt that Fleischer's role in the case should be investigated by freelances like me and Willie Mackey.

88

To keep everything even, I stopped by the Purdue Street station on my way into town. Detective-Sergeant Prince was in a rage so black that his partner Janowski was worried about him. Laurel Smith had died during the night.

Chapter 17

I CLIMBED THE STAIRS to my second-floor office on knees that shook under me. It was a few minutes past ten by the wall clock. I called my answering service. A few minutes before ten, Willie Mackey had called me from San Francisco. I returned the call now, and got Willie in his Geary Street office.

"Nice timing, Lew. I was just trying to phone you. Your man Fleischer checked in at the Sandman about 3 a.m. I put a man on him and made a deal with the night keyboy. The keyboy handles the switchboard after midnight. Fleischer left a call for seven thirty and as soon as he got up he phoned a certain Albert Blevins at the Bowman Hotel. That's in the Mission District. Fleischer came up to the city and he and Blevins had breakfast together in a cafeteria on Fifth Street. Then they went back to Blevins's hotel and apparently they're still there, in his room. Does all this mean anything to you?"

"The name Blevins does." It was the name on Laurel's Social Security card. "Find out what you can about him, will you, and meet me at San Francisco Airport?"

"What time?"

I got a plane schedule out of my desk. "One o'clock, in the bar."

I made an airline reservation and drove out to Los Angeles International. It was a clear bright day at both ends of the flight. When my jet came down over San Francisco Bay I could see the city standing up like a perpendicular dream and past it to the curved dark blue horizon. The endless roofs of the bedroom towns stretched southward along the Peninsula farther than I could see.

I found Willie in the airport bar drinking a Gibson. He was a smart experienced man who copied his style of life from the flamboyant San Francisco lawyers who often employed him. Willie spent his money on women and clothes, and always looked a little overdressed, as he did now. His gray hair had once been black. His very sharp black eyes hadn't changed in the twenty years I'd known him.

"Albert Blevins," he said, "has lived in the Bowman Hotel for about a year. It's a pensioners' hotel, one of the better ones in the Mission District."

"Just how old is he?"

"Maybe sixty. I don't know for sure. You didn't give me much time, Lew."

"There isn't much time."

I told him why. Willie was a money player, and his eyes shone like anthracite coal when he heard about Hackett's wealth. A chunk of it would buy him a new young blonde to break his heart with again.

Willie wanted another Gibson and some lunch, but I steered him to an elevator and out to the parking lot. He backed his Jaguar out of its slot and headed up Bayshore to the city. The aching blue water and the endless mud flats gave me the pang of remembered younger days.

Willie broke into my thoughts. "What's Albert Blevins got to do with the Hackett snatch?"

"I don't know, but there has to be some connection. A woman named Laurel Smith who died last night—homicide victim—used to call herself Laurel Blevins. Fleischer knew her in Rodeo City fifteen years ago. Around the same time, and the same locality, an unidentified man was decapitated by a train. Apparently he was Davy Spanner's father. Deputy Fleischer handled the case, and put it in the books as accidental death."

"And you say it wasn't?"

"I'm suspending judgment. There's still another connection. Spanner was Laurel Smith's tenant and employee, and I suspect they were closer than that, maybe very close."

"Did he kill her?"

"I don't think so. The point is that the people and the

places are starting to repeat." I told Willie about the midnight scene at the railroad crossing. "If we can get Fleischer and Blevins to talk, we may be able to shut the case down in a hurry. Particularly Fleischer. For the past month he's been bugging Laurel's apartment in Pacific Palisades."

"You think he killed her?"

"He may have. Or he may know who did."

Willie concentrated on the traffic as we entered the city. He left his car in an underground garage on Geary Street. I walked up to his office with him to see if the tail on Fleischer had called in. He had. Fleischer had left Blevins at the Bowman Hotel, and at the time of the call was inside the shop of the Acme Photocopy Service. This was Fleischer's second visit to the Acme Photocopy Service. He had stopped there on his way to the Bowman Hotel.

I did the same. The Acme Service was a one-man business conducted in a narrow store on Market Street. A thin man with a cough labored over a copying machine. For five quick dollars he told me what Fleischer had had copied. On his first visit it was the front page of an old newspaper, on his second an even older birth certificate.

"Whose birth certificate?"

"I don't know. Just a minute. Somebody called Jasper, that was the first name, I think."

I waited, but nothing else came. "What was in the newspaper?"

"I didn't read it. If I read everything I copy, I'd go blind."

"You say it was old. How old?"

"I didn't look at the date, but the paper had turned pretty yellow. I had to handle it carefully." He coughed, and lit a cigarette in reflex. "That's all I can tell you, mister. What's it all about?"

I took that question to the Bowman Hotel. It was a grimy white brick building whose four rows of evenly spaced front windows had a view of the railroad yards. Some of the windows had wooden boxes nailed to their outside sills in lieu of refrigerators.

The lobby was full of old men. I wondered where all the old women were.

One of the old men told me that Albert Blevins's room was

on the second floor at the end of the hall. I went up and knocked on the door.

A husky voice said: "Who is it?"

"My name is Archer. I'd like to talk to you, Mr. Blevins."

"What about?"

"Same thing as the other fellow."

A key turned in the lock. Albert Blevins opened the door a few inches. He wasn't terribly old, but his body was warped by use and his seamed face was set in the cast of permanent stubborn failure. His clear blue eyes had the oddly innocent look of a man who had never been completely broken in to human society. You used to see such men in the small towns, in the desert, on the road. Now they collected in the hollow cores of the cities.

"Will you pay me same as the other fellow?" he said.

"How much?"

"The other fellow gave me fifty dollars. Ask him yourself if you don't believe me." A horrible suspicion ravaged his face. "Say, you're not from Welfare?"

"No."

"Thank Jehosophat for that. You get a lucky windfall, they take it off your Welfare and that wipes out your luck."

"They shouldn't do that."

My agreement pleased Blevins. He opened the door wider and beckoned me into the room. It was a ten-foot cube containing a chair, a table, and a bed. The iron fire escape slanted across the single window like a cancellation mark.

There was a faint sour odor of time in the room. So far as I could tell, it came from the leatherette suitcase which lay open across the bed. Some of its contents were on the table, as if Blevins had been sorting through his memories and laying them out for sale.

I could recognize some of the things on sight: a broad-bladed fisherman's knife to which a few old fish scales were clinging like dry tears, a marriage certificate with deep fold-marks cutting across it, a bundle of letters tied together with a brown shoestring, some rifle bullets and a silver dollar in a net sack, a small miner's pick, a couple of ancient pipes, an ineffectual-looking rabbit's foot, some clean folded underwear and socks, a glass ball that filled itself with a miniature snowstorm when you shook it, a peacock feather watching us with its eye, and an eagle's claw.

I sat at the table and picked up the marriage certificate. It was signed by a civil registrar, and stated that Albert D. Blevins had married Henrietta R. Krug in San Francisco on March 3, 1927. Henrietta was seventeen at the time; Albert was twenty; which made him just over sixty now.

"You want to buy my marriage paper?"

"I might."

"The other fellow gave me fifty for the birth certificate. I'll let this one go for twenty-five." He sat on the edge of the bed. "It's of no great value to me. Marrying her was the big mistake of my life. I never should of married any woman. She told me that herself a hundred times, *after* we got hitched. But what's a man to do when a girl comes to him and tells him he got her pregnant?" He spread his hands out incompletely on his faded denim knees. His painfully uncurling fingers reminded me of starfish torn from their moorings.

"I shouldn't complain," he said. "Her parents treated us right. They gave us their farm and moved into town. It wasn't Mr. Krug's fault that we had three straight years of drought and I couldn't afford to bring in water and feed and the cattle died. I don't even blame Etta for leaving me, not any more. It was a miserable life on that dry farm. All we had between us was going to bed together, and that dried up before the baby was born. I delivered him myself, and I guess it hurt her pretty bad. Etta never let me come near her again."

He was talking like a man who hadn't had a chance to reveal himself for years, if ever. He rose and paced the room, four steps each way.

"It made me mean," he said, "living with a pretty girl and not being able to touch her. I treated her mean, and I treated the boy even worse. I used to beat the living bejesus out of him. I blamed him, see, for cutting off my nooky by being born. Sometimes I beat him until the blood would flow. Etta would try to stop me, and then I'd beat her, too."

His calm blue eyes looked down into mine. I could feel the coldness of his innocence.

"One night I beat her once too often. She picked up the kitchen lamp and threw it at my head. I ducked, but the kerosene splashed on the hot stove and set fire to the kitchen. Before I got the fire out, most of the house was gone, and so was Etta."

"You mean she burned to death?"

"No, I don't mean that." He was impatient with me for failing to divine his thoughts. "She ran away. I never saw hide nor hair of her again."

"What happened to your son?"

"Jasper? He stayed with me for a while. This was right at the beginning of the depression. I got a government job working on the roads, and I found some boards and bought some tarpaper and roofed over what was left of the house. We lived there for a couple more years, little Jasper and me. I was treating him better, but he didn't like me much. He was always scared of me, I can't say I blame him. When he was four he started to run away. I tried tying him up, but he got pretty good at untying knots. What could I do? I took him to his grandparents in L.A. Mr. Krug had a watchman job with one of the oil companies and they agreed to take him off my hands.

"I went down to see Jasper a few times after that, but he always got upset. He used to run at me and hit me with his fists. So I just stopped going. I left the state. I mined silver in Colorado. I fished for salmon out of Anchorage. One day my boat turned over and I made it to shore all right but then I came down with double pneumonia. After that I lost my poop and I came back to California. That's my sad story. I been here going on ten years."

He sat down again. He was neither sad nor smiling. Breathing slowly and deeply, he regarded me with a certain satisfaction. He had lifted the weight of his life and set it down again in the same place.

I asked him: "Do you know what happened to Jasper?" The question made me conscious of its overtones. I was fairly sure by now that Jasper Blevins had died under a train fifteen years ago.

"He grew up and got married. Etta's parents sent me a wedding announcement, and then about seven months after that they sent me a letter that I had a grandson. That was close to twenty years ago, when I was in Colorado, but that seven months stuck in my mind. It meant that Jasper had to get married, just the same as *I* did in my time.

"History repeating itself," he said. "But there was one way I didn't let it repeat. I kept away from my grandson. I wasn't going to make him a-scared of me. And I didn't want to get to know him and then get cut off from seeing him either. I'd rather stay alone right on through."

"You wouldn't have that letter, would you?"

"I might. I think I have."

He untied the brown shoelace that held his bundle of letters together. His awkward fingers sorted them and picked out a blue envelope. He took the letter out of the envelope, read it slowly with moving lips, and handed it to me.

The letter was written in faded blue ink on blue notepaper with a deckled edge:

> *Mrs. Joseph L. Krug*
> *209 West Capo Street*
> *Santa Monica, California*
> *December 14, 1948*

Mr. Albert D. Blevins
Box 49, Silver Creek, Colorado

Dear Albert:

> *It's a long time since we heard from you. Here's hoping this finds you at the same address. You never did let us know if you got the wedding announcement. In case you did not, Jasper married a lovely girl who has been staying with us, nee Laurel Dudney. She's only seventeen but very mature, these Texas girls grow up fast. Anyway they got married and now they have a darling baby boy, born the day before yesterday, they called him David which is a biblical name as you know.*

> *So now you have a grandson, anyway. Come and see him if you can, you really should, we'll all let bygones be bygones. Jasper and Laurel and the babe will be staying at our house for a while, then Jasper wants to have a try at ranching. We hope*

you are taking care of yourself, Albert, in those
mines. Your loving mother-in-law,

Alma R. Krug,

P.S. We never hear from Etta.

A.R.K.

"Do you have the wedding announcement?" I asked Blevins.

"I had, but I gave it to the other fellow. I threw it in along with the birth certificate."

"Whose birth certificate?"

"Jasper's. Jasper is the one he's interested in."

"Did he say why?"

"No. This Fleischer fellow plays his cards very close to his vest. Is he really a policeman?"

"An ex-policeman."

"What's in it for him?"

"I don't know."

"You know what's in it for *you*," Blevins said. "You didn't come here to listen to the story of my life."

"I sort of have, though, haven't I?"

"I guess you have." He smiled, so widely I could count his six upper teeth. "This business of Jasper churned up a lot of memories. Why is everybody so interested in Jasper? Why are you fellows willing to pay me money? Or are you?"

Instead of answering his questions, I took three twenties from my wallet and spread them out on a bare part of the table. Blevins opened the front of his shirt and pulled out an oilskin pouch which hung around his neck on a piece of soiled rawhide. He folded the twenties small and put them in the pouch, replacing it against the sparse gray fur of his chest.

"That's twenty-five for the marriage certificate," I said, "twenty-five for the letter, and ten for the autobiography."

"Come again?"

"The life story," I said.

"Oh. Thank you very much. I been needing some warm clothes. Sixty dollars goes a long way at the rummage stores."

I felt a little cheap when he handed me the letter and marriage certificate. I put them in my inside breast pocket. My hand came in contact with the picture Mrs. Fleischer had given me. I showed it to Albert Blevins, remembering with a pang that Laurel was newly dead.

"Do you recognize her, Mr. Blevins?"

"No."

"It's the girl Jasper married."

"I never met her."

Our hands touched as he gave the picture back to me. I felt a kind of short-circuit, a buzzing and burning, as if I had grounded the present in the actual flesh of the past.

Time blurred like tears for an instant. Davy's father had died a violent death. His mother had died in violence. Davy the child of violence was roaring down the trail which led back to Albert Blevins. In the buzzing and the burning and the blur I got my first real feeling of what it was like to be Davy, and it jolted me.

"No," Blevins said, "I never saw Jasper's wife. She's a handsome filly."

"She was."

I took the picture and left before either of us could ask the other more questions.

Chapter 18

I TOOK A CAB back to Willie Mackey's office, buying a paper on the way. Stephen Hackett's disappearance had made the headlines. The story underneath was weak in detail. I did learn from it, though, that Hackett was alleged to be one of the richest men in California.

From Willie Mackey I learned that Jack Fleischer had checked out of the Sandman Motor Hotel and headed south.

Willie's operative had lost Fleischer on the highway above San José.

I talked to the operative when he came in. He was an earnest crew-cut young man named Bob Levine, and he was deeply frustrated. Not only had Fleischer eluded him; Fleischer's car was faster than his. He looked ready to kick Willie's ornate red-upholstered office furniture.

"Don't take it so hard," I told Levine. "I know where Fleischer lives, I can pick him up down south. It would have been a wasted trip for you."

"Really?"

"Really. During the time you tailed him, did Fleischer visit anyone besides Albert Blevins?"

"Not unless you count the Acme copying shop. I haven't had a chance to check back on them."

"I have. You might try the man again. He may have been holding back on me. He may have copies of the newspaper page and the birth certificate that Fleischer took in to him."

"If he had I'll get them," Levine said. "Now is there anything else I can do for you?"

"Drive me to the airport." I looked at my watch. "We've got time to stop at the Sandman Motor Hotel on the way."

It was worth making the detour to Camino Real. The maid was cleaning out Fleischer's room at the Sandman. The only thing he had left behind in the wastebasket was a copy of the same paper I had bought. The Hackett story had been torn out of it.

Whatever Fleischer's interests were, they were steadily converging with mine. At the moment he was a step ahead of me, and I calculated how much time I would have in Los Angeles before Fleischer could possibly get there by car. Three hours, anyway.

I used up nearly all of the first hour driving in slow traffic from Los Angeles International Airport to the Sebastian house in Woodland Hills. I hadn't phoned ahead because I didn't want to be told by Sebastian that I couldn't talk to his daughter. It was daylight when I left the airport, and full night when my overheated engine toiled up Sebastian's hill.

A Los Angeles County sheriff's car was parked in front of Sebastian's house. Its radio was talking brokenly, as if the car itself had developed a voice and begun to complain about the state of the world. When I rang Sebastian's doorbell, it was a grim-looking sheriff's deputy who answered the door.

"Yes sir?"

"I'd like to talk to Mr. Sebastian."

"Mr. Sebastian is busy right now. You the lawyer?"

"No." I told him who I was. "Mr. Sebastian will want to see me."

"I'll ask him."

The deputy closed the door until it clicked. I waited for a couple of minutes, listening to the mutterings of the patrol car. Sebastian opened the door. He kept changing, like a fighter undergoing a fifteen-round beating. The clump of hair on his forehead needed combing. His face was pale. His eyes were hopeless. The deputy stood behind him formally, like a keeper.

"They're taking her away," Sebastian said. "They're going to put her in prison."

"It isn't a prison," the deputy said. "It's a home."

I asked Sebastian: "Can't you get bail?"

"Yes, but I can't raise twenty thousand dollars."

"That's high."

"Assault with intent is a very serious charge," the deputy said. "And then there's the kidnapping charge—"

"It's still high."

"The judge didn't think so," the deputy said.

I said: "Would you go away, please? I want to talk to Mr. Sebastian in private."

"You said you weren't a lawyer. You got no right to give him legal advice."

"Neither have you. Give us a little leeway, officer."

He retreated out of sight if not out of hearing. I asked Sebastian: "Who is your lawyer?"

"I called a man in Van Nuys. Arnold Bendix. He said he'd come out tonight."

"This is tonight. What have you been doing all day?"

"I hardly know." He looked back into the house as if the day was still there waiting for him like a maze or a puzzle. "The D.A. sent two men out. Then we did a lot of talking to Sandy, of course, trying to make sense of this whole terrible mess."

"You won't do that by sitting around talking. Get your

lawyer out here. And a doctor. You should be able to persuade the law to let you keep your daughter overnight. That will give your lawyer time to get back to the court and see if he can get the bail reduced. You can swing ten thousand bail. A bondsman will let you have it for one thousand."

He was appalled by the amount. "How can I possibly raise a thousand dollars? I'm sure to be fired from my job."

"Go to a loan shark. This is what they're for."

"And how much will that cost me?" he said wretchedly.

"A hundred or two more, perhaps. But we're not talking about money. We're talking about keeping your daughter out of jail."

He got the message, dimly at first, as if it had reached him by way of a communications satellite: he was at the crux of his life. The realization entered his eyes and took the place of hopelessness. There were still things he could do.

He went to the telephone and called his family doctor, a Dr. Jeffrey in Canoga Park. Dr. Jeffrey didn't want to come out to the house. Sebastian told him he had to. Then he called the lawyer and told him the same thing.

We went into the living room, accompanied by the deputy sheriff, who seemed to suspect that all of us might be planning a mass getaway. Bernice Sebastian was there, looking strained and gaunt and exceedingly well-groomed in a black sheath. With her was a pert blonde about my age who wore a blue suit that resembled a uniform.

She introduced herself as Mrs. Sherrill from the probation office. I told her I knew Jake Belsize.

"I was talking to him this afternoon," she said. "He's very upset about this whole affair. He blames himself for not keeping closer tabs on Spanner."

"He *should* blame himself," Mrs. Sebastian said.

"That's water under the bridge," I said to both of them; and to Mrs. Sherrill: "Does Belsize have any suggestions?"

"My being here was his suggestion. The girl won't talk to me, unfortunately. I tried to explain to her parents that if Sandy would give some sign of cooperation, it would be a lot easier for her."

Sebastian spoke up: "Sandy's in no condition to be questioned. She's in bed under sedation. Dr. Jeffrey's on his way over. So is my lawyer, Arnold Bendix."

"We can't wait around all night," the deputy said. "We've got a warrant, and it's our duty to take her in."

"No, we better wait, Tom," Mrs. Sherrill said. "See what the doctor has to say."

The deputy sat down in a corner by himself. A heavy silence settled over the room. It was like a funeral, or a death-bed scene. By getting into trouble Sandy had converted herself into an unforgettable presence, a kind of presiding deity of the household. I wondered if that had been her real intention.

Dr. Jeffrey arrived, a young man in a hurry. He went into Sandy's bedroom with her mother. The lawyer came close on the doctor's heels. Between the two of them, they persuaded the deputy and Mrs. Sherrill to let the whole thing lie over until morning.

The doctor was the first to leave: his time was the most expensive. I followed him out to his Rover, and he gave me a reluctant couple of minutes.

"What's Sandy's mental condition?"

"She's frightened and confused, naturally. A bit hysterical, and very tired."

"Is it all right for me to question her, doctor?"

"Is it necessary?"

"A man's life may depend on it. You may not know what's going on—"

"It's in tonight's paper. But it sounds pretty farfetched to me. How could a girl like that be involved in a kidnapping?"

"There's no doubt she is. Can I talk to her?"

"For five minutes, no longer. She needs rest."

"What about psychiatric care?"

"We'll see about that tomorrow. These adolescents have great recuperative powers."

Jeffrey turned to get into his car. But I had more questions for him.

"How long have you been treating her, doctor?"

"Three or four years, since she left her pediatrician."

"Last summer she was treated by a doctor named Converse in Beverly Hills. Did you know that?"

"No." I had succeeded in interesting Jeffrey. "I never heard of any Dr. Converse. What was he treating her for?"

"He wouldn't tell me. But he'd probably tell you. It could have a bearing on this mess."

"Really? Perhaps I'll give him a call."

The deputy and Mrs. Sherrill came out to the patrol car, and Jeffrey's Rover led them down the hill. Bernice Sebastian stood in the open doorway and watched them go.

"Thank God we've got them out of here for tonight. Thank you, too, Mr. Archer, for taking charge."

The expression of feeling came hard to her. Her eyes had a dull overexposed look.

"Your husband took charge. I gave him some advice. I've sat in on quite a few of these family evenings."

"Do you have children of your own?"

"No. I used to feel deprived."

She let me in and closed the door and leaned on it, as if she was countering the pressure of the night outside. "Will they let us keep her?"

"It depends on several things. You have trouble in the family, and Sandy isn't the only source of it. The trouble is between her and you."

"It's Keith she's angry with, mainly."

"That makes it three-way trouble. You've got to resolve it some way."

"Who says so?"

"Probation will say so, if she's lucky enough to be taken on as a risk. What's Sandy got against her father?"

"I don't know." But she veiled her eyes and looked down.

"I don't believe you, Mrs. Sebastian. Do you want to show me Sandy's diary?"

"I destroyed it, as I told you this morning—yesterday morning." She closed her eyes and covered them with her fine narrow hand. She had lost a day, for a moment, and it worried her.

"Tell me what was in it that made you destroy it."

"I can't. I won't. I won't put up with this humiliation."

She tried to rush blindly past me. I stepped sideways, and she ran into me. We stood in close contact, her body taut and elegant against mine. A spreading heat climbed from my groin to my heart and into my head.

We stepped back away from each other by sudden mutual

consent. But there was a difference in our relation now, the difference of a possibility.

"I'm sorry," she said without explaining what she was sorry for.

"It was my fault. We haven't finished." Possibility put a curve on the meanings of the words.

"Haven't we?"

"No. The most important thing in determining what happens to Sandy is what happens to Stephen Hackett. If we can get him back alive—" I let the sentence finish itself in her mind. "Sandy may be able to tell me something. I have the doctor's permission to question her."

"What about?"

"She said last night that Davy Spanner was looking for a place where he used to live. I'm hoping she can pin it down a bit."

"Is that all?"

"It's all for now."

"Very well. You can talk to her."

We passed the door of the living room, where Sebastian and the lawyer were talking about bail. The door of Sandy's room was locked and the key was in the door. Her mother turned the key and gently pushed the door open.

"Sandy? Are you still awake?"

"What do you think?"

"That's not a nice way to answer me." The mother's tone was strangely mixed, as if she was talking to an immensely powerful idiot. "Mr. Archer wants to talk to you. *You* remember Mr. Archer."

"How could I forget him?"

"Sandy, *please* talk like yourself."

"This is the new me. Send in the fuzz."

The girl's toughness was clearly an act, generated by guilt and terror and self-disgust, and a rather bullying contempt for her mother. But for the time, at least, the tough act had taken over her personality. I went in hoping to reach the original girl, the one who collected Ivy League pennants and cloth animals.

She was sitting up in bed with one of the cloth animals hugged to her chest: a brown velvet spaniel with drooping ears, button eyes, a red felt tongue. Sandy was flushed and

103

heavy-eyed. I sat on my heels by the bed, so that our eyes were almost on a level.

"Hello, Sandy."

"Hello. They're going to put me in jail." Her voice was matter-of-fact, wooden. "That should make you happy."

"Why do you say that?"

"It's what you wanted, isn't it?"

Her mother spoke from the doorway: "You mustn't talk like that to Mr. Archer."

"Go away," the girl said. "You give me a headache."

"*I'm* the one with the headache."

"I think I'm getting one, too," I said. "Please let me talk to Sandy alone for a minute."

The woman withdrew. The girl said: "What are we supposed to talk about?"

"You may be able to help me and help yourself at the same time. Everyone will be a lot better off if we can find Davy before he kills Mr. Hackett. Do you have any idea where they are?"

"No."

"You said last night, early this morning, that Davy was looking for a certain place, a place where he used to live. Do you know where it is, Sandy?"

"How should I know? He didn't know himself."

"Did he remember anything about it?"

"It was in the mountains someplace, up north of Santa Teresa. Some kind of a ranch where he used to live before they put him in the orphanage."

"Did he describe the place?"

"Yes, but it didn't sound like much of a place to me. The house burned down a long time ago. Somebody put a roof over part of it."

"The house burned down?"

"That's what he said."

I stood up. The girl recoiled, clutching the velvet dog as if it was her only friend and guardian.

"Why did he want to go back there, Sandy?"

"I don't know. He used to live there with his father. And his mother. I guess he thought it was heaven or something, you know?"

"Was Laurel Smith his mother?"

"I guess she was. She said she was his mother. But she ran out on him when he was a little boy." Sandy took a quick audible breath. "I told him he was lucky to have that happen."

"What have you got against your parents, Sandy?"

"We won't talk about it."

"Why did you throw in with Davy on this? You're not that kind of a girl."

"You don't know me. I'm bad clear through."

The tough act, which she'd forgotten for a minute, was coming on strong again. It was more than an act, of course. Her mind was caught between darkness and light, spinning like a coin she had tossed herself.

Outside in the hallway, where Bernice Sebastian was waiting, I remembered that something was missing from Sandy's room. The silver-framed picture of Heidi Gensler had been taken down.

Chapter 19

WITH BERNICE SEBASTIAN'S permission, I shut myself up in the study and put in a call for Albert Blevins at the Bowman Hotel. The long silence on the line was broken by a succession of voices. Albert would be right down. Albert wasn't in his room but he was being searched for. Albert had apparently gone out, and nobody knew when he was expected back. He'd gone to a triple feature on Market Street, it was thought.

I left a message for Albert, asking him to call my answering service collect, but I doubted that I'd be hearing from him tonight.

There was another possible source of information. I got out the papers I'd acquired from Albert Blevins and laid them on Sebastian's desk. I reread the letter which Alma R.

Krug, Albert's mother-in-law, had sent him in 1948 from her house at 209 West Capo Street in Santa Monica.

"Jasper and Laurel and the babe will be staying at our house for a while," Mrs. Krug had written; "then Jasper wants to have a try at ranching."

I looked for Alma Krug's name in the telephone directory, and tried Information, in vain. Mrs. Krug's letter had been written nearly twenty years ago. The lady must be very old, or dead.

I could think of only one way to find out which. I said good night to the Sebastians and headed back toward Santa Monica. The traffic on the freeway was still heavy but it was flowing freely now. The headlights poured down Sepulveda in a brilliant cataract.

I felt surprisingly good. If Mrs. Krug was alive and able to tell me where the ranch was, I could break the case before morning. I even let a part of my mind play with the question of what I might do with a hundred thousand dollars.

Hell, I could even retire. The possibility jarred me. I had to admit to myself that I lived for nights like these, moving across the city's great broken body, making connections among its millions of cells. I had a crazy wish or fantasy that some day before I died, if I made all the right neural connections, the city would come all the way alive. Like the Bride of Frankenstein.

I left Sepulveda at Wilshire and drove down San Vicente to Capo Street. 209 West Capo was a two-story apartment building. Transplanted palm trees lit by green floodlights leaned across the new-looking stucco front.

I found the manager in Apartment One, a middle-aged man in shirt sleeves with his finger in a book. I told him my name. He said his was Ralph Cuddy.

Cuddy had a Southern accent, probably Texan. There were crossed pistols over the mantelpiece and several moral sayings on the walls. I said: "A Mrs. Alma Krug used to live at this location."

"That's right."

"Do you know where she lives now?"

"In a home."

"What kind of a home?"

"A convalescent home. She broke her hip a few years back."

"That's too bad. I'd like to talk to her."

"What about?"

"Family matters."

"Mrs. Krug has no family left." He added with a self-conscious smirk: "Unless you count me."

"She has a son-in-law in San Francisco." And a great-grandson named Davy, God knows where. "Did she ever mention a ranch she owns in Santa Teresa County?"

"I've heard of the ranch."

"Can you tell me how to find it?"

"I've never been there. They let it go for taxes years ago."

"Are you related to Mrs. Krug?"

"Not exactly. I was close to the family. Still am."

"Can you give me the address of her convalescent home?"

"Maybe. Just what do you want to see her about?"

"I ran into her son-in-law Albert Blevins today."

Cuddy gave me a wise look. "That would be Etta's first husband."

"Right."

"And where does the ranch come in?"

"Albert was talking about it. He lived there once."

"I see."

Ralph Cuddy laid down his open book—its title was *The Role of the Security Officer in Business*—and went to a desk on the far side of the room. He came back to me with the address of the Oakwood Convalescent Home neatly written on a slip of paper.

The Home turned out to be a large California Spanish house dating from the twenties. It occupied its own walled grounds in Santa Monica. The driveway was overarched by Italian stone pines. There were ten or a dozen cars in the lighted parking lot, a drift of music from the main building. You could almost imagine that time had been reversed and there was a party going on.

The illusion faded in the big reception hall. Old people sat around in groups of two or three, chatting, keeping life warm. They made me think of refugees who had been given shelter in some baronial manor.

A very contemporary-looking nurse in white nylon led me

down a corridor to Mrs. Krug's room. It was a spacious and well furnished bed-sitting room. A white-haired old lady wearing a wool robe was sitting in a wheel chair with an afghan over her knees, watching the Merv Griffin Show on television. She held an open Bible in her arthritic hands.

The nurse turned down the sound. "A gentleman to see you, Mrs. Krug."

She looked up with keen inquiring eyes magnified by her glasses. "Who are you?"

"My name is Lew Archer. Remember Albert Blevins, who married your daughter Etta?"

"Naturally I remember him. There's nothing the matter with my memory, thank you. What about Albert Blevins?"

"I was talking to him in San Francisco today."

"Is that a fact? I haven't heard from Albert in nearly twenty years. I asked him to come and see us when Jasper's boy was born, but Albert never answered."

She was silent, listening to silence. The nurse left the room. I sat down and Mrs. Krug leaned toward me, into the present.

"How is Albert, anyway? Is he still the same old Albert?"

"Probably. I didn't know him when he was younger."

"You weren't missing much." She smiled. "My husband always said that Albert was born too late. He should have been an old-time cowpoke. Albert was always a loner."

"He still is. He lives in a hotel room by himself."

"I'm not surprised. He should never have married anybody, let alone Etta. At first I blamed Albert for all the trouble between them, when he threw the lamp and set fire to the house. But when I saw the things that my daughter did later —" She closed her mouth with a click, as if to bite back memory. "Did Albert send you here to me?"

"Not exactly. In the course of our conversation, he mentioned the ranch you gave him, or let him use."

She nodded briskly. "That was in 1927, the year Albert married Etta. I was sick of the ranch myself, if you want the truth. I was a city girl, and a trained teacher. Twenty years of feeding chickens was all I could take. I made Krug move down here. He got a good job, a security job, which he held until he retired. Albert and Etta took over the ranch. They lasted about two years and then they split. It was a bad-luck ranch. Did Albert tell you?"

"Tell me what?"

"The things that happened at that ranch. No." She shook her head. "Albert couldn't tell you because he didn't know, at least not all of them. First he burned down the house, and Etta ran out on him. She left him to look after little Jasper. When that broke down my husband and I took over Jasper and raised him, which wasn't easy, I can tell you. He was a handful.

"Then when Jasper settled down and married Laurel Dudney, he took it into his head to go back to the ranch. He didn't plan to work it, you understand. He thought it would be a cheap place to live while he painted pretty pictures of the countryside. I guess it was cheap enough, for him, with my husband and me sending him money after he used up Laurel's." Her veined hands closed on the arms of the wheel chair. "Do you know how that spoiled grandson of ours showed his gratitude?"

"Albert didn't tell me."

"Jasper took Laurel and the little boy and shook the dust from his heels. I haven't heard from any one of them since. Jasper is like his mother—and I say it even if she is my daughter—an ingrate through and through."

I didn't try to tell Alma Krug about Jasper's death, or Laurel's. The old woman's eyes were getting too bright. They knew too much already. A bitter frozen expression had settled on her mouth like a foretaste of her own death.

After another silence, she turned to me. "You didn't come here to listen to me complaining. Why *did* you come?"

"I want to see that ranch."

"What for? It's wornout land. It never was any better than semi-desert. We raised more buzzards than we did cattle. And after Jasper and Laurel took off into the blue we let it go for taxes."

"I think your great-grandson David may be there."

"Really? Do you know David?"

"I've met him."

She calculated rapidly. "He must be a young man now."

"A very young man. Davy is nineteen."

"What's he doing with himself?" she asked with the kind of

hopeful interest that wasn't betting too heavily on the answer.
"Nothing much."

"I suppose he takes after his father. Jasper always had big
dreams and nothing much to show for them afterwards." She
rotated one wheel of her chair and turned to face me. "If you
know where David is, do you know where Jasper is?"

"No. And I don't know where David is. I was hoping you
could tell me how to find the ranch."

"Sure, if it hasn't blown away, the way that wind comes
roaring down the wash. You know Rodeo City?"

"I've been there."

"Go into the middle of town to the main corner, that's the
Rodeo Hotel with the sheriff's office right across from it.
Take a right turn there and drive out past the rodeo grounds
and over the pass and inland about twenty miles, to a little
settlement called Centerville. I taught school there once.
From Centerville you drive north another twelve miles on a
county road. It's not too easy to find, especially after dark.
Are you thinking of going there tonight?"

I said I was.

"Then you better ask in Centerville. Everybody in Centerville knows where the Krug ranch is." She paused. "It's
strange how the generations of the family keep homing to that
place. It's a bad-luck place, I guess we're a bad-luck family."

I didn't try to deny this. The little I knew of the family—
Albert Blevins' solitary life, the ugly fates of Jasper and Laurel fifteen years apart, Davy's penchant for violence—only
confirmed what Mrs. Krug had said.

She was sitting with her fists pressed against her body, as
if she could feel the memory of labor. She shook her white
head.

"I was thinking, if you see David, you could tell him
where his great-grandma is. But I don't know. I just have
enough for myself. I pay six hundred a month here. Don't
tell him about me unless he asks. I wouldn't want Jasper back
on my hands again. Or Laurel. She was a sweet girl, but she
turned out to be an ingrate, too. I took her into my home and
did my best for her, and then she turned her back on me."

"Was Laurel related to you, too?"

"No. She came from Texas. A very wealthy man was interested in Laurel. He sent her to us."

"I don't understand."

"You're not supposed to. I won't tell on Laurel. She wasn't my daughter or granddaughter, but I liked her better than any of them."

She was whispering. The past was filling the room like a tide of whispers. I got up to leave.

Alma Krug gave me her knobbed, delicate hand. "Turn up the sound on your way out, please. I'd rather listen to *other* people talk."

I turned up the sound and closed her door after me. Behind another door, halfway down the corridor, a quavering old man's voice rose: "Please don't cut me."

The old man pulled the door open and came out into the corridor. His naked body was the shape of an elongated egg. He flung his arms around me, and pressed his almost hairless head into my solar plexus.

"Don't let them cut me to pieces. Tell them not to, Momma."

Though there was nobody else there, I told them not to. The little old man let go of me and went back into his room and closed the door.

Chapter 20

IN THE RECEPTION HALL, the refugees from the war of the generations had dwindled to half a dozen. A middle-aged male orderly was quietly herding them back to their rooms.

"It's bedtime, folks," he said.

Jack Fleischer came in the front door. His eyes, his entire face, were glazed with weariness and alcohol.

"I'd like to see Mrs. Krug," he said to the orderly.

"I'm sorry, sir. Visiting hours are over."

"This is important."

"I can't help that, sir. I don't make the decisions around here. The manager's in Chicago at a convention."

"Don't tell me that. I'm a law-enforcement officer."

Fleischer's voice was rising. His face was swelling with blood. He fumbled in his pockets and found a badge which he showed to the orderly.

"That makes no difference, sir. I have my orders."

Without warning, Fleischer hit the orderly with his open hand. The man fell down and got up. Half of his face was red, the other half white. The old people watched in silence. Like actual refugees, they were more afraid of physical force than anything.

I moved up behind Fleischer and put an armlock on him. He was heavy and powerful. It was all I could do to hold him.

"Is he a friend of yours?" the orderly asked me.

"No."

But in a sense Fleischer belonged to me. I walked him outside and released him. He pulled out an automatic pistol.

"You're under arrest," he told me.

"What for? Preventing a riot?"

"Resisting an officer in the performance of his duty."

He was glaring and sputtering. The gun in his hand looked like a .38, big enough to knock me down for good.

"Come off it, Jack, and put the gun away. You're out of your county, and there are witnesses."

The orderly and his charges were watching from the front steps. Jack Fleischer turned his head to look at them. I knocked the gun from his hand and picked it up as he dove for it. On his hands and knees, like a man changing into a dog, he barked at me: "I put you away for this. I'm an officer."

"Act like one."

The orderly came toward us. He was just a whitish movement in the corner of my vision. I was watching Fleischer as he got up.

The orderly said to me: "We don't want trouble. I better call the police, eh?"

"That shouldn't be necessary. How about it, Fleischer?"

"Hell, I am the police."

"Not in this bailiwick you're not. Anyway, I heard that you were retired."

"Who the hell are you?" Fleischer squinted at me. His eyes gleamed like yellowish quartz in the half light.

"I'm a licensed private detective. My name is Archer."

"If you want to stay licensed, give me back my gun." He held out his thick red hand for it.

"We better have a talk first, Jack. And you better apologize to the man you hit."

Fleischer lifted one corner of his mouth in a snarl of pain. For a spoiled old cop, having to apologize was cruel and unusual punishment.

"Sorry," he said without looking at the man.

"All right," the orderly said.

He turned and walked away with formal dignity. The old people on the steps followed him into the building. The door sucked shut behind them.

Fleischer and I moved toward our cars. We faced each other in the space between them, each with his back to his own car.

"My gun," he reminded me. It was in my pocket.

"First we talk. What are you after, Jack?"

"I'm working on an old case, a fatal accident which happened years ago."

"If you know it was an accident, why did you open it up again?"

"I never closed it. I don't like unfinished business."

He was fencing, talking in generalities. I tried to jolt him. "Did you know Jasper Blevins?"

"No. I never met him," he said levelly.

"But you knew his wife Laurel."

"Maybe I did. Not as well as some people think."

"Why didn't you get her to identify her husband's body?"

He didn't answer for quite a while. Finally he said: "Are you recording this?"

"No."

"Come away from your car, eh, pal?"

We walked down the driveway. The overarching stone pines were like a darker sky narrowing down on us. Fleischer was more voluble in the almost total darkness.

"I admit I made a mistake fifteen years ago. That's the

only thing I'm going to admit. I'm not going to dig up the garbage and spread it all over my own front porch."

"What was the mistake, Jack?"

"I trusted that broad."

"Did Laurel say it wasn't her husband who died under the train?"

"She said a lot of things. Most of them were lies. She conned me good."

"You can't blame her for everything. It was your job to get the body identified."

"Don't tell me what my job was. In the thirty years I worked for the sheriff's department, close to a hundred hoboes died under trains in our county. Some had identification on them, and some didn't. This one didn't. How was I to know it was different from the others?"

"What makes it so different, Jack?"

"You know damn well what makes it different."

"Tell me."

"I've told you all I'm going to. I thought we could have a meeting of the minds. But you're all take and no give."

"You haven't given me anything I can use."

"You haven't given me anything, period," he said. "What's your angle?"

"No angle. I'm working on the Stephen Hackett snatch."

"The what?" He was stalling.

"Don't kid me, you know about Hackett. You read about it in the San Francisco paper."

He made a quarter-turn and faced me in the darkness. "So you're the one that had me tailed in Frisco. What in hell are you trying to do to me?"

"Nothing personal. Your case and mine are connected. Jasper Blevins' little boy Davy, the one who got lost in the shuffle, has grown up into a big boy. He took Hackett yesterday."

I could hear Fleischer draw in his breath quickly, then let it out slowly. "The paper said this Hackett is really loaded." It was a question.

"He's loaded all right."

"And Jasper Blevins' boy is holding him for ransom?"

"There hasn't been any talk of ransom, that I know of. I think he's planning to kill Hackett, if he hasn't already."

"Christ! He can't do that!" Fleischer sounded as if his own life had been threatened.

I said: "Do you know Hackett?"

"I never saw him in my life. But there's money in it, pal. We should throw in together, you and me."

I didn't want Fleischer as a partner. I didn't trust him. On the other hand, he knew things about the case that were unknown to anyone else alive. And he knew Santa Teresa County.

"Do you remember the Krug ranch, near Centerville?"

"Yeah, I know where it is."

"Davy Blevins may be holding Stephen Hackett on the ranch."

"Then let's get up there," Fleischer said. "What are we waiting for?"

We went back to our cars. I handed Fleischer his gun. Facing him in the semi-darkness, I had the feeling that I was looking at myself in a bleared distorting mirror.

Neither of us had mentioned the death of Laurel Smith.

Chapter 21

WE AGREED TO DOUBLE UP in Fleischer's car, which was new and fast. I left mine at an all-night station in Canoga Park, not too far from Keith Sebastian's house. Whatever happened, I'd be coming back there.

I drove while Fleischer dozed in the front seat beside me. Up the San Fernando Valley, over the main pass, back by way of Camarillo to the dark sea. When we crossed the Santa Teresa County line, Fleischer woke up as if he could smell home territory.

A few miles south of Santa Teresa, as we were traversing a lonely stretch of highway, Fleischer told me to stop by a eucalyptus grove. I assumed it was a call of nature. He didn't get out of the car, though, when I pulled off on the shoulder.

He twisted toward me in the seat and chopped at my head with the loaded butt of his gun. I went out, all the way. After a while the darkness where I lay was invaded by dreams. Huge turning wheels, like the interlocking wheels of eternity and necessity, resolved themselves into a diesel locomotive. I was lying limp across the tracks and the train was coming, swinging its Cyclops eye.

It honked its horn at me. It wasn't a train sound, though, and I wasn't lying on a track, and it was no dream. I sat up in the middle of the northbound lane of the highway. A truck lit up like a Christmas tree was bearing down on me, honking repeatedly.

Its brakes were shrieking, too, but it wasn't going to be able to stop before it got to me. I lay down and watched it blot out the stars. Then I could see the stars again, and feel the blood pounding all through my body.

More traffic was coming up from the south. I crawled off the road, feeling small and awkward as a Jerusalem cricket. The eucalyptus trees muttered and sighed in the wind like witnesses. I felt for my gun. It was missing.

Fleischer's treachery had touched a paranoid nerve which twanged and jangled in my injured head. I reminded it and myself that I had been ready to turn on Fleischer when it suited me to. His timing had been a little faster than mine.

By now the driver of the truck had pulled his rig off the road and set out a flare. He ran toward me with a flashlight.

"Hey, are you all right?"

"I think so." I stood up, balancing the angry weight of my head.

He shone the flashlight in my face. I closed my eyes and almost fell under the slap of light.

"Hey, there's blood on your face. Did I hit you?"

"You missed me. A friend of mine knocked me out and left me on the highway."

"I better call the police, eh? You need an ambulance?"

"I don't need anything if you'll give me a lift to Santa Teresa."

He hesitated, his face torn between sympathy and suspicion. The blood on my face cut two ways. Nice people didn't get hurt and left on the highway.

"Okay," he said without enthusiasm. "I can do that much for you."

He drove me to the outskirts of Santa Teresa. The Power Plus station was still lit up, and I asked the driver to let me off there.

Fred Cram, the attendant with the special boot, was on duty. He didn't seem to recognize me. I went into the men's room and washed my face. There was a swollen cut above my temple, but it had stopped bleeding.

Someone had printed on the wall: MAKE SENSE NOT WAR. I laughed. It hurt my head.

I went outside and asked Fred Cram for permission to use the phone. He recognized me now.

"Did you find the girl?"

"I found her. Thanks very much."

"You're welcome. Is there anything I can do for you?"

"Just let me use the phone, for a local call."

The electric clock in the office had its hands straight up on midnight. Midnight was my time for calling the Langstons. I looked up their number in the directory, and dialed it. Henry Langston answered, in a muffled voice:

"Langston residence."

"Archer. You're going to hate me."

His voice brightened. "I've been wondering about you. Davy is all over the local paper."

"I think I know where he is, Hank. So does Fleischer— he's on his way there now. Do you feel like another midnight drive?"

"Where to?"

"A ranch near Centerville in the northern part of the county."

"And Davy's there with Hackett?"

"I'd say there's a fifty per cent chance of it. Bring a gun."

"All I have is a .32 target pistol."

"Bring it. And bring a flashlight."

I told him where I was. While I was waiting outside the office, Fred Cram locked the pumps and turned out the overhead lights.

"I'm sorry," he said to me. "It's time to close."

"Go right ahead. I expect to be picked up in a few minutes."

But the young man lingered, eying my head wound. "Did Davy Spanner do that to you?"

"No. I'm still looking for him."

"That was him with the girl last night. I didn't know him at first, he's changed so much. But when I read about him in the paper—he really did have somebody in the trunk."

"He really did. Do you know Davy?"

"I knew him in high school one year. He was a freshman and I was a senior. He wasn't a delinquent back in those days. He was real little and small, before he got his growth, which is why I didn't recognize him last night."

"If you see him again let me know, Fred." I gave him my card. "You can call my answering service any time, collect."

He took the card, but the look on his face rejected it. "That isn't really what I had in mind."

"What did you have in mind?"

"The way things turn out in life. I mean, here I am pumping gas for a living and Davy's turned into a criminal."

Having put himself on record, he turned out the office lights and locked the door. He stayed around, politely, until Langston's station wagon came in off the highway and pulled up beside his jalopy.

I said good night to Fred and climbed into the wagon. Langston's sensitive eyes took in my face and head.

"You've been hurt. Do you need a doctor?"

"Not now. I'm at least half an hour behind Fleischer already."

"How did he get into this?"

"He's been in it from the beginning. You know that. I made the mistake of trying to work with him. That lasted about an hour. He knocked me out and left me on the highway."

Hank whistled. "Shouldn't you tell the police?"

"Then we'd never get away. Did you bring your flashlight and pistol?"

"In the dash compartment. I feel like a crimebuster's apprentice."

His humor sounded a little forced, but I went along with it. "Let's go, apprentice."

Langston turned onto the highway and headed north. He'd caught a few hours' sleep before I called, and was full of energy and curiosity. He wanted to talk at length about Davy and his psychological problems. I was weary of such palaver. My answers got shorter and shorter. After a while I crawled into the back seat and tried to sleep. But every time a truck went by I woke up with a start.

Where the highway looped inland, we ran into a spatter of rain. Above the mountains to the north, the sky was very black, lit by occasional stabs of lightning. The highway brought us back to the coast. Here the night sky was still clear, and the moon's white eye peered over the rim of the sea. I recognized the crossroads where we had picked up Sandy the night before.

The thought of the girl was heavy on my mind. She was swinging through all the changes of the moon. The moon was white and shining, the very symbol of purity, but it had its dark side, too, pocked and cold and desolate and hidden. The girl could turn either way, depending on the outcome of our journey.

If we could bring Hackett out alive, she'd have a chance for probation. If Hackett died, her future died with him.

Chapter 22

IT WAS AFTER ONE when we got to Rodeo City. It was a seaside motel town strung out between the highway and the shore. We went down a ramp to the main street, which ran parallel to the highway and just below it. Three motorcyclists in bowler hats roared past us down the middle of the street. Girls with blowing hair clung to their backs like succubi.

We found the turning and the sign: CENTERVILLE 20 MIS., and we turned inland. The blacktop road passed rodeo stands which loomed like an ancient amphitheater in the darkness. Gradually it looped up through the foothills, then more abruptly into a mountain pass. Before we reached the summit of the pass we were in a dense cloud. It gathered like rain on the windshield, and slowed us to a crawl.

On the far side of the summit actual rain began to pound on the roof. The windshield and the windows fogged up. I climbed into the front seat and wiped them every few minutes, but it was slow going.

It rained all the way to Centerville. Every now and then a flash of lightning would show the timbered walls of the valley slanting up above us.

Centerville was one of those Western hamlets that hadn't changed much in two generations. It was a street of poor frame houses, a general store with a gas pump, closed for the night, a schoolhouse with a bell housing on the roof-peak, and a small white steepled church shining wetly in our headlights.

The only lighted building was a lunch counter with a beer sign, beside the general store. The place had its CLOSED sign out, but I could see a white-aproned man swinging a mop inside. I ran through the downpour and knocked on the door.

The aproned man shook his head, and pointed at the CLOSED sign. I knocked some more. After a while he leaned his mop against the bar and came and opened up.

"What is this, anyway?" He was a man past middle age with a foxy weathered face and a talker's mouth.

I stepped inside. "I'm sorry to bother you. Can you tell me how to get to the Krug ranch?"

"I can tell you, but it doesn't mean you'll get there. Buzzard Creek will be running by now."

"So?"

"The wash crosses the road to the ranch. You can try it if you want to. The other fellow made it, leastwise he hasn't come back."

"You mean Jack Fleischer?"

"You know Jack, do you? What's going on up at the ranch?" He nudged me confidentially. "Has Jack got a woman up there? It wouldn't be the first time."

"Could be."

"It's a hell of a night for a party, and a hell of a place."

I called Hank Langston in from the car. The man in the apron introduced himself. His name was Al Simmons, and he made it very clear that he owned the place, as well as the store next door.

Simmons spread out a paper napkin on the bar and drew a crude map for us. The entrance to the ranch was twelve miles north of Centerville. Buzzard Creek ran, when it ran, just this side of the ranch. It rose very quickly in a heavy rain. But we might make it across, since it hadn't been raining long.

Simmons said as we were leaving: "If you get stuck, I have a tractor that can pull you out. Of course that will cost you money."

"How much money?" Hank wanted to know.

"Depends on how long it takes. I generally get ten an hour with the tractor. That's portal to portal. But if your car gets carried away downriver, there's nothing anybody can do. So don't let that happen, eh?"

We drove forever up a gravel road that badly needed resurfacing. The rain came hissing down from the sky. The lightning made frightening meaningless signs.

We crossed several small streams which ran through dips in the road. Exactly twelve miles from Centerville by the odometer, we came to the creek. It flowed across the road, sliding brown and steady under the headlights, dappled by falling rain. It looked at least a hundred feet wide.

"Do you think you can make it, Hank?"

"I don't know how deep it is. I'd hate to lose the car."

"We might do better wading. I'll try first."

I got out my gun and flashlight and put them in the inside breast pockets of my jacket. Then I removed my shoes and socks and trousers and left them in the wagon. When I stepped out in front of the headlights, jacketed but trouserless, Hank laughed out loud at me.

The water was cold, and the gravel hurt my feet. Still I felt a certain pleasure which went back a long way, to my first infantile wades in Long Beach, holding my father's hand.

I could have used a hand to hold on to now. Though the water never rose higher than my thighs, it pulled at my legs and made it hard to walk. At the deepest part, in the middle of the stream, I had to brace my legs apart and lean into it. It was like a second force of gravity pulling me at right angles to the first.

When I got beyond the middle I paused for a moment to

rest and get my bearings. Peering ahead to the far shore, I could see a grayish bundle lying beside the road. I moved closer. It was a man, or the body of a man, wearing gray clothes. I splashed toward him and got the flashlight out.

It was Hackett, lying face up to the rain. His face was so badly battered that he was hardly recognizable. His clothes were sodden. There was mud in his hair.

He responded to the light, though, by trying to sit up. I got down and helped him, with an arm around his shoulders.

"I'm Archer. Remember me?"

He nodded. His head lolled against me.

"Can you talk?"

"Yes, I can talk." His voice was thick, as though he had blood in his mouth, and pitched so low I had to lean close to hear it.

"Where's Davy Spanner?"

"He ran away. Shot the other one and ran away."

"He shot Jack Fleischer?"

"I don't know his name. An older man. Spanner blew his head off. It was terrible."

"Who beat you, Mr. Hackett?"

"Spanner did. He beat me unconscious and left me for dead, I guess. The rain brought me to. I got this far, but then I pooped out."

Hank shouted at me from the other bank. The headlights of the station wagon blinked. I yelled at him to cool it, and told Hackett to wait where he was.

He said in utter dismay:" You're not going to leave me here?"

"Just for a few minutes. We'll try and bring the station wagon across. If Spanner's gone, there's nothing to be afraid of."

"He's gone. Thank God for that."

Hackett's bad experience seemed to have humbled him. I felt a sympathy for him which had been lacking before, and I lent him my jacket.

I started back across the river with the flashlight in one hand and the gun in the other. Then I remembered Fleischer's car. If he was dead, I might as well use it.

I came back to Hackett. "Where's the dead man's car?"

"I think I saw a car beside the barn."

Waveringly, he pointed off to the right.

I walked up the road a hundred yards or so and came to a lane branching off to the right. Rains past and present had worn it down to bare rocks. I went up the lane, dreading what I would find at the end of it.

The barn was the first building I came to. It was sagging and old, with great holes in its walls. I shone my flashlight around. A barn owl flew out of one of the holes: a blank flat oddly human face flying on silent wings through the beam of light. It startled me, as if it had been Jack Fleischer's ghost.

His car was parked below the barn, unlocked, with no key in the ignition. This probably meant the key was in Fleischer's pocket. I almost gave up my plan to use his car. But I forced myself to go on up to the house.

Apart from one small flat-roofed section, there was nothing left of the building but its old stone foundations. Even the part still standing had taken a beating from the weather. Torn roofing paper flapped in the wind, and the warped door hung ajar.

When I found Jack Fleischer inside, prone on the wet concrete floor, he had become a part of the general ruin. In the weak flashlight beam, his face and head seemed to have been partly rusted away. Water dripped down on him from the leaking roof.

I found when I went through Fleischer's pockets that his body was still warm. His car keys were in his trousers, and in the breast pocket of his jacket were the documents he had had copied at the Acme shop in San Francisco. I kept a copy of each of them.

Before leaving the shack, I took a final look around with the flashlight. Built into one corner was a two-level board bed like those you see in old Western bunkhouses. There was a sleeping bag in the lower bunk. The only other furniture was a chair made from a cut-down wooden barrel. Looped and coiled beside this chair was a lot of used adhesive tape. Some cigarette butts lay on the floor by the bunk.

I left Fleischer where he was, for the police, and made my way down the muddy slope to his car. The engine started on the first try. I drove in low gear down the gullied lane to the road, and back to the spot where Hackett was waiting. He sat with his head leaning forward on his knees.

I helped him to his feet and into the front seat. Hank shouted from the other bank:

"Don't try it, Lew. It's too deep."

I had to try it. I couldn't leave Hackett where he was. I didn't trust myself to carry him across. One slip and he'd be gone downriver, and all our efforts lost.

I eased the car forward slowly into the water, aiming straight for Hank Langston's headlights and trusting there were no curves in the road. For one frightening instant in the middle, the car seemed to be floating. It shifted sideways, then jarred to rest on a higher part of the invisible road.

We got across without further incident. Supporting Hackett between us, Langston and I transferred him to the back seat of the wagon. After putting on my trousers I took back my jacket and wrapped Hackett in a car rug. Fortunately the wagon had a good heater.

I locked the doors of Fleischer's car and left it in the road. Then I went back to it and searched the trunk. No tapes. I slammed the trunk lid down. We made the slow twelve-mile journey back to Centerville.

We must have been gone about two hours, but the lights were still on in Al Simmons' place. He came to the door yawning. He looked as if he'd been sleeping in his clothes.

"I see you made it back."

"We did. Jack Fleischer didn't. He's been shot."

"Dead?"

"Half his head was blasted away with a sawed-off shotgun."

"At the Krug place?"

"That's correct."

"What do you know? I always reckoned that place would get him in the end."

I didn't take time to ask Simmons what he meant. He showed me his telephone at the back of the counter, and gave me the number of the nearest sheriff's office, in Rodeo City. The officer on duty was a Deputy Pennell. I told him that Jack Fleischer had been killed by a shotgun blast.

"Jack?" he said in a shocked voice. "But I was just talking to Jack tonight. He dropped by earlier in the evening."

"What did he say?"

"Said he was on his way to the old Krug ranch. He

wouldn't tell me what was on his mind. But he said if he didn't come back by morning, I was to come up after him, with a couple of extra men."

"You better do just that. Don't wait for morning."

"I can't. I got no patrol car available. My car broke down, and the county won't budget another till January." Pennell sounded upset and confused. "I'll have to have a car sent up from Santa Teresa."

"What about an ambulance?"

"That has to come up from Santa Teresa, too. But if Jack's dead he don't need an ambulance."

"Not everybody's dead. I have an injured man with me." I didn't mention Hackett's name, since I was hoping somehow to get him home before the news broke. "I'll bring him into Rodeo City. We'll meet the ambulance and the patrol car at your office."

Al Simmons sat at the counter listening openly to my end of the conversation. When I hung up he spoke in a meditative tone:

"It's funny how things turn out in a man's life. Jack held that same post in Rodeo for over fifteen years. Rory Pennell was his sidekick."

"What was Jack's connection with the Krug ranch?"

"I don't hardly like to say." But his eyes were bright with desire to deliver his story. "Jack's dead and all, and he's—he was a married man. I wouldn't want it to get back to Mrs. Fleischer."

"Another woman?"

"Yeah. Jack had his good qualities, I guess, but he was always a skirt-chaser. Back in the early fifties, he was chasing the woman who lived on the Krug place. I think he caught her, too," Simmons said with a sideways grin. "He used to stop off here for a case of beer, and then he'd go up and spend the night with her. I can't hardly blame him. Laurel Blevins was a pretty piece."

"Didn't her husband object?"

"I don't think he knew. Blevins was gone a lot of the time. He killed all his own meat. When he wasn't hunting, he was tramping around the hills with a painter's whatever-you-call-it."

"Easel?"

"Yeah. He pretended to be some kind of an artist. But him and his wife, and the little boy, they lived like Digger Indians in that burned-out old ranchhouse. You can't hardly blame the woman for going for Jack. He was a good-looking fellow fifteen years ago, and he always had money from the Rodeo houses. After Blevins left her, he kept the woman in Mamie Hagedorn's house. I got that from Mamie Hagedorn herself."

"What happened to Blevins?"

"He traveled on. He was a born loser."

"And the little boy?"

"I don't know. He got lost in the shuffle."

He should have stayed lost, I was thinking, instead of coming back to revenge himself on a past he couldn't change even with a shotgun.

I questioned Al Simmons about Davy, and Simmons remembered him. At least he'd seen a man or boy, driving a green compact, take the turn to the ranch early the previous morning. No, he hadn't seen or heard him come out tonight.

"Is there another way out?"

"There's the northwest pass. But it takes a four-wheel drive, 'specially in weather like this."

Langston was honking outside. I had one more thing to do. I phoned Hackett's house in Malibu and got Ruth Marburg on the line and told her I was bringing her son home.

She burst into tears. Then she started to ask me questions, which I cut short. I told her we were coming down by ambulance. While Hackett didn't seem to be seriously hurt, he was exhausted and suffering from exposure. She'd better have a doctor on hand when we got there.

I gave her six a.m. as our E.T.A.

Chapter 23

DEPUTY RORY PENNELL was a rawboned man of forty or so with a heavy chestnut mustache and a bad stammer. The stammer had probably been intensified by Jack Fleischer's death. Pennell seemed genuinely upset. As we talked, his big right hand kept going back to the butt of the gun he wore on his hip.

I would have liked to spend more time in Rodeo City, talking to Pennell and Mamie Hagedorn and anyone else who might help me to reconstruct the past. It was beginning to look as though Jack Fleischer had been deeply implicated in the death of Jasper Blevins. But the question was fairly academic now, and it would have to wait. The important thing was to get Stephen Hackett home.

The two sheriff's men from Santa Teresa would have been glad to escort him. It was a relatively safe and easy job, high in publicity value. I reminded them that Jack Fleischer's body was lying alone on the Krug place. Somewhere in the hills north of there the boy who killed him was probably stuck in the mud.

I said good-bye to Hank and rode the ambulance south, sitting on the floor beside Hackett's pallet. He was feeling better. He had had some first aid on his face, and sucked a cup of broth through a straw. I asked him a few of the questions that had to be asked.

"Did Sandy Sebastian hit Lupe?"

"Yes. She knocked him out with a tire iron."

"Did she use violence on you?"

"Not directly. She did tape me while the boy held the shotgun on me. She taped my wrists and ankles and mouth, even my eyes." He raised his hand from the blanket and touched his eyes. "Then they put me in the trunk of her car. It was

127

hellish being shut up like that." He lifted his head. "How long ago did it start?"

"About thirty-six hours. Did she have any special grudge against you?"

He answered slowly. "She must have. But I can't understand what."

"What about the boy?"

"I never saw him before. He acted crazy."

"In what way?"

"He didn't seem to know what he was doing. At one point he laid me out across a railroad track. I know it sounds like Victorian melodrama. But he clearly intended to kill me, by letting a train crush me. The girl ran away, and he changed his mind. He took me up to the—the other place and kept me prisoner there.

"For most of the day—yesterday?—he treated me pretty well. He took the tape off and let me move around some. Gave me water to drink, and some bread and cheese. Of course the shotgun was always in evidence. He lay on the bunk and held the gun on me. I sat in the chair. I'm not a coward, ordinarily, but it got pretty nerve-wracking after a while. I couldn't understand what he had in mind."

"Did he mention money, Mr. Hackett?"

"I did. I offered him a good deal of money. He said he didn't want it."

"What did he want?"

Hackett took a long time to answer. "He didn't seem to know. He seemed to be living out some kind of a dream. In the evening he smoked marijuana, and he got dreamier. He seemed to be hoping for some kind of mystic experience. And I was the burnt offering."

"Did he say so?"

"Not directly. He said it as a joke, that he and I should form a musical group. He suggested several names for it, such as The Human Sacrifice." His voice faded. "It was no joke. I believe he meant to kill me. But he wanted to see me suffer as long as possible first."

"Why?"

"I'm not a psychologist, but he seemed to regard me as a substitute father. Toward the end, when he got high on marijuana, he started calling me Dad. I don't know who his real dad is or was, but he must have hated him."

"His dad died under a train when he was three. He saw it happen."

"Good Lord!" Hackett sat up partly. "That explains a lot of things, doesn't it?"

"Did he talk about his father?"

"No. I didn't encourage him to talk. Eventually he dozed off. I was planning to jump him when the other chap—Fleischer?—came in. He must have thought there was nobody there. The boy let him have both barrels. He had no chance at all. I ran outside. The boy caught me and beat me unconscious."

He fell back onto the pallet and raised both elbows defensively, as if Davy's fists were in his face again. We rode the rest of the way in silence. Hackett's hoarse breathing quieted down, lengthening out gradually into the rhythms of sleep.

I spread a blanket on the vibrating floor and slept, too, while the world turned toward morning. I woke up feeling good. Stephen Hackett and I had come back together and alive. But he was still full of fear. He moaned in his sleep and covered his head with his arms.

The red sun was coming up behind the Malibu hills. The ambulance stopped in West Malibu near a sign which said "PRIVATE COLONY: NO TRESPASSING." The driver didn't know where to make his turn, and he gestured through the window.

I went up front with him. The other attendant got into the back with Hackett. We found our left turn and climbed through the hills to Hackett's gate.

It was just a few minutes past six. Coming over the pass we were met by the full blaze of the morning sun, like an avalanche of light.

Ruth Marburg and Gerda Hackett came out of the house together. Ruth's face was lined and bleary-eyed and joyful. She ran heavily toward me and pressed my hands and thanked me. Then she turned to her son, who was being lifted out of the ambulance by the attendants. She bent over him and hugged him, crying and exclaiming over his wounds.

Gerda Hackett stood behind her. She looked a little piqued, as if she felt upstaged by Ruth's display of emotion.

But she got her hug in, too, while Sidney Marburg and Dr. Converse stood and watched.

There was a third man, fortyish and heavy-shouldered, with a square unsmiling face. He acted as if he was in charge. When Hackett stood up shakily and insisted on walking into the house, instead of being carried, the heavy-shouldered man assisted him. Dr. Converse followed them in, looking rather ineffectual.

Ruth Marburg surprised me. I'd temporarily forgotten about the money she'd promised. She hadn't. Without having to be reminded, she took me into the library and wrote a check.

"I've postdated this a week." She stood up, waving the check to dry the ink. "I don't keep this much in the bank. I'm going to have to transfer some funds and sell some securities."

"There's no hurry."

"Good." She handed me the little yellow slip. It was for the amount she had promised.

"You're an unusual rich woman," I said. "Most of them scream bloody murder over a nickel."

"I haven't always been rich. Now I have more money than I can spend."

"So have I, now."

"Don't let it fool you. A hundred grand is chicken feed these days. Uncle Sam will cut it in half for you. If you take my advice you'll put the rest in real estate and watch it grow."

Somehow, I didn't think I would. I put the check away in my wallet. It excited me in a way I didn't quite like. Underlying the excitement was a vague depression, as if I belonged to the check in a way, instead of having it belong to me.

Ruth Marburg reached up and touched my cheek. It wasn't a pass, but it was a gesture of possession. "Aren't you happy, Lew? May I call you Lew?"

"Yes and yes."

"You don't look happy. You should be. You've done a wonderful thing, for all of us. I'm eternally grateful to you."

"Good." But it wasn't so good. Even her repeated thanks were a subtle form of possession, taking and not giving.

"How on earth did you pull it off?" she said.

I told her, very briefly, about the series of leads, from Fleischer to Albert Blevins and Alma Krug, which took me to the shack where her son was held; and what I found there.

"You've had a terrible night. You must be exhausted." She touched my cheek again.

"Don't do that please."

She withdrew her hand as if I'd tried to bite it. "What's the matter?"

"You bought your son with this check. Not me."

"I didn't mean anything by it. It was a friendly gesture. Heavens, I'm old enough to be your mother."

"The hell you are."

She chose to take this as a compliment, and it soothed her injured feelings. "You really are tired, aren't you, Lew? Did you get any sleep at all?"

"Not much."

"I'll tell you what. Why don't you go to bed and get some sleep now? Stephen and Gerda have plenty of room."

The invitation sounded so good that I started yawning, like an addict for a fix. But I told her I preferred my own bed.

"You're very independent, aren't you, Lew?"

"I guess I am."

"I feel the same way myself. I only wish Sidney had some of the same spirit."

She sounded like a mother talking about her backward little boy.

"Speaking of Sidney, I wonder if I can get him to drive me. My car's over in the Valley."

"Of course. I'll tell him. There's just one thing before you leave," she said. "Mr. Thorndike will want to talk to you."

She went and got the heavy-shouldered man. Thorndike introduced himself as a special agent of the FBI. Ruth left us together in the library and Thorndike debriefed me, recording what I said on a portable tape recorder.

"I don't mean to be critical," he said, "since it all worked out. But that was kind of a wild idea, going up against a kidnapper with nobody but a high-school counselor to back you up. You could have got what Fleischer got."

"I know that. But this is a peculiar kind of kidnapper. I don't believe he'd shoot Langston."

"Anyway, he didn't get a chance to."

Thorndike's manner was a little superior, like a teacher giving an oral quiz to a not very apt pupil. I didn't mind. I had brought Hackett in. He hadn't.

Chapter 24

CAPTAIN AUBREY of the sheriff's department arrived, and Thorndike went to talk to him. I closed the door of the library behind Thorndike and pushed the button in the knob which locked the door. It was the first time I'd been alone in a lighted place since I took the photocopies from Jack Fleischer's body.

I spread them out on a table by the windows and pulled back the drapes. The copy of the birth certificate stated that Henrietta R. Krug had been born in Santa Teresa County on October 17, 1910, the daughter of Joseph and Alma Krug. It was signed by Richard Harlock, M.D., of Rodeo City.

The other photocopy was more interesting. It showed a part of the front page of the *Santa Teresa Star* for May 28, 1952. Under the heading "Oil Tycoon Slaying Still Unsolved" and the subheading "Youth Gang Sought," was the following short account, datelined Malibu:

"The May 24 beach shooting of Mark Hackett, well-known Malibu citizen and Texas oil millionaire, is still under investigation by the police. According to Deputy Robert Aubrey of the sheriff's Malibu substation, more than a dozen suspects have been arrested and released. A gang of motorcyclists which was reported in the Malibu area on the night of May 24 is being sought for questioning.

"Hackett was shot to death while walking on the beach on the evening of May 24. His wallet was taken. Police have recovered a revolver which has been identified as the murder weapon. The dead man is survived by his widow and his son, Stephen."

On the same page there was a story, with the dateline "Rodeo City (by Special Correspondent)," under the heading "Death on the Rails Strikes Again":

"Riding the rails, which is reputed to be the cheapest way to travel, is costing some travelers their lives. Over the past several years, the lonely stretch of tracks south of Rodeo City has been the scene of a number of fatal accidents. Beheadings, dismemberments, and other mutilations have occurred.

"The most recent victim of the railroad jinx, and the second to die this year, was found early this morning by Sheriff's Deputy Jack Fleischer of the Rodeo City substation. The body, which bore no identification, was that of a man in his middle twenties. His head had been severed from his body.

"According to Deputy Fleischer, the man's clothes marked him as a transient laborer. He had more than twenty dollars in his pockets, ruling out suspicion of foul play.

"A touching aspect of the accident was revealed by Deputy Fleischer to this reporter. The victim was accompanied by a small boy, approximately three years old, who apparently spent the night by his father's body. The child has been placed in Children's Shelter pending further investigation."

Besides confirming what I already knew, this second story suggested that Fleischer had deliberately closed off the investigation. He must have known who the victim was; possibly he removed identification. The money in the dead man's pockets didn't rule out the possibility of murder, or the possibility that Fleischer himself had committed it.

I was struck by the sequence of the two deaths, three or four days apart. It could have been a coincidence, but it was clear enough that Fleischer hadn't thought so. Also it seemed very likely that Captain Aubrey was that same Deputy Aubrey who had dealt with Mark Hackett's murder fifteen years ago.

I found Captain Aubrey in the living room with Thorndike and Dr. Converse. Hackett wasn't seriously injured, the doctor was telling them, but he was suffering from a certain degree of shock. He didn't feel that his patient should be questioned any further until he'd had some rest. The policemen didn't argue.

When Converse had finished, I drew him into the next room, out of earshot.

"What is it now?" he said impatiently.

"The same old question, about Sandy Sebastian. What did you treat her for last summer?"

"I can't possibly tell you. It wouldn't be ethical without the patient's permission." Converse paused, and his eyebrows went up. "Did you put Dr. Jeffrey up to calling me last night?"

"Not exactly. I asked him the same question I'm asking you."

"Well, I'm not answering either of you," Converse said flatly. "The girl's in enough trouble as it is."

"I'm trying to get her out of trouble."

"You're going about it rather strangely, aren't you?"

I threw him a question from left field. "Was she taking drugs last summer, something like that?"

"I refuse to answer." But his clever eyes flickered in a way that said yes.

"Psychedelic drugs?"

His curiosity overcame his ethics, or whatever they were. "What makes you suggest that?"

"I heard she was suicidal. A bad trip on LSD sometimes has that effect. I'm sure you know that, doctor."

"Of course."

"Will you sit down and talk about it with me?"

"No sir, I will not. I have no right to discuss my patient's private affairs."

"Sandy's affairs are pretty public now. And I'm on her side, remember."

Converse shook his head. "You really must excuse me. I have hospital rounds to make."

"How's Lupe?"

"He's doing fine now."

"Is Lupe on drugs by any chance?"

"How on earth should I know?"

Converse turned abruptly and went away.

Captain Aubrey was waiting for me in the living room. Thorndike had filled him in on my report, but he had some further questions.

"You've been close to this case from the beginning," he said. "How do you think it all started?"

"It started the day that Davy Spanner and Sandy Sebastian

got together. They're both badly alienated, young people with a grudge."

"I know something about Spanner. He's a psycho with a record. He shouldn't have been out on the streets." His eyes were a cold gray. "Fortunately he won't be out much longer. I've been in touch with Rodeo City. They found the Sebastian girl's car north of the ranch, hub-deep in the mud. Spanner won't get far without it. The Santa Teresa County authorities expect to take him today."

"Then what?"

"Spanner's their baby." Aubrey's phrase hit me queerly, and broke into multiple meanings. "They want him for first-degree murder, and that takes care of him. The problem of the girl is more complicated. For one thing, she's a juvenile, with a clean record. Also she ran out on Spanner before the Fleischer murder was committed. Lucky for her."

"Sandy's no criminal. She wanted to quit as soon as she saw crime was for real."

"You've talked to her, haven't you? What gets into a girl like that?" Aubrey was genuinely disturbed. "I've got a daughter sixteen. She's a good girl. So was this one apparently. How do I know my own daughter won't walk up to somebody some fine day and crack his skull with a tire iron?"

"I think Sandy had a grudge against Lupe. The case may have started right there."

"What did she have against him?"

"I better not say until I can prove it, Captain."

He leaned toward me, red in the face, remembering his own daughter. "Did he have sexual congress with her?"

"Not that I know of. Whatever happened between them will all come out in the wash. The probation people will be going over her with a fine-tooth comb."

Aubrey gave me an impatient look, and turned to leave.

I detained him. "There's another thing I wanted to talk to you about. Let's go out to your car. It's more private."

He shrugged. We went outside. Aubrey got in behind the wheel of his unmarked car, and I slid in beside him.

"Are you the same Aubrey who used to work out of the Malibu station?"

"I am. It's why I was assigned to this one."

"This is the second major crime in the Hackett family, I've been told."

"That's right. The senior Mr. Hackett—his name was Mark—was shot on the beach."

"Did you ever get a line on the killer?"

"No. These hit-and-run crimes are hard to solve." Aubrey sounded apologetic. "The trouble is there's generally no provable connection between the robber and his victim."

"Was robbery the motive?"

"Apparently. Hackett's wallet was taken, and he carried a lot of money. Which wasn't the wisest thing to do under the circumstances. He had a hideaway cottage on the beach, and he made a habit of walking down there at night, all by himself. Some thief with a gun caught onto the habit, and took him for his roll."

"Did you arrest anyone?"

"We picked up dozens of suspects. But we couldn't pin the crime on any one of them."

"Do you remember any of their names?"

"Not at this late date."

"I'll try one on you, anyway. Jasper Blevins."

He shook his head. "I'm afraid it rings no bell. Who is Jasper Blevins?"

"Davy Spanner's father. According to an old Santa Teresa newspaper, he died under a train near Rodeo City, about three days after Mark Hackett was murdered."

"So?"

"It's an interesting coincidence."

"Maybe. I run into these coincidences all the time. Sometimes they mean something, other times they don't."

"This one does."

"Do you mean there's a causal connection between these two crimes—Mark Hackett's murder and his son's kidnapping?"

"Some kind of a connection, anyway. According to a newspaper account, you recovered the revolver Mark Hackett was shot with."

Aubrey turned and looked at me appraisingly. "You do your homework, don't you?"

"Did you ever trace the revolver to its owner?"

Aubrey was slow in answering. "The queer thing is," he

said finally, "the gun belonged to Hackett himself, in a sense—"

"That suggests a family affair."

Aubrey lifted the flat of his hand above the wheel. "Let me finish. The gun belonged to Hackett in the sense that one of his oil companies had purchased it. They stored it in an unlocked drawer in their Long Beach office. It wasn't kept proper track of, and it simply disappeared, apparently some time before the murder."

"Disgruntled employee?"

"We went into that pretty thoroughly. But we didn't come up with anything tangible. The trouble was, Hackett had quite a number of disgruntled employees. He'd recently moved here from Texas, and he was riding herd on them Texas style. He was very unpopular with his people. But we couldn't prove that any one of them killed him. He had nearly five hundred employees in Long Beach alone, and a good half of them hated his guts."

"What was the name of his company?"

"Corpus Christi Oil and Gas. Mark Hackett originally came from Corpus Christi. He should have stayed there."

Aubrey punched my arm in a friendly way, and turned his ignition key. I wandered into the house.

Chapter 25

GERDA HACKETT was in the picture gallery, standing absorbed in front of a painting. It showed a man in a geometrical maze, and seemed to show that the man and the maze were continuous with each other.

"Are you interested in painting, Mrs. Hackett?"

"Yes. Particularly in Klee. I sold this picture to Mr. Hack —to Stephen."

"Really?"

"Yes. I worked in a gallery in München, a very good gallery." Her voice was thick with nostalgia. "It was how I met my husband. But if I had a second chance I would stay in Germany."

"Why?"

"I don't like it here. Such dreadful things happen to people."

"At least you got your husband back."

"Yes." But this failed to cheer her. She turned to me with a vague ambiguous light in her blue eyes. "I'm very grateful, really. You saved his life and I want to thank you. *Vielen Dank.*"

She pulled my face down and kissed me. This gesture was unexpected, perhaps even by her. It may have started out as a thank-you kiss, but it turned into something more involved. Her body leaned into me. Her tongue pushed into my mouth like a blind worm looking for a home.

I didn't like the woman that well. I took her by the arms and released myself. It was like handling a soft statue.

"Am I no good?" she said. "Am I not attractive?"

"You're very attractive," I said, stretching the truth a little. "The trouble is, I work for your husband and this is his house."

"He wouldn't care!" The ambiguous light in her eyes crystallized in a kind of helpless anger. "Do you know what they're doing? She's on the bed beside him feeding him soft-boiled eggs with a spoon."

"That sounds like an innocent pastime."

"It's no joke! She is his mother. He has an Oedipus fixation on her, and she encourages it."

"Who told you that?"

"I can see it with my own eyes. She is the seductive mother. The soft-boiled eggs are symbolic. Everything is symbolic!"

Gerda was disheveled and close to tears. She was one of those women who dishevel easily, as if the fronts they turned to the world were precarious to begin with. She would never be the equal of her mother-in-law.

But that was not my problem. I changed the subject: "I understand you're a friend of Sandy Sebastian's."

"No more. I helped her with her languages. But she is a little ingrate."

"Did she spend any time with Lupe?"

"Lupe? Why do you ask?"

"Because it may be important. Did she see much of him?"

"Certainly not, not in the way you mean. He used to go and get her sometimes, and drive her home."

"How often?"

"Many times. But Lupe isn't interested in girls."

"How do you know?"

"I can tell." She flushed. "Why do you ask?"

"I'd like to have a look at Lupe's room."

"For what reason?"

"Nothing to do with you. Does he have a room in the house?"

"His apartment is over the main garage. I don't know if it's open. Wait, I'll get our key."

She was gone for a few minutes. I stood and looked at the Klee, and found that it grew on me. The man was in the maze; the maze was in the man.

Gerda Hackett came back carrying a key with a tab attached: "Garage apt." I went out to the garage and used the key to open Lupe's door.

It was what is called a studio apartment, consisting of one large room with a pullman kitchen. It was furnished in bold colors with Mexican fabrics and artifacts. Some pre-Columbian masks hung over the serape-covered bed. If Lupe was a primitive, he was a sophisticated one.

I went through the chest of drawers and found nothing unusual except some pornographic pictures of the handcuff school. The bathroom medicine cabinet yielded only a jar of something labeled Psychedelic Love Balm. But some of the sugar cubes in the bottom of the bowl in the pullman kitchen were amateurishly wrapped in aluminum foil.

There were six wrapped cubes. I took three, tied them in my handkerchief, and put them away in an inside pocket.

I hadn't heard anyone coming up the stairs, and was mildly surprised by the door opening behind me. It was Sidney Marburg, wearing tennis shoes.

"Gerda said you were out here. What's with Lupe?"

"Just checking."

"Checking what?"

"His morals and his manners. He's no ordinary houseman, is he?"

"You can say that again. Personally I think he's a creep." Marburg walked toward me silently. "If you get something on him, I'd like to know about it."

"Are you serious?"

"You're bloody right I'm serious. He puts on a show of being interested in art, because my wife is, but she's the only one that's taken in."

"Is there something between the two of them?"

"I think there is. He comes to our house in Bel-Air sometimes when I'm away. Our houseboy keeps me posted."

"Are they lovers?"

"I don't know," Marburg said in pain. "I do know she gives him money, because I've seen some of the canceled checks. According to the houseboy, Lupe tells her everything that goes on here in her son's house. It isn't a healthy situation, and that's putting it mildly."

"How long have they known each other?"

"Practically forever. He's worked here, if you can call it work, as long as I can remember."

"How long is that?"

"Fifteen—sixteen years."

"Did you know the Hacketts when Mark was still alive?"

For some reason, the question irritated him. "I did. That's hardly relevant to what we were talking about. We were talking about Lupe."

"So we were. What do you suspect him of, besides spying for your wife? Does he mess around with drugs?"

"I wouldn't be surprised," Marburg said, a little too readily. "I've seen him high more than once. He was either manic or on drugs."

"Did you ever see him with the Sebastian girl?"

"I never did."

"I understand he chauffeured her quite a bit."

"No doubt he did. She spent a lot of time here in the summer." He paused, and gave me a questioning look. "You think he tampered with her?"

"I haven't come to any conclusion about it."

"Boy, if you can get that on him—!"

I didn't like his eagerness. "Slow down. I'm not going to shove the facts around to suit you."

"Nobody asked you to." But he sounded angry. I suspected he was angry with himself for talking to me too freely. "If you're finished here, I'll drive you bloody well home."

"Since you put it so charmingly."

"I don't have to be charming. I'm a serious painter, and that's all I have to be."

In spite of his lousy manners, I felt a certain liking for Sidney Marburg, or a tolerance bordering on liking. Perhaps he had sold out for money in marrying Ruth, who was nearly twenty years older. But like a shrewd agent he'd held back a percentage of himself.

"That sounds like a declaration of independence," I said.

His angry grimace changed to a smile, but there was self-deprecation in it. "Come on, let's go. I didn't mean to take it out on you." We went out to his Mercedes. "Where do you live?"

"In West Los Angeles, but I'm not going home. My car's in Woodland Hills."

"That's where the Sebastian girl lives, isn't it?"

"Yes."

"What's the matter with her? Schitzy?"

"I'm trying to find out."

"More power to you. Excuse my little flareup a minute ago. I'm glad to drive you. But this place has bad associations for me."

As if he hoped to leave them behind forever, he started the Mercedes' engine with a roar. We rocketed along the shore of the lake, across the dam, and down the long winding grade to the gate, where Marburg braked the car to a jarring halt.

"Okay," I said, "you win the Distinguished Flying Cross."

"Sorry if I alarmed you."

"I've had a rough two days. I was hoping this one would be some improvement."

"I said I was sorry."

Marburg drove more carefully down to the coastal highway and turned north. At Malibu Canyon he turned inland again. In a few minutes we were surrounded by the hills.

I said that they would make a pretty picture.

Marburg corrected me. "No. Anything that would make a

pretty picture makes a bad picture. The picturesque things have all been done. You have to do something new. Beauty is difficult, as somebody said."

"That Klee in the gallery, for instance?"

"Yes. I advised Stephen to buy Klee ten years ago." He added: "Stephen needs advice. His taste is terrible, in everything."

"Women?"

Marburg groaned. "Poor Gerda. When she came back from Germany with him, she thought she was going to live *la vie en rose*. She had a rude awakening. They live like recluses, never go anywhere, never see anyone."

"Why?"

"I think he's frightened—frightened of life. Money does that to some people. And then of course there's what happened to his father. It's strange, for fifteen years Stephen's been acting as if the same thing was going to happen to him. And it almost did."

"Almost."

"You've had considerable experience, Mr. Archer. Is it possible for people to bring disaster down on their own heads? You know, by assuming a disaster-prone posture?"

"It's an interesting idea."

"You haven't answered my question."

"Ask me again when I've finished with this case."

He gave me a swift startled look, during which the car almost left the road. He concentrated on driving for a minute, slowing down.

"I thought you *had* finished."

"Not with Spanner still at large, and several unsolved murders."

"Several?"

I let the question hang. We passed the Probation Camp, off the road to the left. Marburg looked at the buildings in a worried way, as if I might be tricking him into custody.

"Did you say several murders?"

"There are at least two others besides Mark Hackett."

Marburg drove until we were out of sight of the camp. He found a turnout point, pulled off the road, and stopped the car.

"What about these other murders?"

"One was a woman named Laurel Smith. She owned a small apartment building in the Palisades. She was beaten to death there the day before yesterday."

"I read about her in this morning's *Times*. The police think she was beaten by a kook—some sadist who didn't even know her."

"I don't think so. Laurel Smith was once married to a man named Jasper Blevins. He died under a train fifteen years ago —just a few days after Mark Hackett was killed. As far as I can make out, Laurel Smith and Jasper Blevins were Davy Spanner's parents. I think all these crimes, including the one against Stephen, are tied together."

Without moving, except for his fingers drumming on the wheel, Marburg gave the impression of squirming. His eyes came up to mine and gave me a quick unguarded look, like a spurt of darkness. "Am I being paranoid, or are you accusing me of something?"

"Maybe I am. What am I accusing you of?"

"It isn't so funny," he said in an aggrieved tone. "This isn't the first time I've been accused of something I didn't do. The cops gave me a really bad time after Mark was killed. They took me down to the station and questioned me most of the night. I had a perfectly good alibi, but to them it looked like one of those open-and-shut cases—you know, the standard triangle. I don't deny, and I didn't deny then, that Ruth and I were very close and I adore her passionately," he said in a rather perfunctory way. "But the fact is she was planning to divorce Mark."

"And marry you?"

"And marry me. So I had nothing to gain by Mark's death."

"Ruth had."

"Not really. He left her as little as he legally could. Mark changed his will, on account of me, shortly before he died, and left the bulk of his estate to Stephen. Anyway, Ruth had a perfectly good alibi, just as I had, and I resent your imputation for both of us."

But there was no real force in Marburg's anger. Like his passion, it belonged to the part of himself he had sold. He was watching me and talking carefully, like a hired advocate for himself.

"Tell me about the alibis, just for fun."

"I don't have to, but I will. Gladly. At the time that Mark was killed, Ruth and I were having dinner with some friends in Montecito. It was a large dinner party, with over twenty guests."

"Why didn't the police accept your alibi?"

"They did when they got around to checking it out. But that wasn't until the next day. They wanted me to be guilty, I know how their minds work. They were afraid to tackle Ruth directly, but they thought they could get at her through me."

"Whose side was Stephen on?"

"He was out of the country, had been for several years. At the time of his father's death he was studying economics at the London School. I'd never even met him at that time. But he was close to his father, and Mark's death hit him hard. He actually broke down and wept on the transatlantic phone. That was about the last time I ever knew him to show any real emotion."

"When was this?"

"Ruth called him immediately after Lupe phoned her, before we left her friends' house in Montecito. As a matter of fact I put in the call to London for her, and then she took it on another extension. The news came as a terrible blow to Stephen. Frankly, I felt sorry for him."

"How did he feel about you?"

"I don't think Stephen even knew I existed, at that time. And I kept out of sight for nearly a year afterwards. That was Ruth's idea, and it was a good one."

"Why? Because she's financially dependent on Stephen?"

"That may have played a part in it. But the fact is she's very fond of him. She wanted to arrange her life so she could have us both, and that's what she's done." Marburg spoke of his wife as if she was some kind of natural force, a demiurge or deity. "She gave me a—well, a kind of personal scholarship, at San Miguel de Allende. A few minutes after Stephen flew in from London, I flew out for Mexico City. Ruth kept us separate at the airport, but I caught a glimpse of Stephen when he got off the plane. He was a lot less conventional in those days. He wore a beard and a mustache and had let his hair grow long. By the time I finally met him he'd stiffened up a good deal—money ages a man."

"How long were you gone?"

"Nearly a year, as I said. Actually that year was the making of me. I'd never had any decent instruction before, or painted from a model, or had a chance to talk to genuine painters. I loved the light in Mexico, and the colors. And I learned to paint them." The part of Marburg that belonged to himself was talking to me now. "I changed from a Sunday painter into an artist. And Ruth made it possible for me."

"What did you do before you became an artist?"

"I was a geological draftsman. I worked for a—an oil company. It was dull work."

"Corpus Christi Oil and Gas?"

"That's right, I worked for Mark Hackett. It's how I met Ruth." He paused, and hung his head in depression. "So you have been researching me?"

I answered him with another question; "How do you and Stephen get along?"

"Fine. We follow our separate courses."

"Night before last, you suggested it would be nice if he never came back. You'd own his art collection then, you said."

"I was joking. Don't you recognize black humor?" When I failed to reply, he peered into my face. "You don't think I had anything to do with what happened to Stephen?"

I still didn't answer him. He sulked the rest of the way to Woodland Hills.

Chapter 26

I WENT INTO a chain restaurant on Ventura Boulevard and ordered a rare steak for breakfast. Then I reclaimed my car from the station where I had left it and drove up the long hill to Sebastian's street.

It was Saturday, and even at this time in the morning the

fairways beyond the street were sprinkled with golfers. A mailbox bearing the name Gensler stopped me before I reached Sebastian's house. I knocked on the door of the Gensler house instead.

A fair-haired man of about forty came to the door. He had an anxious vulnerable look which was accentuated by prominent blue eyes and almost invisible eyebrows.

I explained who I was, and asked if I could see Heidi.

"My daughter isn't here."

"When will she be back?"

"I don't really know. I've sent her out of town to stay with relatives."

"You shouldn't have done that, Mr. Gensler. The probation people will want to talk to her."

"I don't see why."

"She's a witness."

His face and neck reddened. "She certainly is not. Heidi's a nice clean-living girl. Her only connection with the Sebastian girl is that we happen to live on the same street."

"It's no disgrace to be a witness," I said. "Or even to know someone in trouble."

Gensler closed the door abruptly in my face. I drove my car up the street to Sebastian's house, thinking that Heidi must have told her father something that frightened him.

Dr. Jeffrey's Rover was parked in front of the house. When Bernice Sebastian let me in, I could see that her face reflected some further disaster. Its flesh was being eaten away from inside so that the bones had become more prominent: her eyes were like lights in a cage.

"What happened?"

"Sandy attempted suicide. She hid one of her father's razor blades in her dog."

"Her dog?"

"Her little cloth spaniel. She must have got the blade when she went to the bathroom. She tried to cut her wrist with it. Fortunately I was listening at the door. I heard her cry out and I stopped her before she hurt herself too terribly."

"Did she say why she did it?"

"She said she didn't deserve to live, that she was a terrible person."

"Is she?"

"No."

"Did you tell her that?"

"No. I didn't know what to say."

"When did all this happen?"

"Just now. The doctor's still with her. Please excuse me."

It was her daughter, but my case. I followed her to the door of Sandy's room and looked in. Sandy was sitting on the edge of her bed. She had a gauze bandage on her left wrist, a sprinkling of blood on the front of her pajamas. She had changed in other ways in the course of the night. Her eyes were darker in color. Her mouth was set hard. She wasn't very pretty now.

Her father was sitting beside her, holding her hand in an unreal sort of way. Dr. Jeffrey was standing over them, telling them both that Sandy would have to be hospitalized:

"I recommend the Psychiatric Center in Westwood."

"Isn't that terribly expensive?" Sebastian said.

"No more so than other hospitals. Good psychiatric treatment is always expensive."

Sebastian shook his head: his face swung loosely. "I don't know how I'm going to pay for it. It was all I could do to raise bail money."

Sandy lifted her heavy eyes. Barely moving her lips, she said: "Let them take me to jail. That doesn't cost anything."

"No," her mother said. "We'll sell the house."

"Not on this market," Sebastian said. "We wouldn't even get our equity out."

His daughter pulled her hand away from his. "Why didn't you let me die? That would solve all the problems."

"The hard way," Jeffrey said. "I'll order an ambulance."

Sebastian got to his feet. "Let me drive her. Ambulances cost money."

"I'm sorry, this is an ambulance case."

I followed Jeffrey to the telephone in the study. He made his call and hung up.

"Yes?" His look was hard and questioning.

"How sick is she?"

"I don't know. There's been some slippage, obviously. But I'm not a psychiatrist. That's why I want to get her to one right away. She needs security precautions."

"You think she'll try again?"

"We have to go on that assumption. I'd say she's very likely to repeat. She told me she's been planning this for months. She took some LSD last summer and had a bad reaction. She's still not over it."

"She told you this?"

"Yes. It may account for the change in her personality over the last few months. One dose can do it if it hits you wrong. She claims that's all she had—one dose in a sugar cube."

"Did she tell you where she got it?"

"No. Obviously she's covering up for somebody."

I got out the sugar cubes I'd taken from Lupe's kitchen and handed one of them to the doctor. "This almost certainly came from the same source. Can you have it analyzed?"

"I'll be happy to. Where did you find it?"

"In Lupe Rivera's apartment. He's the man she clobbered the other night. If I can prove that he fed her LSD—"

Jeffrey rose impatiently. "I get the point. Why don't I ask her?"

We went back to Sandy's bedroom where the little family sat frozen in each other's company. The girl, who was in the middle, looked up at us.

"Did you send for the wagon to the booby hatch?"

"As a matter of fact I did," Jeffrey said unexpectedly. "Now it's my turn to ask you a question."

She waited in silence.

"That sugar cube you took last August—did Lupe Rivera give it to you?"

"What if he did?"

The doctor put his hand under her chin, very gently, and tipped it up. "Did he? I want a yes or no answer, Sandy."

"Yes. I freaked out. I blew my mind."

"Did he do anything else to you, Sandy?"

She withdrew her chin from the doctor's hand and hung her head. Her face was impassive, her eyes very dark and fixed. "He said he would kill me if I told anyone."

"Nobody's going to kill you."

She looked at the doctor in disbelief.

"Did Lupe take you to Dr. Converse?" I said.

"No, Gerda—Mrs. Hackett—took me. I tried to jump out

of the car on the freeway. Dr. Converse put me in a strait-jacket. He kept me in his clinic all night."

Bernice Sebastian groaned. When the ambulance came for her daughter, she rode along.

Chapter 27

I WENT BACK to the freeway, where I seemed to live. I was running out of initiative, and sorely tempted to go home. Instead I drove to Long Beach on the bleakest stretch of pavement in the world.

The Corpus Christi Oil building was a massive four-story structure overlooking the waterfront and its slums. I was born and raised in Long Beach, within walking distance of the waterfront, and I could remember when the building had been put up, the year after the earthquake.

I parked in a visitor's slot and went into the lobby. Just inside the front door, a uniformed security officer sat behind a counter. When I gave him a second look I found that I knew him. He was Ralph Cuddy, who managed Alma Krug's apartment building in Santa Monica.

He knew me too. "Couldn't you find Mrs. Krug?"

"I found her, thanks."

"How is she? I haven't had a chance to visit her this week. My two jobs keep me humping."

"She seems to be doing pretty well for her age."

"Good for her. She's been like a mother to me all my life. Did you know that?"

"No."

"She has been." His emotional gaze narrowed on my face. "What sort of family matters did you discuss with her?"

"Various relatives of hers. Jasper Blevins, for instance."

"Hey, do you know Jasper? Whatever happened to him?"

"He died under a train."

"I'm not surprised," Cuddy said moralistically. "Jasper was always in trouble. He was a trouble to himself and a trouble to other people. But Alma was good to him anyway. Jasper was always her favorite." His eyes grew small and grudging, in a kind of rivalry.

"What kind of trouble?"

Cuddy started to say something and then decided not to. He was silent for a moment, his face groping for an alternative reply.

"Sex trouble, for example. Laurel was pregnant when he married her. I almost married her myself, till I found out she was in trouble." He added in mild surprise, as if he hadn't thought of the fact for some years: "I never did marry. Frankly, I never found a woman worthy of my standards. I've often said to Alma Krug, if only I wasn't born too late—"

I interrupted him: "How long have you worked here, Mr. Cuddy?"

"Twenty years."

"In security?"

"After the first three, four years, yep."

"Do you remember the summer when Mr. Hackett was killed?"

"I sure do." He gave me a rather worried look. "I had nothing to do with it. I mean, I didn't even know Mr. Hackett personally. I was just an underling in those days."

"Nobody's accusing you of anything, Mr. Cuddy. I'm trying to find out what I can about a certain revolver. Apparently it was stolen from this office and used to shoot Mr. Hackett."

"I wouldn't know anything about that."

His face closed up into a stiff mask of righteousness. I suspected he was lying.

"You have to remember the search for the gun if you were in security at the time."

"Don't tell me what I have to remember." He manufactured a quick rage and stood up full of it. Cuddy was wearing a sidearm, which added weight to his rage. "What are you trying to do, force thoughts into my head?"

"That would be a hopeless task," I said unfortunately.

He put his hand on his gun butt. "You get out of here.

You got no right to come in here and brainwash and insult me."

"I'm sorry if I said the wrong thing. I take it back. Okay?"

"No, it's not okay."

"You seem to think I'm after your scalp or something. The man I'm interested in is Sidney Marburg. He worked here as a draftsman."

"I never heard of him. And I'm not answering any more questions."

"Then I'll try personnel." I started toward the elevator. "What floor is the personnel manager on?"

"He's out to lunch."

"It's only the middle of the morning."

"I mean he hasn't come in yet. He isn't coming in today."

I turned and faced Cuddy. "This is ridiculous. What do you know that you don't want me to know?"

He lifted a hinged section of the counter and came out, pulling his gun. His mouth was mean.

"Go away," he said in a yammering voice. "You're not going to smear my friends, see."

"Is Marburg a friend of yours?"

"There you go again, twisting the thoughts in my mind. I never even heard of any Marburg. Is he a Jew?"

"I don't know."

"I'm a Christian. You can thank the Lord I am. If I wasn't a religious man, I'd shoot you down like a dog."

Righteous anger and a loaded gun: the combination scared me: it always had. I went.

My office on Sunset was beginning to look abandoned. A spider was working in the corner of the waiting room. Flies drowsed in the window, making a noise like time running down. A thin patina of dust had gathered on all the horizontal surfaces.

I wiped the top of my desk with a piece of Kleenex and sat and looked at the check Ruth Marburg had given me. Since I couldn't deposit a postdated check in the bank, I put it in my safe. It didn't make me feel rich.

I called Corpus Christi Oil in Long Beach and got in touch with the head of the drafting department, a man named Patterson. He remembered Sidney Marburg but was careful in what he said about him. Sid was a good worker, talented draftsman, always wanted to be a painter, glad he made it.

"I understand he married the former Mrs. Hackett."

"So I heard," Patterson said noncommittally.

"Did he work for you at the time of Mark Hackett's death?"

"Yeah, he quit about that time."

"Why did he quit?"

"Told me he had a chance to go to Mexico, on an art scholarship."

"Do you remember a gun that was missing? A gun that was used in the killing of Mark Hackett?"

"I heard something about it." His voice was getting fainter, like a receding spirit. "It wasn't the responsibility of the drafting department. And if you're pointing a finger at Sid, you couldn't be wronger, mister. Sid wouldn't kill anybody."

"I'm glad to hear it. Whose responsibility was that gun?"

"It belonged to security. It was their responsibility to look after it. But don't go running to them and quoting me. I don't want any trouble with the head security man."

"You mean Ralph Cuddy?"

"Listen, you've made me say more than I should already. Who is this calling, anyway? Did you say you were with the L.A. police?"

"I said I was working with them. I'm a private detective."

Patterson hung up.

I sat and tried to do some thinking. My mind went around in a circle, and I had the frustrating feeling that there was a missing connection just beyond the circle. Or deep inside the circle, at its center, buried as deep as the dead.

I dug and groped for the missing connection, sure that it was in my memory if I could only recognize it. But you can't force your unconscious mind to rap out information like a computer. It only retreats growling further into its lair.

I was stoned with weariness and frustration. I stretched out on the settee in the waiting room. I tried to stretch out, that is. The settee was a foot too short, and I lay with my legs hanging over the wooden arm, as usual.

I watched the spider in the corner of the ceiling, and wished my case was as neat and controlled as his web. I dropped off to sleep and dreamed that I was caught in a larger web, whose radii were hung with the husks of dead men. The web spun like a roulette wheel, and the spider at the center of the web had a croupier's rake in each of his eight hands. He raked me in toward him.

I woke up wet under my shirt. The spider was still working in the corner of the ceiling. I got up, intending to kill him, but both my feet were asleep. By the time they came awake, my mind was awake, too. I let the spider be. Perhaps he'd catch the flies buzzing in the window.

My brief, nightmare-ridden sleep had somehow refreshed me. I discarded my damp shirt, shaved with an electric razor, and put on a fresh shirt that I kept in the closet. Then I went to the window to see what the weather was like.

It was fair and clear, only faintly tinged with smog. Early noon traffic was roaring along the boulevard.

Detective-Sergeant Prince and his partner Janowski got out of a police car on the far side of the street. I hoped they weren't coming to see me; I was aware that I hadn't been co-operating with them. But of course they were coming to see me.

They crossed the boulevard as if they were invulnerable or oblivious to traffic. Prince walked a step ahead, like a keen dog pulling Janowski along on a kind of moral leash.

I put on a jacket, and met them at the outside door of my office. They came in without being asked. Prince was wan with barely controlled anger. Even Janowski's fair skin was blotched with feeling. He said:

"You haven't been taking us into your confidence, Archer. We decided to come and ask you why."

"I had other things to think about."

"Such as?" Prince said unpleasantly.

"Such as trying to save a man's life. His life got saved, in-cidentally."

"Lucky for you it did," Prince said. "Your neck was out a mile. It still is."

I was getting tired of being sounded off at. The blood was pounding in my stomach and my sore kidneys.

"Moderate your tone, Sergeant."

Prince looked ready to slug me. I almost wished he would. Like most Americans, I was a counter-puncher.

Janowski stepped between us. "Let me do the talking," he said to his partner. He turned to me: "We won't cry over spilt milk, but we'd like to have your cooperation now. There are places you can go, things you can do, that we can't."

"What do you want done?"

"This retired deputy sheriff, the one who was knocked off in the snatch—"

"Jack Fleischer."

"Right. You probably know all this, but I'll tell you anyway. Fleischer has had Laurel Smith's apartment under electronic surveillance for several weeks. Apparently he recorded it all on tapes. Anyway, we know he bought the tapes and the other equipment. Those tapes could be very helpful to us, I think."

"I think so, too."

Prince spoke across Janowski: "Do you have them?"

"No."

"Where are they?"

"I don't know. They may be in Fleischer's house in Santa Teresa."

"That's our opinion, too," Janowski said. "His widow denies it, but that doesn't prove anything. I talked to her on the phone, and she was pretty evasive. I tried to get some action from the Santa Teresa police, but they won't touch it. Fleischer had political connections, or so I gather, and now that he's dead he's a hero. They won't even admit the possibility that he was bugging the dead woman's apartment. Of course we could kick it up to the higher echelons—"

"Or kick it down to the lower," I said with a smile. "You want me to go to Santa Teresa and talk to Mrs. Fleischer?"

"That would be very cooperative of you," Janowski said.

"It's no chore. I was planning to see her anyway."

Janowski shook my hand, and even Prince smiled a little. They had forgiven me, to the extent that policemen ever forgive anything.

Chapter 28

I GOT TO SANTA TERESA shortly after one o'clock. I had a cold sandwich in a restaurant near the courthouse, and walked from there to Fleischer's house, slowly. I wasn't looking forward to another interview with Fleischer's widow.

The drapes pulled over the front windows gave the house a shut and deserted look. But there was life inside of it. Mrs. Fleischer answered the door.

She was drinking again, or still, had passed through various stages of drunkenness into a kind of false sobriety. She was decently clothed in a black dress. Her hair was brushed and in place. The tremor in her hands wasn't too obvious.

But she didn't seem to remember me at all. Her eyes looked right through me, as if there was someone behind me and I was a ghost.

I started over. "You may not remember me. I was working with your husband on the Davy Spanner case."

"He killed Jack," she said. "Did you know that? He killed my husband."

"Yes. I'm sorry."

She glanced at the neighbor's house, and leaned toward me, conspiratorially, twitching at my sleeve. "Didn't you and I have a talk the other night? Come in, I'll pour you a drink."

I followed her into the house reluctantly. The lights were on in the living room, as if she preferred to live in permanent evening. The drinks she brought were gin faintly tinctured with tonic. We seemed to be picking up where we had left off.

She drank most of hers down. "I'm glad he's dead," she said without gladness. "I mean it. Jack only got what was coming to him."

"How so?"

"You know as well as I do. Come on, drink up your drink."

She finished hers. I drank a little of the oily mixture in my glass. I like to drink but that particular drink, in Jack Fleischer's house and his widow's company, reminded me of taking castor oil.

"You say you were working with Jack," she said. "Did you help him make the tapes?"

"Tapes?"

"Don't try to kid me. A policeman called me from L.A. this morning. He had a funny name, a Polish name, Junkowski, something like that. Know him?"

"I know a Sergeant Janowski."

"That's the name. He wanted to know if Jack left any tapes around the house. He said they could be important in a homicide. Laurel got it, too." She thrust her face toward me, as though to affirm her own continued existence. "Did you know that?"

"I found it out."

"Jack beat her to death, didn't he?"

"I don't know."

"Of course you do. I can see it in your face. You don't have to be so tight-mouthed with me. I was married to Jack, remember. I lived with him and his wildness for thirty years. Why do you think I started drinking? I was a teetotaler when we got married. I started drinking because I couldn't bear the thought of the things he did."

She leaned so close her eyes crossed. She had a cool way of saying outrageous things, but her version of events was too subjective to be entirely true. Still I wanted to hear more from her, and when she told me to finish my drink I did.

She went out to the kitchen and returned with another dose of the stuff for me, and another for her.

"What about those tapes?" she said. "Are they worth money?"

I made a quick decision. "They are to me."

"How much?"

"A thousand dollars."

"That isn't very much."

"The police won't pay you anything for the tapes. I might

raise my offer, depending on what's on them. Have you played them back?"

"No."

"Where are they?"

"I'm not telling. I need much more than a thousand. Now that Jack is dead and gone, I'm planning to do some traveling. He never took me anywhere, not once in the last fifteen years. And you know why? Whenever he went someplace, *she* was there waiting for him. Well, now she isn't waiting any more." After a moment, she added in mild surprise: "Jack isn't waiting, either. They're both dead, aren't they? I wished it on them so often I can't believe it happened."

"It happened."

"Good."

She went through the motions of drinking a toast and stood swaying, tangle-footed. I took the glass from her hand and put it down on the table inset with stones.

"Sanctuary muchly."

She did a little dance step to inaudible music. She seemed to be trying hard to find something to do that would make her feel human again.

"I never thought I'd feel sorry for *her*," she said. "But I kind of do feel sorry for her. She resembled me, did you know that? I was much more beautiful when I was young, but Laurel had fifteen years on me. I used to pretend to myself that I was her in bed with Jack. But it wasn't all fun and frolic even for her. He put her through the ropes and over the jumps just like he did with any of his women. And in the end he caved in her pretty face for her."

"Do you really believe your husband did that?"

"You don't know the half of it." She plopped down on the settee beside me. "I could tell you things that would make your flesh crawl. It's a terrible thing to say, but I hardly blame that boy for blowing his head off for him. You know who the boy is?"

"His father was Jasper Blevins. His mother was Laurel."

"You're smarter than I thought." She gave me a crinkled look. "Or did I tell you all this the other night?"

"No."

"I bet I did, though, didn't I? Or did they tell you in the north county? It's common knowledge in Rodeo City."

"What is, Mrs. Fleischer?"

"Jack and his tricks. He was the law, there was no way they could stop him. He killed that Blevins man, shoved him under a train so he could have his wife. He got Laurel to say it wasn't her husband's body. He put their little boy in the orphanage, because he got in the way of the big romance."

I didn't believe her. I didn't disbelieve her. Her words hung in the unreal room, perfectly at home there, but unconnected with the daylight world.

"How do you know all this?"

"Some of it I figured out for myself." One of her eyes gave me a wise look: the other was half closed and idiotic. "I have friends in law enforcement, or used to have. Other deputies' wives—they did some whispering."

"Why didn't their husbands bring your husband to book?"

The idiotic eye closed entirely in a frozen wink; she peered at my face with the wise one. "Jack knew where too many bodies were buried. The north county's rough territory, mister, and he was the king of it. Anyway, what could they prove? The woman Laurel said the body didn't belong to her husband. Said she never saw him before in her life. The head was all smashed up, unrecog—" She stumbled over the word —"unrecnizable. They put it down as just another accidental death."

"Do you know for a fact it wasn't?"

"I know what I know." But her one closed eye seemed to mock her seriousness.

"Are you willing to pass this on to the police?"

"What would be the use? Jack's dead. Everybody's dead."

"You're not."

"I wish I was." The statement surprised or alarmed her. She opened both eyes and glared at me, as if I'd threatened her with loss of life.

"And Davy Spanner isn't dead."

"He soon will be. There's a fifty-man posse out after him. I talked to Rory Pennell on the phone this morning. He promised they'd shoot to kill."

"You want them to?"

"He killed Jack, didn't he?"

"But you said you hardly blamed him."

"Did I?" The question was directed to herself as well as me. "I couldn't have. Jack was my husband."

This was where I came in. Her single life and mind were as deeply split as her marriage had been. I got up to leave.

She followed me to the door. "What about the tapes?"

"What about them? Do you have them?"

"I think I can put my hands on them."

"For a thousand?"

"It isn't enough," she said. "I'm a widow now, I have to look out for myself."

"Let me play the tapes. Then I'll make you another offer."

"They're not here."

"Where are they?"

"That's for me to know and you to find out."

"Okay, sit on them. I'll be back, or I'll phone you. Do you remember my name?"

"Archer," she said. "Jack Archer."

I left it at that. She went back into the artificial twilight of her living room.

Chapter 29

BEFORE I LEFT Santa Teresa I called Henry Langston's house from a gas-station telephone booth. His wife answered, formally: "This is the Langston residence."

"Is your husband at home?"

"Who is calling, please?" But she probably knew my voice. Her voice was hostile.

"Lew Archer."

"No, he isn't here, and you're responsible. He's still up in the north county, trying to save that precious murderer of his. He'll end up getting shot himself."

She was semi-hysterical, and I tried to soothe her. "That isn't very likely, Mrs. Langston."

"You don't know," she said. "I have this terrible feeling of fatality, that nothing will ever go right for us again. And it's your fault, you got him into this."

"Not really. He's been involved with Davy Spanner for years. He made a commitment to him, and he's trying to follow through."

"What about *me?*" she cried.

"Is there something specific bothering you?"

"There's no use telling you," she said in a kind of angry intimacy. "You're not a doctor."

"Are you ill, Mrs. Langston?"

She answered by hanging up on me. I was tempted to go to her house, but that would only lead to further involvement and loss of time. I sympathized with her but I couldn't help her. Only her husband could do that.

I got onto the freeway headed north. My body was beginning to rebel against continuous action without enough rest. It felt as if my right foot on the accelerator pushed the car uphill all the way to Rodeo City.

Deputy Pennell was in the back room of his office, listening to his dispatcher's radio. I gathered he had been sitting there ever since I talked to him in the middle of the night. His mustache and his eyes gave the impression that they were taking over his face, which was paler and thinner and needed a shave.

"What's the word, Deputy?"

"They lost him." His voice was edged with disgust.

"Where?"

"There's no telling. The rain washed out his tracks. It's still raining in the north pass."

"Where does that lead to?"

"He'd have to come back to the coast. Inland there's nothing but more mountain ranges. It's snowing in the back country above five thousand feet."

"So?"

"We head him off when he hits the highway. I'm requesting the highway patrol to set up roadblocks."

"Is there any chance that he's still in the valley?"

"Could be. The p-professor seems to think so, anyway."

"Do you mean Henry Langston?"

"Yeah. He's still hanging around the old Krug ranch. He's

got a theory that Spanner is kind of cracked on the subject of that place, and that he'll head back there."

"But you don't buy that theory?"

"Naw. I never saw a p-professor yet that knew what he was talking about. They get soft in the head from reading too many books."

I didn't argue, and this encouraged Pennell to go on. Langston had upset him, it appeared, and he needed reassurance.

"You know what the professor tried to tell me? That Spanner had j-j-justification for doing what he did to poor old Jack. On account of Jack putting him in the orphanage."

"Didn't that happen?"

"Sure, but what else could Jack do with the kid? His father got killed by a train. Jack wasn't responsible for him."

I could hear a little slippage, a trace of double-talk. "Jack wasn't responsible for what, Deputy?"

"For either of them, father *or* son. I know there were dirty rumors at the time, and now this Langston is trying to start them up again, before old Jack is even in his grave."

"What kind of rumors?"

He raised his hot sorrowful eyes. "I wouldn't even pass them on, they're so crazy."

"Rumors that Jack killed the man himself?"

"Yeah. That's all a lot of malarkey."

"Would you swear to it, Deputy?"

"Sure I would," he said with some bravado, "I'd swear to it on a stack of Bibles. I told the p-professor that, but he wasn't satisfied."

Neither was I. "Would you take a lie-detector test?"

Pennell was disappointed in me. "So you think I'm a liar. And that poor old Jack was a murderer."

"Who killed Jasper Blevins if he didn't?"

"Plenty of people could have."

"Who were the suspects?"

"There was a wild-looking character with a beard hanging around the ranch. He looked like a Russian, I heard."

"Come on now, Deputy. I'm not buying any bearded anarchists. I know Jack hung around the ranch. Later, I've been told, he stashed the woman at Mamie Hagedorn's place."

"What if he did? Blevins didn't want his wife; he made that clear."

"Did you know Blevins?"

"I saw him once or twice."

"Did you see him after he was dead?"

"Yeah."

"Was it Blevins?"

"I couldn't swear to it, one way or the other." He added with a shifty look in his eye: "Mrs. Blevins said it wasn't. She ought to know."

"What did the little boy say?"

"Never said a word. He couldn't talk; he was just a dummy."

"That was convenient, wasn't it?"

Pennell stood up with his hand on his gun butt. "I've heard enough of that kind of t-talk. Jack Fleischer was like an older b-brother to me. He t-taught me to shoot and drink. He g-got me my first woman. He m-made a m-man of me."

"I was wondering who to blame."

Pennell cursed me and got his gun out. I retreated. He didn't follow me out of the office, but I was a little shaken. This was the second gun that had been pulled on me today. Sooner or later one was bound to go off.

I walked across the street to the Rodeo Hotel and asked the desk clerk where Mamie Hagedorn lived.

He looked up brightly. "Mamie retired from business."

"Good. My intentions are social."

"I see. She lives up the road a piece, on the way to Center-ville. It's a big red-brick house, the only red-brick house on that side of town."

I drove out of town past the rodeo grounds and up into the hills. The red-brick house stood high on one of them, com-manding the whole scene. It was a gray overcast day, and the sea was like a wornout mirror reflecting the sullen sky.

I went up the gravel drive and knocked on the door of the big house. It was answered by a Spanish American woman wearing a black uniform and white cap with a black velvet bow. She was the first maid in uniform I'd seen in quite a while.

She started to give me an oral quiz on who and what I was, and why I was here. It was interrupted by a woman's voice which came from the front parlor: "Send him in! I'll talk to him."

The maid took me into a room filled with ornate Victorian furniture, complete with antimacassars. It underlined the feeling I had when I came to the north county, though the gantries of Vandenberg were just over the county line, that I was stepping back into prewar time.

Mamie Hagedorn sustained the illusion. She was sitting on a couch, a small woman whose gold-slippered feet dangled clear of the parquet floor. She was wearing a rather formal high-necked dress. She had a pouter pigeon bosom, a rouged and raddled face, hair or a wig which was a peculiarly horrible shade of iridescent red. But I liked the way her smile broke up her face.

"What's on your mind?" she said. "Sit down and tell Mamie."

She raised her hand, on which a diamond winked. I sat beside her.

"I was talking to Al Simmons last night in Centerville. He mentioned that you once knew Laurel Blevins."

"Al talks too much for his own good," she said cheerfully. "As a matter of fact I knew Laurel very well. She lived with me after her husband died."

"Then it was her husband who died under the train?"

She thought about this. "I'm not *sure* it was. It never came out officially."

"Why not?"

She moved uneasily. Her dress rustled and gave off a whiff of lavender. To my stretched nerves she seemed like the past itself stirring in its shroud.

"I wouldn't want to queer things for Laurel. I always liked Laurel."

"Then you'll be sorry to hear that she's dead."

"Laurel? She's just a young woman."

"She didn't die of old age. She was beaten to death."

"Holy cripes!" the woman said. "Who did that?"

"Jack Fleischer's a prime suspect."

"But he's dead, too."

"That's right. You can't hurt either of them by talking, Mrs. Hagedorn."

"*Miss.* I never married." She put on horn-rimmed glasses

which made her look severe, and studied my face. "Just who are you, anyway?"

I told her. Then she asked me about the case. I laid it out for her, with the names and the places.

"I knew most all of those people," she said in a rusty voice, "going all the way back to Joe Krug and his wife Alma. I liked Joe. He was a fine figure of a man. But Alma was a Bible-thumping sobersides. Joe used to come and visit me sometimes—I ran a house in Rodeo City in case you didn't know—and Alma never forgave me for leading him astray. I think I was one of the main reasons she made him move to Los Angeles. Cripes, that was forty years ago. What happened to Joe?"

"He's dead now. Alma's alive."

"She must be old. Alma's older than I am."

"How old is that?"

She answered with her broken smile: "I never tell my age. I'm older than I look."

"I bet you are."

"Don't flatter me." She took off her glasses and wiped her eyes with a lace handkerchief. "Joe Krug was a good man, but he never had any luck in this neck of the woods. I heard he had a little before he died, after he moved to Los Angeles."

"What kind of luck?"

"Money luck. Is there any other? He got himself a job with some big company and married his daughter Etta to the boss."

"Etta?"

"Henrietta. They called her Etta for short. She was married before to a man named Albert Blevins. And he was the father of Jasper Blevins who married Laurel, poor dear." The old woman seemed to take pride in her genealogical knowledge.

"Who killed Jasper, Miss Hagedorn?"

"I don't know for sure." She gave me a long shrewd look. "If I tell you what I do know, what do you plan to do with it?"

"Open up the case and let the daylight in."

She smiled a little sadly. "That reminds me of a hymn, an old revival hymn. I was converted once, would you believe it?

164

It lasted until the boy evangelist ran away with the week's offerings and my best friend. What are you after, Mr. Evangelist? Money?"

"I'm being paid."

"Who by?"

"Some people down south."

"Why are they paying you?"

"It would take all day to explain."

"Then why not drop it, leave it lay? Let the dead people rest in peace."

"There are getting to be too many of them. It's been going on for a long time now. Fifteen years." I leaned toward her and said in a quiet voice, "Did Laurel kill her husband? Or was it Jack Fleischer?"

She countered with another question, which seemed to contain an answer hidden in it: "You said Laurel is dead. How do I know you're telling me the truth?"

"Call the L.A.P.D., Purdue Street Station. Ask for Sergeant Prince or Sergeant Janowski."

I recited the number. She slid off the couch, with the help of a needlepoint footstool, and left the room. I heard a door close down the hall. A few minutes later I heard the same door open.

She came back much more slowly. The rouge stood out on her slack cheeks. She climbed back onto the couch, reminding me for an instant of a child dressed up in attic finery, wearing an ancestor's wig.

"So Laurel really is dead," she said heavily. "I talked to Sergeant Prince. He's going to send somebody up here to interview me."

"I'm here now."

"I know that. With Laurel dead, and Jack, I'm willing to answer your question. The answer is yes. She killed Jasper Blevins, smashed in his head with the blunt end of an ax. Jack Fleischer got rid of the body under a train. He put it down on the books as an accident, victim unknown."

"How do you know all this?"

"Laurel told me herself. Before she left here Laurel and I were as close as mother and daughter. She told me how she killed Jasper, and she told me why. I didn't ever blame her for a minute." Mamie Hagedorn took a deep shuddering breath. "The only thing I blamed her for was leaving the little boy the way she did. That was a terrible thing to do. But she was bound to travel light and make her way in the world. The little boy was evidence against her."

"She came back to him finally," I said. "By that time it was too late for either of them."

"You think her own boy killed her?"

"I didn't until now. He had no motive. But if he found out that she killed his father—" I left the sentence unfinished.

"She didn't, though."

"You just said she did."

"No, I said she killed her husband Jasper Blevins. He wasn't the little boy's father."

"Who was?"

"Some rich fellow in Texas. Laurel got herself pregnant by him before she ever left there. His family gave her some money and shipped her off to California. Jasper married her for that money, but he never had normal relations with her. I never could respect a man who didn't like normal meat-and-potatoes—"

I interrupted her. "How do you know all this?"

"Laurel told me after she killed him. He did things to her that no woman has to put up with. That was why she killed him, and I don't blame her."

Chapter 30

I THANKED MAMIE HAGEDORN and went out to my car. I'd let some daylight into the case, all right. But the main effect had been to change the color of the daylight.

I headed over the pass toward the Krug ranch. It was the place where all the trouble had started, where Albert Blevins had thrown a lamp at his wife (or vice versa) and ruined his house and his marriage and his son Jasper, where Jasper's marriage had ended in murder, where Davy Spanner was born and Jack Fleischer died. I wanted to see the place in the different-colored daylight.

It wasn't raining in the valley. The cloud cover was breaking up, letting the sky show through in places.

I went through Centerville and made my turn without pausing. I didn't stop till I got to Buzzard Creek.

Henry Langston's station wagon was parked on the side of the road. The creek had shrunk to a shallow stream meandering across the road through several channels cut in the mud it had deposited.

I waded through the mud, following footprints which were probably Langston's, and climbed the rocky lane to the old ranch. The fields around it looked fresh and new. Each blade of grass, each oak leaf, was brilliantly distinct. The sky was luminous, and even the scattering clouds were like floes of light.

Only the human structures were dilapidated. They were dwarfed by the sky, which seemed to arch like a great span of time across the valley.

Henry Langston's footsteps led past the barn to the ruined house. Before I reached the house, he came out carrying his .32 target pistol in his left hand and a sawed-off shotgun on his right arm. For a moment I entertained the wild idea that he intended to shoot me.

Instead, he waved the shotgun at me in a friendly way and spoke my name with pleasure. "I found the murder weapon."

"In the house?"

"No. He threw it in the river. I saw it sticking out of the mud when I came across."

I took the shotgun out of his hands and broke it. There were two expended cartridges in the breech. The short ugly double muzzle was choked with mud.

"Any other sign of him?"

Hank shook his head. "I had a hunch that he might come back to the ranch here. It seemed to be the place he was looking for. But I was wrong."

"Where's the posse?"

Hank pointed toward the mountains in the northeast. Over them I could see black clouds whose trailing edges were ragged with rain.

"They may be bogged down," he said with some satisfaction.

"You don't want him caught, do you, Hank?"

"I'm of two minds about Davy. Of course I want him caught. He's dangerous. But I don't want him shot and killed without a trial. There are mitigating circumstances, remember."

I knew that. It was one of my reasons for going on with the case. There wasn't much chance of saving Davy from a first-degree conviction, but I hoped the girl was still reclaimable.

"Let's get out of here," I said. "I stopped in Santa Teresa, by the way, talked to your wife on the phone."

Hank gave me a quick guilty look. "Is Kate all right?"

"No, she isn't. She's worried about you and worried about herself."

"What's the matter with her?"

"It may be only nerves. She said she wouldn't tell me because I wasn't a doctor."

"She's concerned about losing the baby," he said gravely. "She was bleeding a little before I left last night."

He started walking with long strides past the barn toward the road. The barn owl flew out, his eyes wide in his flabbergasted face. Hank took a shot at the owl with his target pistol. He missed the bird, but I didn't like the action. It reminded me of Lupe's shot at the mud hen.

We drove to Centerville in separate cars. Hank parked his wagon in front of Al Simmons's beer and sandwich place. When I followed him in, he was already talking into the bar telephone: "Make it collect, please. My name is Henry Langston."

There was a long silence, stitched by the telephone ringing at the far end of the line, and the mutter of a turned-down radio at this end. Al Simmons leaned across the bar:

"More trouble?"

"I hope not."

The operator's voice came over the line like a second answer to Al's question: "Your party does not answer, sir. Do you wish me to try again?"

"I'll try again myself, thanks." Hank hung up and turned

to me: "She must be at the nursery school picking up Henry, Jr. It's early for that, though."

Moving abruptly, as if he was pulled or driven, he started for the door. Al Simmons detained me.

"What's on your friend's mind?"

"He's worried about his wife."

"On account of the shotgun killer?"

"Yes."

"I guess a lot of people will be worried. He made it out over the north pass, did you know that? The radio said he hitched a ride on a truck."

"Headed which way?"

"South. The truck driver says he dropped him in Santa Teresa."

I went outside to tell Hank. He was already roaring up the county blacktop. By the time I reached the summit of the pass, his car was far down the twisting road, crawling like a flea on the mountain's scarred flank.

Perhaps I should have stopped in Rodeo City. The trouble was that I didn't trust Pennell's judgment. Assuming that Davy had holed up in Langston's house, the last thing needed was the kind of shoot-out in which innocent people could get hurt.

Once on the highway and past the roadblock which Pennell had ordered too late, I pushed the speedometer up to ninety and held it till I reached the outskirts of Santa Teresa. I took the first off-ramp and drove to the Langstons' neighborhood.

Hank's wagon was standing in the road with steam blowing out from under the hood. Hank was halfway between the wagon and his front door, running with his pistol in his hand.

He shouted: "Kate! Are you all right?"

Kate Langston came out screaming. She lunged toward her husband, fell on the flagstone walk before she reached him, got up bloody-kneed and crying piteously: "I'm going to lose the baby. He's making me lose the baby."

Hank gathered her against him with his left arm. Davy appeared in the doorway. He was muddy and unshaven, and awkward, like an actor dying of stage fright.

Hank raised his right arm, pointing the pistol like a dark elongated finger. Davy looked at him shyly, and opened his mouth to speak. Hank shot him several times. The third shot broke his left eye. He sat down on the threshold and died there very quickly.

An hour or so later, I was inside the house with Hank. The local police had come and, after getting a statement from Hank and congratulating him, had taken the body away. Kate was in the emergency ward of the hospital under sedation for shock.

With the same general idea in mind, I was pouring whisky for Hank but not drinking much myself. On top of everything else, the whisky hit him hard. He wandered around the living room, looking for something that probably wasn't there. He paused at the grand piano, with closed fists began to hammer the keys.

I yelled at him: "Is that necessary?"

He turned with his fists raised. His eyes were dark and wild, as wild as Davy's had been.

"I shouldn't have killed him, should I?"

"I'm not your conscience. There is a kind of economy in life. You don't spend more than you have, or say more than you know, or throw your weight around more than necessary."

"He was wrecking my marriage, driving my wife crazy. I had to make a decision, do something decisive."

"You certainly did that."

"The police didn't blame me."

"They're not your conscience either."

He sat swaying on the piano bench. I was disappointed in Hank, and worried about him. The second self that most of us have inside of us had stepped into the open and acted out its violence. Now he had to live with it, like an insane Siamese twin, for the rest of his life.

The telephone rang. I answered it: "Langston residence."

"Is that you, Mr. Langston?" a woman said.

"I'm a friend of the family. There's illness in the family."

"I was wondering why Mrs. Langston didn't pick up Junior."

"Is that the nursery school?"

The woman said it was, and that she was Mrs. Hawkins.

"Just keep the boy for now. Keep him overnight."

"We can't do that. We don't have the facilities."

"Give it a try, will you? Mrs. Langston's in the hospital."

"What about Mr. Langston?"

"He's not well, either."

I hung up and went back to him. His eyes had a dark used look, like burned ends. He was beginning to feel the change in himself and in his life.

I said good-bye and left the house, stepping wide over the threshold where some of Davy's blood was turning brown in the sun that had rejected him now forever.

Chapter 31

BEFORE HEADING BACK to Los Angeles, I paid a final visit to Mrs. Fleischer. She came to the door wearing a black hat and coat. Her face was freshly made up but under the makeup it looked pasty and inert.

She seemed almost completely sober, but very nervous. "What do you want?"

"The tapes."

She spread her gloved hands. "No havey, no savvy."

"Don't give me that, Mrs. Fleischer. You said they're where you could put your hands on them."

"Well, they're not any more."

"Did you turn them over to the police?"

"Maybe I did and maybe I didn't. You've got to let me go now. I'm expecting a taxi."

She started to close the door on me. I leaned against it casually but firmly. Her eyes moved sluggishly up to my face.

"What is this, anyway?"

"I've decided to raise my offer. I'll give you two thousand."

She laughed joylessly. "That's peanuts. Chicken feed. If I wasn't a lady I'd tell you what you can do with your lousy two thousand."

"Who have you been talking to?"

"A very nice young man. He treated me like a gentleman, which is more than some people do." She gave the door a fretful shove, which my shoulder blocked. "And he told me how much those cans of tape were really worth."

"How much?"

"Ten grand," she said with the pride of a daily-double winner putting down a loser.

"Did he buy them from you?"

"Maybe he did."

"I know. And maybe he didn't. Can you describe him to me?"

"He's very good-looking, with nice brown curly hair. Much better looking than you are. And quite a few years younger," she added, as if she could score off her husband through his old buddy Jack Archer.

Her description failed to evoke anyone, unless it was Keith Sebastian, which seemed unlikely. "What name did he use?"

"He didn't mention his name."

That probably meant she had been paid in cash, if she had been paid. "Ten grand is a lot of cash," I said. "I hope you're not planning to carry it around loose."

"No, I'm gonna—" She bit her lower lip and got lipstick on her front teeth. "It's none of your business what I'm gonna do. And if you don't lay off me, I'll call the police."

That was the last thing she was likely to do. But I was weary of her, and of myself talking to her. I drove around the block and parked at the corner. After a while a yellow cab came from the other direction. It stopped in front of her house and honked gently.

Mrs. Fleischer came out carrying a light-blue traveling bag. She got into the taxi. I followed it across town to the freeway and north along the freeway to the local airport.

I didn't try to find out where Mrs. Fleischer was flying to. I didn't care. She wouldn't be leaving town if she hadn't sold the tapes.

I drove south to Woodland Hills, feeling empty and light and futile. I think I'd been harboring a secret wish that I could somehow pull it out for Davy, save his life at least, give him a long-term chance for rehabilitation.

Such wishes for other people were always going sour.

Langston's wish for Davy had turned into a secret triangle which meant the opposite of what it seemed to mean. I was beginning to worry about my wish for the girl.

Bernice Sebastian let me into her house. She was sallow and desolate, with black glittering eyes. Her grooming was coming apart for the first time that I'd seen. She had cigarette ashes down the front of her dress, and her hair needed combing.

She took me into the living room and seated me in a golden drench of late afternoon sunlight which came in through the high glass.

"Would you like some coffee?"

"No thanks. A glass of water would taste good."

She brought it to me formally, on a tray. She gave the impression of trying to hold together, by such formalities, all the centrifugal pieces of her life. I drank the water and thanked her.

"Where's your husband?"

"Off on one of his missions," she said dryly.

"He didn't go to Santa Teresa, by any chance?"

"I don't know where he went. We had a quarrel."

"Do you want to talk about it?"

"No. It isn't the sort of talk I'd care to repeat, to anyone. Essentially we were blaming each other, for this disaster."

She sat down on a hassock facing me, folding her knees and holding them with locked fingers. Nothing she did was graceless, as she knew. She turned her pretty, disheveled head self-consciously under my eyes.

"I'll tell you what our quarrel was about, if you promise not to do anything."

"What do you want me not to do?"

"I don't want you to do anything to stop Keith. That would be treachery."

"Stop him doing what?"

"Promise first."

"I can't, Mrs. Sebastian. I will promise this: I won't do anything that would harm your daughter."

"But not Keith?"

"If their interests turn out to be separate, I'll do my best for Sandy."

"Then I'll tell you. He's planning to take her out of the country."

"Jump bail?"

"I'm afraid so. He's talking in terms of South America."

"It isn't a good idea. She'd have a hard time ever coming back, and so would he."

"I know that. I told him that."

"How is he planning to finance the trip?"

"I'm afraid he's thinking about embezzling money. Keith seems to be breaking up. He simply can't bear the idea of Sandy standing trial and possibly going to jail."

"She's still in the Psychiatric Center, isn't she?"

"I don't know."

"Call them and find out."

Bernice went into the study and closed the door behind her. I heard her talking, too dimly to know what she said. She came out with a frightened grimace pulling at her mouth.

"He took her out of the Center."

"When?"

"About an hour ago."

"Did he say where he was taking her?"

"No."

"Or give you any clue?"

"This morning he talked about flying to Mexico City, and then perhaps on to Brazil. But he wouldn't go without telling me first. He expects me to go along."

"Do you want to?"

She shook her head. "I don't think any of us should go. We should stay here and fight it out."

"You're a good girl."

Her eyes filled up with feeling but what she said was: "No. If I were a good person, my family wouldn't have got into this mess. I made all the mistakes in the book."

"Do you feel like naming them?"

"If you can bear to listen." She sat quiet for a minute, ordering her thoughts. "I don't really want to talk it out at any length. This isn't the time, and I doubt that you're the person."

"Who is?"

"Keith should be. He's still my husband. The trouble is we stopped talking years ago. We started a game of let's pretend, without ever admitting it to each other. Keith was to be the rising young executive and I was to be his model homemaker, making him feel like a man, which is hard for Keith. And Sandy was to make us both feel good by doing well in school and never doing or saying anything wrong. What that boils down to is exploitation. Keith and I were exploiting each other and Sandy, and that's the opposite of loving each other."

"I still say you're a good girl."

"Don't try to make me feel better. I have no right to."

But she closed her eyes and leaned her face toward me. I held it between my hands. I could feel her mouth and her breathing warm on my fingers.

After a while she straightened up. Her face was more composed. It had recovered some of the pride that made it beautiful.

She said: "Are you hungry? Let me fix you something to eat."

"It wouldn't be a good idea."

"Why not?"

"You said it yourself just now. People shouldn't play let's pretend."

"Is that what I'd be doing?"

"That's what I'd be doing, Bernice. There's something else we should be doing."

She misunderstood me, and gave me a quick-frozen quizzical look. "Really?"

"That wasn't a pass. But I have to ask you a question that may embarrass you. It has to do with Sandy's sex experience."

She was startled. She stood up and walked away from me, to the far side of the room.

"How much did your daughter know about sex?"

Slowly, she turned to face me. "I haven't the faintest idea. We never discussed the matter."

"Why not?"

"I assumed she learned all about it in school. She took a course on the subject. Anyway, I didn't feel qualified."

"Why?"

She looked at me angrily. "I don't know why you're insisting on this catechism. It has nothing to do with anything."

"People are always telling me that about their central concerns."

"Sex is *not* one of my central concerns. I can take it or leave it. Keith and I—" She heard herself, and paused.

"What about you and Keith?"

"Nothing. You have no right to ask me these questions."

I moved toward her. "Tell me one thing. What happened to Sandy last summer—the incident you've been suppressing in her diary?"

"It hardly matters any more."

"Everything matters."

She looked at me with a kind of incredulity. "You really believe that, don't you? I never met a man like you before."

"Let's not get off on the personal. Did she write about her LSD experience?"

"That was part of it. Incidentally, I forgot to tell you, the doctor left a message for you. The substance you gave him for analysis was LSD of a poor quality. He said that helped to account for Sandy's reaction."

"I'm not surprised. What else helped to account for it?"

"He didn't say."

"I'm asking you, Bernice. What was the rest of it?"

Her face darkened. "I can't tell you. Honestly I can't."

"If Sandy could do it or have it done to her, you should be able to say it. Are we talking about her sexual relations with Lupe?"

She bowed her head. "There were more than one of them: They took turns at her, doing—different things."

"And she spelled this out in her diary?"

"Yes."

"May I see it?"

"I destroyed it. Honestly. I was so terribly ashamed."

"Why do you suppose she wrote it out?"

"To shame me. She knew I read her diary."

"Don't you think she may have been asking you for help?"

"I don't know. It came as such a shock, I couldn't think clearly about it. I still can't." Her voice was hurried and monotonous, with a shrill note of panic running through it.

"Why, Bernice?" I wondered if the same sort of thing had ever happened to her.

She raised her head and looked at me with black dislike. "I don't want to talk to you any more. Go away."

"Promise me one thing first. Let me know when you hear from Keith. All I want is a chance to talk to him and Sandy."

"I'll call you. I promise that much."

I told her I would wait for her call in my office, and went outside. Late afternoon sunlight spilled over the mountains to the west. The light had a tarnished elegiac quality, as if the sinking sun might never rise again. On the fairway behind the house the golfers seemed to be hurrying, pursued by their lengthening shadows.

Chapter 32

I BOUGHT a plastic basket of fried chicken and took it to my office. Before eating it, I checked in with my answering service. The girl on the switchboard told me I'd had a call from Ralph Cuddy.

I called the Santa Monica number that Cuddy had left for me. He answered the phone himself:

"Good evening. This is Ralph Cuddy."

"Archer here. I wasn't expecting to hear from you again."

"Mrs. Krug asked me to call you." His voice was stiff with embarrassment. "I told her Jasper was dead. She wants to talk to you about it."

"Tell her I'll get in touch with her tomorrow."

"Tonight would be better. Mrs. Krug is very anxious to see you. You know that missing gun you were asking me about? She has some information on that, too."

"How could she have?"

"Mr. Krug was security chief at Corpus Christi Oil at the time the gun was stolen."

"Who stole it? Jasper Blevins?"

"I'm not authorized to tell you anything. You better get it direct from Mrs. Krug."

I drove through heavy early-evening traffic to the Oakwood Convalescent Home. As the nurse conducted me down the corridor, I got a whiff of some patient's dinner. It reminded me of the chicken I had left untouched on my desk.

Alma Krug looked up from her Bible when I entered the room. Her eyes were grave. She dismissed the nurse with a movement of her hand.

"Please shut the door," she said to me. "It's good of you to visit me, Mr. Archer." She indicated a straight chair, which I took, and turned her wheel chair to face me. "Ralph Cuddy says my grandson Jasper was killed in a train wreck. Is that true?"

"His body was found under a train. I've been told he was murdered somewhere else, and that Laurel did the killing. That's hearsay evidence, but I'm inclined to believe it."

"Has Laurel been punished?"

"Not directly and not immediately. The local sheriff's man covered up for her, or so I'm told. But Laurel was killed herself the other day."

"Who killed her?"

"I don't know."

"This is terrible news." Her voice had a rustling sibilance. "You say that Laurel was killed the other day. You didn't tell me that when you came to see me before."

"No."

"And you didn't tell me Jasper was dead."

"I wasn't sure, and I didn't want to hurt you unnecessarily."

"You should have told me. How long ago did he die?"

"About fifteen years. Actually his body was found on the tracks near Rodeo City in late May of 1952."

"A bad end," she said.

"Other bad things have happened." I went on slowly and carefully, watching her face. "Three or four days before Jasper was killed, Mark Hackett was shot on Malibu Beach. Perhaps we've both been holding back, Mrs. Krug. You didn't tell me your husband was security officer for Mark Hackett's oil company. I admit I should have been able to work it out for myself, but for some reason I didn't. I think you're the reason."

Her eyes flinched. "I have a lot on my conscience. It's why I asked you to come here, Mr. Archer. The still small voice wouldn't let me rest, and now that my grandson Jasper's dead—" She let the sentence trail off into silence.

"Did Jasper steal the gun from Hackett's company?"

"Joe always thought so. Jasper had stolen before—I had to lock up my purse when he was with us. And he visited Joe at the office that same day."

"The day Mark Hackett was killed?"

She nodded very slowly. "The day before that he had a terrible quarrel with Mr. Hackett."

"How do you know?"

"He told Joe. He wanted Joe to intercede for him with Mr. Hackett."

"What was the problem?"

"Money. Jasper thought he had a legitimate claim on Mr. Hackett, for raising the boy. Actually Mr. Hackett gave Jasper a good deal of money at the time he married Laurel. That was all part of the bargain."

"Are you telling me that Davy was Mark Hackett's illegitimate son?"

"His grandson," she corrected me soberly. "Davy was Stephen Hackett's natural son. Laurel Dudney was one of the Hacketts' servants back in Texas. She was a pretty little thing, and Stephen got her with child. His father sent him off to study in Europe. He sent Laurel out to us, to find a husband before she got too big.

"Jasper decided to marry her himself. He was barbering at the time, and he hardly made enough to keep body and soul together. Mr. Hackett gave them five thousand dollars for a wedding present. Later, Jasper thought he should get more. He was badgering Mr. Hackett the day before—" Her precise mouth closed without completing the sentence.

"The day before he killed him?"

"That's what Joe always thought. It shortened my husband's life. Joe was an honest man, but he couldn't bring himself to accuse his own daughter's son. He asked me if he should, and I told him not to. That's on my conscience, too."

"You did what most grandparents would do."

"That isn't good enough. But we were in the habit of making excuses for Jasper. From the time that he was a little boy and first came to us, he was a Tartar. He stole and fought and tortured cats and got in trouble at school. I took him to a head doctor once and the doctor said he should be sent away. But I couldn't bear to do that to him, the poor boy wasn't all bad." She added after some thought: "He had some artistic talent. He got that from his mother."

"Tell me about his mother."

Mrs. Krug was confused for a moment. She looked at me with displeasure. "I prefer not to talk about my daughter. I have some right to the privacy of my feelings."

"I already have some facts, Mrs. Krug. Your daughter was born in 1910 in Rodeo City. Oddly enough, I have a copy of her birth certificate. She was christened Henrietta R. Krug. You called her Etta, but at some point in her life she dropped that name."

"She always hated it. She started using her middle name after she left Albert Blevins."

"Her middle name is Ruth, isn't it?"

The old woman bowed her head in assent. Her eyes refused to meet mine.

"And her second husband was Mark Hackett."

"There was another one in between," she said with an old woman's passion for accuracy. "She took up with a Mexican boy from San Diego.

"What was his name?"

"Lupe Rivera. They only stayed together a few months. The police arrested him for smuggling, and Etta got a divorce from him. Then came Mark Hackett. Then came Sidney Marburg." Her voice rang harshly, as if she was reciting an indictment.

"Why didn't you tell me Ruth Marburg was your daughter?"

"You didn't ask me. It makes no difference, anyway. I haven't had much to do with Etta since she threw herself at Mr. Hackett and rose in the world and became a great lady. She never comes to see me, and I know why. She's ashamed of the life she leads, with young men half her age. I might as well not have a family. I never even see my grandson Stephen."

I said I was sorry, and left her warming her hands at her Bible.

Chapter 33

I DROVE TO MALIBU, forgetting that I was hungry and tired. Just before I reached the Hacketts' gate, I passed a car going in the other direction. The man at the wheel looked like Keith Sebastian. I turned in the entrance to the Hacketts' driveway and chased him down the hill.

I caught him at the highway STOP sign. He turned right on the highway and then left on a secondary road that looped down along the beach. He parked behind a lighted beach house and knocked on the back door. For an instant, as she opened the door for him, his daughter was silhouetted against the light.

I got out of my car and approached the house. The blinds and drapes were closed. A good deal of light leaked out but I couldn't hear anything because of the waves marking time on the beach.

The name on the mailbox was Hackett. I knocked on the back door, trying the knob at the same time. It was locked.

Keith Sebastian said through the door: "Who is it?"

"Archer."

There was another wait. Inside the house a door closed. Sebastian unlocked the outer door and opened it.

I stepped in past him without waiting to be asked. "What are you doing, Keith?"

He had no decent cover story. "I decided I better get away from it all for a day or two. Mr. Hackett loaned me the use of his private cottage."

I moved from the kitchen into the next room. There were

dirty dishes, set for two, on a round poker table. One of the coffee mugs had a half-moon of lipstick at the rim.

"Do you have a girl with you?"

"As a matter of fact I have." He looked at me with hopeful foolish guile. "You won't tell Bernice now, will you?"

"She knows, and so do I. It's Sandy, isn't it?"

He picked up Sandy's coffee mug. For a moment his face was open. I think he was planning to brain me, and I stepped back out of close range. He set the mug down on the table.

"She's my daughter," he asserted. "I know what's best for her."

"Is that why her life is working out so beautifully? This is a lousy substitute for treatment."

"It's better than jail. She'd get no treatment at all."

"Who's been telling you horror stories?"

He wouldn't answer me. He stood there shaking his stupid handsome head. I sat down at the table uninvited. After a minute he sat down opposite me. We faced each other like bluffing poker players.

"You don't understand. Sandy and I aren't planning to stay *here*. Everything's all worked out."

"To leave the country?"

He frowned. "Bernice told you then."

"It's a good thing someone did. If you skip you'll virtually lose your citizenship. Sandy will, anyway. And how will you support yourself in a foreign country?"

"That's all taken care of. If I look after what I've got, and live in the right place, I'll never have to work again."

"I thought you were flat broke."

"Not any more. The whole thing's working out." He spoke with the deaf and blind assurance of terrible anxiety. "So please don't try to stop me, Mr. Archer. I know exactly what I'm doing."

"Is your wife going with you?"

"I hope so. She hasn't decided. We're flying out tomorrow, and she's going to have to make up her mind in a hurry."

"I don't think either of you should decide in a hurry."

"Nobody asked for your advice."

"You did, though, in a way, when you brought me into this case. I'm afraid you're stuck with me."

We sat and looked at each other, two poker players with

lousy hands who were too far behind to quit. For a moment I could hear the sea more clearly, and a cold draft touched my ankles. Something jarred in another part of the house, and the draft was cut off.

"Where is your daughter?"

He crossed the room and opened a door. "Sandy!"

I followed him into a lighted bedroom. It was a strange room, as strange as Lupe's. Wild color exploded on the walls and ceiling. A round bed stood like an altar in the middle. Sandy's clothes were scattered across the bed.

Sebastian opened the sliding glass door. We ran down to the water. The girl was out past the surf line, swimming for her life, or for her death.

Sebastian waded in in his clothes, then turned to me helplessly. "I can't swim very well."

A wave knocked him down. I had to drag him out of the sucking water.

"Go and call the sheriff."

"No!"

I slapped him. "Call the sheriff, Keith. You have to."

He floundered up the beach. I tore off my shoes and most of my clothes, and went in after the girl. She was young, and hard to catch. By the time I reached her, we were a long way out and I was tiring.

She didn't know I was there until I touched her. Her eyes were wide and dark as a seal's. "Go away. I want to die."

"I'm not going to let you."

"You would if you knew all about me."

"I almost do, Sandy. Come on in with me. I'm too tired to drag you."

The eye of a searchlight winked open on the beach. It roved the sea and found us. Sandy swam away from me. Her body was white and faintly phosphorescent, shimmering like moonlight in the water.

I stayed close to her. She was the only one left. A man in a black rubber wet-suit came out on a paddleboard and took her in unresisting through the surf.

Sebastian and Captain Aubrey were waiting for us with blankets. I rescued my clothes from under the feet of the onlookers and followed Sebastian and his daughter toward the beach cottage. Captain Aubrey walked with me.

"Suicide attempt?" he said.

"She's been talking about it for months. I hope this gets it out of her system."

"Don't count on it. Her family better take security precautions."

"I've been telling them that."

"You say it's been on her mind for months. That means it antedates the current mess."

"Correct."

We had reached the cottage. I was shivering in my blanket, but Aubrey detained me outside. "What made her suicidal in the first place?"

"I want to talk to you about that, Captain. First I need a hot shower and a chance to get Sebastian squared away. Where will you be in the next hour?"

"I'll wait for you in the substation."

I opened the glass door and stepped up into the colored bedroom. Sebastian was on the far side of the room. He stood like a sentry beside an open door through which I could hear a shower running. His clothes were dripping. He had wet sand in his hair, and in his eyes a look of maniacal dutifulness.

"What do you plan to do for the next five or ten years, Keith? Stand suicide watch?"

He gave me a puzzled look. "I don't quite follow."

"We almost lost her just now. You can't go on taking chances with her life. And you can't stand around and watch her twenty-four hours a day."

"I don't know what to do."

"Take her back to the Psychiatric Center tonight. Forget about South America. You wouldn't like it."

"But I made a promise."

"To Sandy? She'd rather die than go on this way. Literally."

"She isn't the only one involved," he said miserably. "I don't have any choice about South America. It's part of the whole ball of wax."

"You'd better explain that."

"I can't. I promised not to talk about it."

"Who did you make these promises to? Stephen Hackett?"

"No. It wasn't Mr. Hackett."

I moved around the bed toward him. "I can't do anything more for you, if you won't open up. I think you're being taken for a ride, you and your daughter both."

He answered me doggedly: "I know what I'm doing. I don't want or need your help."

"You may not want it, but you certainly need it. Are you going to take Sandy back to the Center?"

"No."

"Then I'll have to make you."

"You can't. I'm a free citizen."

"You won't be for long. Captain Aubrey is waiting to talk to me now. When he finds out that you've been buying and selling evidence in a murder case—"

"What do you mean?"

"I mean the tapes you bought from Mrs. Fleischer."

It was a guess, but an educated one, that the tapes were part of the ball of wax he'd referred to. His face confirmed my guess.

"Who did you buy them for, Keith?"

He didn't answer.

"Who's paying you to take your daughter out of the country?"

He still refused to answer. Sandy appeared in the doorway behind him. She had on a clean yellow terrycloth robe and was rosy from her shower. Clearly the night swim had been good for her. I found this hard to forgive.

She said to her father: "Is somebody paying you to leave? You didn't tell me that. You said your company was giving you some separation money."

"That's what it is, dear, separation money." He stood between us, looking from one to the other.

"How much money?"

"That's none of your business, dear. I mean, let me handle the business. You don't have to trouble your mind—"

"Gee thanks. Is Mr. Hackett giving you this money?"

"You might say so. It's his company."

"And you get the money if you take me to South America? Is that right? Otherwise you don't?"

"I don't like this cross-questioning," Sebastian said. "After all I am your father."

"Sure you are, Dad." Her voice was sardonic, darkened by

the authority of experienced pain. "But I don't want to go to South America."

"You said you did."

"I don't any more." Brusquely she turned her attention to me. "Get me out of here, will you? I've had it with this scene. This is where I freaked out last summer, right here in this very room. This is the bed where Lupe and Steve took turns at me. In the vulva and the anus." She touched those parts of herself like a child showing where she'd been hurt.

The words and gestures were addressed to me but meant for her father. Sebastian was appalled. He sat on the bed, then stood up quickly and brushed away the sand he had deposited.

"You can't mean Mr. Hackett."

"Yes I can. I blew my mind and I hardly knew what was happening. But I know old Steve Hackett when I see him."

Like lenses in a sophisticated camera, Sebastian's eyes were changing. He wanted not to believe her, to find a credibility gap in her story. But the truth was there, and we both knew it.

"Why didn't you tell me, Sandy?"

"I'm telling you now."

"I mean last summer, when it happened."

She regarded him with scorn. "How do you know it happened last summer? I haven't mentioned that tonight."

He looked around rather wildly, and rushed into speech: "Your mother said something, I don't mean she spelled it out. But there was something in your diary, wasn't there?"

"*I* spelled it out," she said. "I knew Bernice read my diary. But neither of you ever said a word to me. Never ever a word."

"I took your mother's lead in that, Sandy. After all I'm only a man and you're a girl."

"I know I'm a girl. I found it out the hard way."

She was angry and troubled, but she sounded more like a woman than a girl. She wasn't afraid. It occurred to me that she had suffered a sea-change into a woman, and that her storm would pass.

I went into the bathroom for a hot shower. The stall was warm and fragrant from Sandy's use of it.

Then, while Sebastian took a shower, I talked to his daughter across the poker table.

We both had our clothes on now, and they seemed to impose a certain formality on the conversation. Sandy started out by thanking me, though, which wasn't a bad sign.

I told her not to mention it, I'd been dying for a swim. "Have you decided to give life a try?"

"I'm not making any promises," she said. "It's a stinking world."

"You don't improve it by committing suicide."

"I do for me." She was still and silent for a while. "I thought I could break away from it all with Davy."

"Whose idea was that?"

"It was his. He picked me up on the Strip because somebody told him that I knew the Hacketts. He needed a way to get to Steve, and I was glad to help."

"Why?"

"You know why. I wanted to get back at him and Lupe. But it didn't really make me feel any better. It only made me feel worse."

"What did Davy want?"

"It's hard to tell. He always has three or four reasons for everything, three or four different versions. It isn't his fault. Nobody ever told him the truth, about who he was, until Laurel did. And even then he didn't *know* it was true. Laurel was drunk when she told him."

"Told him that Stephen Hackett was his father?"

"I don't know what she told him. Honestly." It was her mother's word, and she said it with her mother's intonation. "Davy and I weren't talking much at the end. I was afraid to go with him, and afraid to quit. I didn't know how far he would go. Neither did he."

"He's gone further now." I thought it was time to tell her, before the changes of the night had crystallized. "Davy was shot dead this afternoon."

She looked at me dully, as if her capacity to react was used up for the time being. "Who shot him?"

"Henry Langston."

"I thought he was a friend of Davy's."

"He was, but he had troubles of his own. Most people do."

I left her with the thought and went into the bedroom

where her father was trying on clothes. He settled for a turtleneck sweater and a pair of slacks. The sweater made him look young and bold, like an actor.

"What's on the agenda, Keith?"

"I'm going up to Hackett's place and give him back his check."

His statement astonished me. He looked slightly astonished himself.

"I'm glad you feel that way. But you better let me have the check. It's evidence."

"Against me?"

"Against Hackett. How much money is involved?"

"The check is for a hundred thousand."

"Plus how much cash for the tapes?"

He barely hesitated. "Ten thousand cash. I paid it over to Mrs. Fleischer."

"What story did Hackett give you about the tapes?"

"He said Fleischer was trying to blackmail him."

"For doing what?"

"He didn't say. I gather he was having an affair, though."

"When did you deliver the tapes to him?"

"Just now. Just before you came."

"Who was there, Keith?"

"Mr. Hackett and his mother were the only ones I saw."

"Do they have a tape recorder?"

"Yes. I saw them try the tapes on it for size."

"How many tapes are there altogether?"

"Six."

"Where did you put them?"

"I left them with Mrs. Marburg in the library. I don't know what they did with them after that."

"And they gave you a check? Right?"

"Yes. Hackett did."

He took the yellow slip out of his wallet and handed it over. It was very like the one in my office safe, except that it was signed by Stephen Hackett instead of his mother, and not postdated.

The moral force required to part with the money generated more of the same in Sebastian. He followed me into the living room, moving eagerly. "I'll go along with you. I want to tell that Hackett creep what I think of him."

"No. You've got better things to do."

"What do you have in mind?"

"Taking your daughter back to the Center," I said.

"Can't I just simply take her home?"

"It's too soon for that."

"It always will be," Sandy said. But she was looking at her father with changing eyes.

Chapter 34

CAPTAIN AUBREY was waiting for me at the wicket which opened onto the porch of the Sheriff's substation. We talked in the dingy hallway of the old building, out of hearing of the officer on duty. Aubrey, when I sketched out what I knew and some of what I guessed, wanted to go along to the Hackett place.

I reminded him that he'd have to get a search warrant, and that might take some doing. Meanwhile Hackett could be destroying the tapes or erasing the sound from them.

"What makes the tapes so important?" Aubrey wanted to know.

"The death of Laurel Smith. I found out tonight that Stephen Hackett had an affair with her about twenty years ago. Davy Spanner was their illegitimate son."

"And you think Hackett killed her?"

"It's too early to say. I know he paid ten grand for the tapes."

"Even so, you can't just go in and seize them."

"I don't have to, Captain. I've been working for Mrs. Marburg. I can get into the house."

"Can you get out again?" he said with a grim half-smile.

"I think I can. I may need some backstopping though. Give me some time alone with them first."

"Then what?"

"We'll play it by ear. If I need help I'll holler."

Aubrey followed me out to my car and leaned in at the window:

"Watch out for Mrs. Marburg. At the time of her second husband's death I—" he cleared his throat and edited the slander out of his warning—"there was some suspicion that she was involved."

"She may have been. Mark Hackett was killed by her son by her first husband—a man named Jasper Blevins."

"You know this for a fact?"

"Just about. I got it from Jasper Blevins's grandmother, and it cost her some pain to tell me. She held back until she knew Jasper was dead."

"Too many people have been dying," Aubrey said. "Don't you be one of them."

His unmarked car followed me to the Hacketts' gate. I drove on up the private road to the pass and across the dam. The house beyond the lake had lights in it, faint behind drawn curtains. As I knocked on the door I felt I was coming there for the last time.

Gerda Hackett answered the door. She looked anxious and lonely, like an overweight ghost haunting the wrong house. She brightened up unnervingly when she saw me:

"Mr. Archer! *Kommen Sie nur 'rein.*"

I stepped inside. "How's your husband?"

"Much better, thank you." She added in a disappointed tone: "It's Stephen you wish to see?"

"And Mrs. Marburg."

"They're in the library. I'll tell them you're here."

"Don't bother. I know where it is."

I left her standing like a stranger at the doorway of her house. Moving through the massive building with its institutional feeling, I could guess why Hackett had married a girl from another country. He didn't want to be known.

The library door was closed. I could hear a voice behind it, a woman's voice, and when I pressed my ear against the oak door I recognized the voice of Laurel Smith. It made the hair on the back of my neck bristle. Then my heart began to pound with the crazy hope that Laurel had survived.

I was close to breaking down, like a man coming near to the end of a long climb: an inverted downward climb into the past. I could hardly breathe the air there, and I leaned against the library door.

"Thank you, Mrs. Lippert," Laurel was saying. "You want me to give you a receipt?"

"It isn't necessary," another woman's voice said. "I'll be getting the check back from the bank."

"How about a little drink?"

"No thanks. My husband doesn't like it when he comes home and I have liquor on my breath."

"You can't smell vodka," Laurel said.

"*He* can. He's got a nose like a beagle. Good night now."

"Take care."

A door closed. Laurel began to hum an old song about whistling in the dark. She must have been moving around her apartment, because her voice faded and returned.

I started to turn the knob of the library door. Ruth Marburg said:

"Who is that out there?"

I had to go in, smiling. Mrs. Marburg was sitting beside the telephone. There was no revolver in sight.

Hackett was sitting at the table where the tape recorder stood. His battered smile looked as ghastly from the outside as mine felt from the inside. He switched off Laurel's singing.

"Mrs. Hackett told me where to find you. I hope I'm not interrupting anything."

Hackett started to tell me that I wasn't, but Mrs. Marburg's voice overbore his: "As a matter of fact you are interrupting something. My son and I are playing some old family tapes."

"Go right ahead."

"You wouldn't be interested. They're very nostalgic, but just to members of the family." Her voice sharpened: "Do you want something?"

"I came to give you my final report."

"This is a bad time. Come back tomorrow, eh?"

"I'd like to hear what he has to say." Hackett looked uneasily at his mother. "As long as we're paying him so much we might as well get the benefit of it."

"I'd rather hear what Laurel has to say."

Mrs. Marburg flapped her false eyelashes at me. "Laurel? Who on earth is Laurel?"

"Jasper's wife. You've just been listening to her. Let's all listen."

Mrs. Marburg leaned toward me urgently. "Close the door behind you. I want to talk to you."

I closed the door and leaned on it, watching them. Mrs. Marburg rose heavily, using her arms as well as her legs. Hackett reached for the tape recorder.

"Leave it alone."

His hand hovered over the controls, and then withdrew. Mrs. Marburg walked toward me.

"So you've dug up a little dirt and you think you can raise the ante. You couldn't be more wrong. If you don't watch yourself you'll be in jail before morning."

"Somebody will."

She thrust her face close to mine. "My son and I buy up people like you two for a nickel. That check I gave you is postdated. Are you too stupid to know what that means?"

"It means you didn't trust me to stay bought. Nobody's staying bought these days." I got out Keith Sebastian's check and showed it to her. "Sebastian gave me this."

She snatched at the check. I held it out of her reach and put it away. "Don't be grabby, Etta."

Her whole face scowled under its mask of paint. "You mustn't call me that name. My name is Ruth."

She went to her chair. Instead of sitting down she opened the drawer of the telephone table. I reached her before she got the revolver out and ready to fire, and tore it out of her hands.

I backed away from her and turned to Hackett. He was on his feet, moving on me. I didn't have to fire the gun. He started to walk backwards, rather tentatively, toward the table where he'd been sitting.

"Get away from the table, Hackett. I want you on the other side of the room, near your mother."

He crossed in front of her and leaned against all of Dickens, then sat on a three-stepped stool in the corner, like a dunce. Mrs. Marburg stood resistant, but eventually sank back into her chair.

I took her son's place on the chair by the tape recorder, and switched it on. Fleischer's recording apparatus must have been noise-activated: there were no long breaks or lacunae in the sound. Laurel's singing was followed by the small noise of Laurel making herself a drink, then by the larger noise of her making another drink.

She sang a song of her own invention, with the refrain of "Davy, Davy, Davy."

The door of her apartment opened and closed, and Davy himself was in the room. "Hi, Laurel."

"Call me Mother."

"It doesn't sound right. Hey, you don't have to kiss me."

"I have a right to. Haven't I treated you like a mother?"

"Lately, you have. Sometimes I wonder why."

"Because I *am* your mother. I'd cut off my right hand to prove it."

"Or your head?"

She cried out, "Ah!" as if he had hurt her physically. "It isn't very nice of you to talk like that. I didn't have anything to do with killing your father."

"But you know who did kill him."

"I told you the other night, it was the young man—the beatnik with the beard."

"They didn't have beatniks in those days." Davy's voice was flat and incredulous.

"Whatever you want to call him—he was the one."

"Who was he?"

After some hesitation she said: "I don't know."

"Then why did you cover up for him?"

"I didn't."

"Yes, you did. You told Fleischer and the law that the dead man wasn't my father. But you told me he was. Either you lied to them or you're lying to me. Which is it?"

Laurel said in a small voice: "You mustn't be so hard on me. I didn't lie either time. The man the train ran over—"

Mrs. Marburg groaned, so loudly that I missed the end of Laurel's sentence. I switched the recorder off as Mrs. Marburg started to speak:

"Do I have to sit here all night and listen to this soap opera?"

"It's a family tape," I said. "Very nostalgic. Your grandson and his mother are talking about what happened to your son. Don't you want to know what happened to him?"

"That's nonsense! I only have the one son."

She turned to Hackett in his corner and showed her teeth in what was probably meant to be a maternal smile. He moved uneasily under it. Finally he spoke, for the second time, very carefully:

"There's not much use pretending, Mother. He can find out about Jasper quite easily. I think he already has. I also think it's time I made a clean breast of it."

"Don't be a fool!"

"A clean breast of what?" I said.

"The fact that I killed my half-brother, Jasper Blevins. If you'll give me a chance to explain what happened, I think you'll take a different view of the matter. Certainly no jury would convict me."

"Don't be too sure of that," his mother said. "I say you're making a big mistake if you trust this s.o.b."

"I have to trust someone," he said. "And this man saved my life. I don't agree with you, by the way, that we should stop payment on his check. He earned the money."

I cut in: "You were going to tell me how you killed Jasper."

He took a deep breath. "Let me start with why I killed him. Jasper murdered my father. My father and I had been very close, though I hadn't seen him for a long time. I was living in London, studying economics in preparation for taking over the business eventually. But Dad was a man in his prime, and I didn't expect him to die for many years. When I got the word that he'd been murdered, it just about pushed me over the edge. I was still very young, in my early twenties. When I flew home I was determined to track down my father's murderer."

Hackett was talking like a book, which made it hard to believe him. "How did you track him down?"

"It turned out to be quite easy. I found out Jasper had quarreled with Dad."

"Who told you?"

He looked at his mother. She pushed air away with the flat of her hand. "Leave me out of this. If you take my advice, you'll shut up here and now."

"What are you afraid of, Mrs. Marburg?"

"You," she said.

Hackett went on with a faint whine in his voice: "I want

to finish what I had to say. I learned that Jasper was at the ranch with his wife, and I drove up there. This was the second or third day after he murdered Dad. I accused him of the crime. He came at me with an ax. Fortunately I was stronger than he was, or luckier. I got the ax away from him and crushed his skull with it."

"So you were the man with the beard?"

"Yes. I'd grown a beard when I was a student in London."

"Was Laurel there when you killed Jasper?"

"Yes. She saw it happen."

"And the boy Davy?"

"He was there, too. I can hardly blame him for what he did to me." Hackett touched his swollen mouth and discolored eyes.

"What happened between you and Davy?"

"He gave me a very bad time, as you know. At first he meant to put me under a train. Then he changed his mind and forced me to show him the way to the ranch. He seemed to be trying to reconstruct what happened, and he made me confess what I've just told you. He gave me a terrible beating. He talked as if he meant to kill me but he changed his mind again."

"Did you tell him you were his father, his natural father?"

A one-sided grin of surprise pulled up the corner of Hackett's mouth and narrowed one eye. It resembled the effects of a mild paralytic stroke. "Yes, I did. I am."

"What happened after you told him that?"

"He untaped my wrists and ankles. We had a talk. He did most of the talking. I promised him money, and even recognition, if that was what he wanted. But he was mainly interested in getting at the truth."

"The fact that you killed Jasper?"

"Yes. He didn't remember me consciously at all. He'd blacked out on the whole thing."

"It isn't entirely clear to me," I said. "The way you tell it, you killed Jasper in self-defense. Even without that, I agree that no jury would have convicted you, of anything worse than manslaughter. Why did you cover up, and go to such lengths to dispose of the body?"

"That wasn't my doing. It was Laurel's. I suppose she felt guilty about our affair in Texas. And I admit I felt guilty, about that and everything else. Don't forget that Jasper was my brother. I felt like Cain himself."

He may have felt like Cain, once long ago, but at the moment he sounded phony to me. His mother stirred and erupted again:

"Talk is expensive. Haven't you learned that yet? You want this s.o.b. to own you outright?"

Hackett watched my face as he answered her: "I don't believe Mr. Archer is a blackmailer."

"Hell, he doesn't call it that. None of them do. They call it investigation, or personal research, or scratch-my-back-and-I'll-scratch yours. So we buy him an apartment house to live in, and an office building to keep his files in, and he pays us five cents on the dollar." She stood up. "What's the ante, this time, you s.o.b.?"

"Don't keep saying that, Etta. It spoils the maternal image. I've been wondering where Laurel got her apartment building and where your mother got hers."

"Leave my mother out of this, my mother has nothing to do with this." I seemed to have touched Mrs. Marburg on a nerve. "Have you been talking to Alma?"

"A little. She knows a lot more than you think she does."

For the first time in our acquaintance, Mrs. Marburg's eyes reflected real fear. "What does she know?"

"That Jasper killed Mark Hackett. And I think she thinks that you put Jasper up to it."

"The hell I did! It was Jasper's own idea."

Mrs. Marburg had blundered, and she knew it. The fear in her eyes began to spill across the rest of her face.

"Did Jasper tell you he killed Mark?" I said.

She considered the long-term consequences of her answer and finally said: "I don't remember. It was a long time ago, and I was very upset."

"So you're taking the Fifth. Maybe the tape will remember." I reached for the recorder, intending to switch it on.

"Wait," Mrs. Marburg said. "What will you take to stop right here? Just walk out and forget about us? How much?"

"I haven't given the matter any thought."

"Think about it now. I'm offering you a million dollars." She held her breath, and added: "Tax-free. You could live like a king."

I looked around the room. "Is this the way kings live?"

Hackett spoke from his dunce's stool: "It's no use, Mother. It's going to be our word against his. So we better stop talking to him, just as you said."

"You hear that?" Mrs. Marburg said to me. "A million, tax-free. That's our final offer. You don't have to do a thing for it. Just walk away."

Hackett was watching my face. "You're wasting your time," he said. "He doesn't want our money. He wants our blood."

"Be quiet both of you."

I switched on the recorder, turned the tape back a little, and heard Davy's voice say again: "—or you're lying to me. Which is it?"

Then Laurel's voice: "You mustn't be so hard on me. I didn't lie either time. The man the train ran over really was your father."

"That's not what you said the other night. You said that Stephen Hackett was my father."

"He was."

I looked at Hackett. He was listening intently, his eyes still focused on my face. His own face seemed queerly starved. The scorn in his eyes had changed to a chilly loneliness.

Davy said: "I don't understand."

"I don't want you to, Davy. I don't want to dig up the past."

"But I have to know who I am," he said in a chanting rhythm. "I have to, it's important to me."

"Why? You're my son and I love you."

"Then why won't you tell me who my father was?"

"I have. Can't we leave it at that? We'll only stir up trouble."

The door opened.

"Where are you going?" Laurel said.

"My bird is waiting. Sorry."

The door closed. Laurel cried a little, then made a drink. She yawned. There were night movements, an inner door closing. Night sounds, cars in the street.

I speeded up the tape and jumped it ahead and heard a voice which had to be my own, saying: "—sounds like a poolroom lawyer to me."

Laurel's voice answered mine: "Davy's more than that. He's more than just a talker. And he isn't the poolroom type. He's a serious boy."

"What's he serious about?"

"He wants to grow up and be a man and do something useful."

"I think he's conning you, Mrs. Smith," I heard my strange voice say, a long time ago.

I moved the tape ahead again and heard the familiar noise of the apartment door being opened. Laurel said: "What do you want?"

No answer, except the sound of the door being closed. Then Hackett's voice:

"I want to know who you've been talking to. I had a phone call last night—"

"From Davy?"

"From Jack Fleischer. Who the hell is Davy?"

"Don't you remember, Jasper?" Laurel said.

The sound of a blow on flesh was followed by Laurel's sigh, then other blows until the sighing changed to snoring. I was watching the man who called himself Stephen Hackett. He sat tense on his stool. He seemed to be excited by the noises, emotionally transported to Laurel's apartment.

I broke the spell: "What did you hit her with, Jasper?"

He let his breath out in a kind of soughing whine. Even his mother had turned her eyes away from him.

I said to her: "What did he hit her with?"

"How in God's name should I know?"

"He went to you immediately afterward. He probably disposed of the weapon at your house. But mainly I think he wanted moral support. When he came back here that afternoon he brought you along with him."

"That doesn't make me responsible."

"You are, though. You can't profit from murder without taking part of the blame."

"I didn't *know* he killed Laurel," she said with some force.

"You knew he killed Mark Hackett. Didn't you?"

"I found out about it."

"But you didn't turn him in."

"He was my son," she said.

"Stephen was your son, too. But your maternal instincts

didn't work for him. You conspired with Jasper to kill Stephen and put Jasper in his place."

She gave me a shocked look, as if the truth of what they had done was just occurring to her, fifteen years too late. "How could I possibly do a thing like that?"

The sentence was meant to be a denial, but it was also a question; which I answered. "You were headed for the rocks. Mark Hackett knew about your affair with Sidney Marburg. He was going to divorce you and cut you off financially. Simply killing Mark wouldn't help you very much. The bulk of his estate was going to Stephen. So Stephen had to go.

"Nobody in California knew Stephen. He'd been out of the country for several years, and at the time he left for Europe you were all living in Texas. But your lover Sid had sharp eyes, and you didn't want to have to knock him off, so you sent him to Mexico for the transition period. Sid caught one glimpse of Stephen wearing a beard when Stephen flew in from England.

"You shunted Stephen off to the ranch where Jasper was waiting for him. Jasper had more than money to gain from Stephen's death. His brother's identity was a perfect mask for the murderer of Mark Hackett. He killed Stephen and shaved his beard off." I looked past Mrs. Marburg to her son. "You were a barber at one time, weren't you, Jasper?"

He looked back at me with eyes as empty as a skull's. I said to him: "You left Laurel behind to con the local law and came down here and took your brother's place. It couldn't have been too hard, with your mother vouching for you. I imagine the hardest part was learning to forge your brother's signature. But then you were a bit of an artist, too. You were a bit of just about everything. But you found your real *métier* as a killer and conman."

The man in the corner spat at me and missed. His role as a rich and lucky man had ended. The room with its books and pictures no longer belonged to him. He was Albert Blevins's son, alone in blank space.

"For fourteen or fifteen years," I said, "nothing much happened to threaten your success. You lived quietly in seclusion, developed a taste for good pictures, visited Europe. You even got up nerve enough to make a bigamous marriage.

"No doubt you were paying off Laurel all those years. You

owed her a lot, really, for keeping Jack Fleischer off your trail. Unfortunately she got lonely with nothing but a little money to keep her company. And she had some pangs of conscience about the boy she'd abandoned.

"In the end she made a move toward the boy. It was enough to tip Jack Fleischer off. I'm sure he'd been suspicious of both of you from the start. His retirement freed him to act. He put Laurel's apartment under surveillance, and started to dig into the whole background.

"We know from the tape what happened after that. Fleischer called you. You silenced Laurel. Later you got your chance to silence Fleischer. Do you want to talk about that?"

Hackett made no response of any kind. He was leaning forward with his hands on his knees. I went on:

"It isn't hard to imagine what happened. Davy believed he had found his father, that his life was just beginning. He laid the shotgun down and untied you. You made a grab for the gun and got hold of it. But Davy got away.

"Jack Fleischer was older and not so quick. Or maybe he was paralyzed by the sudden confrontation. Did he recognize you, Jasper, and know in the moment before he died who shot him? We know, anyway. You killed Fleischer and threw the gun in the creek. Then you collapsed on the creek bank and waited to be rescued."

"You can't prove any of this," Mrs. Marburg said.

Her son was doubtful. He slid off the stool and tried to rush me, clumsy and almost reluctant, trotting in slow motion toward his own revolver in my hand.

I had time to decide where to shoot him. If I had liked the man I might have shot to kill. I shot him in the right leg.

He fell at his mother's feet, clutching his knee and moaning. She didn't reach out to touch him or comfort him. She sat looking down at him in the way I imagine the damned look down, with pity and terror only for themselves, into lower circles than their own.

The sound of the shot brought Aubrey into the house. He arrested both of them and took them in on suspicion of conspiracy to commit murder.

Later I made my way through the crowds of night-blooming young people on the Strip and climbed the stairs to my office. The basket of cold chicken, washed down with a slug of whisky, tasted better than I expected it to.

I had a second slug to fortify my nerves. Then I got Mrs. Marburg's check out of the safe. I tore it into small pieces and tossed the yellow confetti out the window. It drifted down on the short hairs and the long hairs, the potheads and the acid heads, draft dodgers and dollar chasers, swingers and walking wounded, idiot saints, hard cases, foolish virgins.

ABOUT THE AUTHOR

ROSS MACDONALD was born near San Francisco in 1915. He was educated in Canadian schools, traveled widely in Europe, and acquired advanced degrees and a Phi Beta Kappa key at the University of Michigan. In 1938 he married a Canadian girl who is now well known as the novelist Margaret Millar. Mr. Macdonald (Kenneth Millar in private life) taught school and later college, and served as communications officer aboard an escort carrier in the Pacific. For over twenty years he lived in Santa Barbara and wrote mystery novels about the fascinating and changing society of his native state. Among his leading interests were conservation and politics. He was a past president of the Mystery Writers of America. In 1964 his novel *The Chill* was given a Silver Dagger award by the Crime Writers' Association of Great Britain. Mr. Macdonald's *The Far Side of the Dollar* was named the best crime novel of 1965 by the same organization. Recently, he was presented with the Mystery Writers of America's Grand Master Award. *The Moving Target* was made into the highly successful movie *Harper* in 1966. *The Goodbye Look* (1969), *The Underground Man* (1971), *Sleeping Beauty* (1973) and *The Blue Hammer* (1976) were all national bestsellers. Ross Macdonald died in 1983.